VERONA COMICS

JENNIFER DUGAN

G. P. PUTNAM'S SONS

G. P. Putnam's Sons

An imprint of Penguin Random House LLC, New York

First published in the United States of America by G. P. Putnam's Sons, an imprint of
Penguin Random House LLC, 2020
First paperback edition published 2021

Visit us online at penguinrandomhouse.com

THE LIBRARY OF CONGRESS HAS CATALOGED THE HARDCOVER EDITION AS FOLLOWS:
Names: Dugan, Jennifer, author.
Title: Verona comics / Jennifer Dugan.
Description: New York: G. P. Putnam's Sons, [2020] | Summary: Told in two voices,
cellist Jubilee and anxiety-ridden Ridley meet at a comic con where both of their families
have booths, and begin a relationship they must hide from their parents.
Identifiers: LCCN 2019034212 | ISBN 9780525516286 (hardcover) | ISBN 9780525516293
Subjects: CYAC: Dating (Social customs)—Fiction. |
Anxiety disorders—Fiction. | Musicians—Fiction. | Cello—Fiction. |
Comic-book stores—Fiction. | Lesbian mothers—Fiction.
Classification: LCC PZ7.1.D8343 Ver 2020 | DDC [Fic]—dc23
LC record available at https://lccn.loc.gov/2019034212

Printed in the United States of America
ISBN 9780525516309
1 3 5 7 9 10 8 6 4 2

Design by Suki Boynton
Text set in Dante MT Pro

To RJP, who always cheered the loudest.
I miss you every day.

CHAPTER ONE

Jubilee

"YOU LOOK LIKE you're being tortured," Jayla says. "This is supposed to be fun."

Easy to say when you're the one on the other side of the tweezers. I squeeze my eyes shut as she picks them up again, a tinge of fear washing over me when I smell the glue. I can't move my head while Jayla's working on my eyelashes, something she's stressed to me about a dozen times already in increasingly frustrated tones, so I try to distract myself by practicing the prelude from Bach's Fifth Cello Suite in my head. I tap my fingers against the cold bathroom counter, pressing imaginary strings and feeling homesick for my instrument.

Feather eyelashes and fancy dresses are worlds apart from the chunky sweaters and ballet flats that I prefer. But this is for the greater good, a part of my weekend of "pushing the boundaries and embracing life for the sake of my music," which has somehow turned into letting my best friend dress me up for FabCon prom after an already long day at the convention, selling comics with my parents.

"Can I open my eyes yet?"

"No," she says. "You have to relax. Remember what Mrs. G said."

Right. I've been instructed (read: forced) by my private instructor, Mrs. Garavuso; the school orchestra teacher, Mrs. Carmine; and *both* my parents to "let go" and take a weekend off from my instrument. On a technical level, Mrs. Garavuso says I'm the best cellist she's ever had. But apparently I've been, and this is a direct quote, "playing with the passion of a robot lately." Mrs. Carmine, traitor that she is, agreed wholeheartedly. Not exactly what I want to hear as I prepare for the biggest audition of my life—the summer program at the Carnegie Conservatory, where I'll get to study with Aleksander Ilyashev. He's been my dream teacher ever since I heard him play Beethoven's Triple Concerto with the Boston Symphony. And if I want a shot at getting into Carnegie for real after high school, a summer of his advice and guidance is the biggest boost I could possibly get.

"You think too loud." Jayla sighs, so close I can feel her breath on my cheek. "Seriously, get out of your head."

"I'm not in my head."

"Lies," she says, but I can hear the smile in her voice. "Respect the rules. I bet you're breaking at least two right now."

The rules, right. Jayla and I made a list of them on our way to the con. I've been mostly focusing on the first three, with varying degrees of success. Rule One: I can't practice cello, nor can I do any homework this entire weekend. (Half credit; I've been practicing this whole time, but only in my head.) Rule Two: When not helping my parents in their booths, I can't sit in my room obsessing over the audition. (Okay, she's got me there; I'm totally failing at this one.) Rule Three: I have to try a new food at each restaurant we eat at. (Switching from Sprite to Cherry Coke counts. Fight me.)

"You're going to flip when you see yourself," Jayla squeals, pressing another feather to my eyelid.

"In a good way, or . . . ?" I fake cringe, and she smacks my arm.

"Yes, in a good way. Now sit still."

Not that I really doubted it. Jayla is to makeup and fashion what I am to music—top tier, the best of the best, no apologies—except nobody would *ever* say her work lacks passion. She's been planning on going to FIT her entire life, and her new obsession with cosplay has given her an extra excuse to flex her fashion muscles.

"Annnnnd done," Jayla says, and I open my eyes.

I blink twice. I look . . . *amazing*. My dark brown hair is piled high on my head in an elaborate updo with long feathers streaming out in different directions. She's blended shimmery teal and green eye shadows together around my eyes and added little dots of eyeliner to accentuate the corners, and then there are the feathers. The feathers! Tiny little teal things, curled to perfection, adorn each eyelid, transforming me into something more akin to a magical forest creature than a cellist. I've disappeared completely into Mora, the badass peacock-inspired leader from my stepmom's famous *Fighting Flock* comic series.

Jayla turns back to putting the finishing touches on her

own makeup in the mirror, gently dabbing bright white spots onto her dark brown skin. "Go get your dress on. I'm almost done."

"Yes, ma'am," I say, hopping off the counter. I grab my emerald-green dress off the hook and disappear into the bedroom to get changed. I bought this dress for a school dance a few months ago—Jayla said the color "really popped" against my fair skin—but she's modified it pretty heavily since then, changing the cut, adorning it with feathers, and just generally turning it into a gown fit for peacock royalty.

I glance at the time and groan. "Prom started fifteen minutes ago."

"We're supposed to be fashionably late," Jayla calls back through the bathroom door.

"If you don't hurry, we're going to be the unfashionable kind," I mutter, zipping up my dress. I'm still struggling to tie the crisscrossing green and purple ribbons up my arms when Jayla finally steps out of the bathroom.

"Here, let me," she says, coming over, and I do a double take. Gone is Jayla, and in her place stands the best Shuri cosplay I have ever seen in my life. She's wrapped her braids into a massive bun on her head, and while it's not quite Wakandan-princess level, it's close. Add in the makeup and the warrior outfit she's been crafting for months and—

"Holy crap," I say, and she laughs.

"Yeah," she says, holding her arms out and twirling.

"You're definitely going to win tonight. You know that, right?"

She shrugs. "I better, after what happened earlier." Meaning when her Harley Quinn cosplay came in second place, which she rates as a major underperformance, even though there were nearly 150 people competing and there was no way she was beating someone in a life-size replica of Hulkbuster armor.

"Stop, you did awesome," I say, but she shakes her head.

Jayla's always intense with this stuff, partially because she's super competitive (see also: only being a junior and already the co-captain of her club's soccer team), and partially because people will find any excuse to tear down a black girl that dares to also cosplay white characters. Jayla can't just be good; she has to be *great*, and even when she's great, she still gets crap for it. It's gross and annoying and one of the things I hate most about the comics community.

"Ready?" she asks, cinching the last ribbon.

"Yeah, I just have to strap myself into these death traps," I say, sliding my foot into a shiny green stiletto. I thought Jayla was kidding when she showed up to my house with them. Spoiler alert: she was not.

Jayla offers me her arm as we head out when it becomes clear that an ultra-plush carpet adds an additional degree of difficulty to super-high heels. "Everybody's gonna love those death traps." She laughs. "There is absolutely no way you're leaving that dance without checking off Rule Four."

Ah yes, Rule Four, aka the Final Rule, aka the only thing I have yet to even attempt, despite the fact it would probably be the most inspiring for my music: I must experience a con crush.

Con crushes are kind of Jayla's thing—find somebody

nice, spend the weekend flirting, and then go back home, no muss, no fuss—or they were, before she started casually seeing the *other* co-captain of the soccer team, Emily Hayes, a few weeks ago. I was supposed to pick up her slack on that front, but no luck so far. It's not that I'm not open to it . . . it's just that nobody has caught my eye.

Jayla stops at the door next to ours and I knock. My mom opens the door, her bright red hair shining in the hallway light as she blinks hard. She's probably just waking up from a nap, and I don't blame her. After working in the shop booth all day so Vera could sketch and talk to fans in Artist Alley, she's got to be beat.

"Hey, Jubilee." She yawns, but I can tell the second she really looks at me, because her eyes widen and then her eyebrows scrunch together the way they do whenever she's pissed. "Nope."

"Is everything okay?" Jayla asks all innocently, like she doesn't already know.

"Vera," Mom yells over her shoulder, pulling the door open wider. "Look at these kids!"

Vera's sitting on the edge of the bed, pointing the remote at the TV and lazily flipping through channels. She looks over at me and Jayla and nods appreciatively. "Are you evening-gown Mora? Amazing! And wow, Jayla, incredible detailing on the Shuri chest plate. That must have taken forever!" She sounds utterly delighted. My mom is going to kill her.

"Thank you so much," Jayla says with the most wholesome smile she can muster.

"Vera." I can only see the back of Mom's head now, but I

know that tone. I get that tone from her all the time. It's the "you're lucky I love you, because you make my life nearly impossible" tone. "Jubilee cannot go out dressed like that."

"It's prom," Vera says. "Give the kid a break."

"It's not real prom—it's comic-book-people prom, which is worse. And she looks twenty-five."

"It's my winter-formal dress," I point out. "You were fine with it in December."

"See, it's her winter-formal dress, Lillian. It's fine." Vera smirks like that solves everything. I hope it does, but I also know Mom way, way better than that—and Vera should too. They've been together four years now, which means she's had forty-eight months to learn what I've known for as long as I can remember: when Mom stands with her hands on her hips, her pinky finger tapping ever so slightly, it means trouble's definitely brewing.

"No, it *used* to be her winter-formal dress, but now the back goes down to her butt and the leg slit goes up to her elbow! What message does it send to have the creator's own kid turning Mora into some kind of pinup girl?"

Vera drops her head back, pulling her jet-black hair into a ponytail that shows off her undercut before walking over and kissing Mom on the temple. Even when they bicker, I swear they're still the poster children for happily ever after. It's perfect and gross all at once.

"Lil," she coos, and my mom visibly softens. "So they took a little artistic license; it's fine. And the message it sends, if that's *really* your concern, is that people shouldn't have to choose between being feminine or strong; they can be both. And may I remind you that this is an all-ages, dry event—"

"Exactly. *All* ages, Vera," Mom interrupts. "Which means it's not just kids that will be there. All the pervy dinosaurs might show up too."

"They're not going to let people in to party with the kids," Vera says. "You were there last year; the only adults allowed were sponsors and chaperones."

"I still think she should at least wear a shirt over it," Mom says, crossing her arms. "You know what teenage boys are like."

Vera arches an eyebrow. "And I think it's bullshit to make women cover up instead of holding men accountable for their actions."

Mom purses her lips. "I hate when you're right."

"You know, I could have just stayed home and happily rehearsed all weekend."

"You needed some sunlight, kid," Vera says. I don't bother pointing out that there is literally no natural daylight in this hotel–slash–casino–slash–convention center. "Go. Enjoy yourselves. Let me take care of your mom." She winks, which makes my mom blush, and ugh, gross. Shouldn't the lovey-dovey newlywed stage be over by now?

"Okay, yuck, bye," I say, grabbing Jayla's hand.

"Bye!" Jayla calls as I drag her down the hall, and we hear my mom giggle and say "Vera!" as she shuts the door. "Wow," Jayla says. "You know they're probably gonna—"

"Don't even finish that sentence."

By some miracle, the elevator doors are open as we

round the corner, but thanks to these ridiculous shoes, we don't have a prayer of making it in time . . . which means potentially being trapped on this floor for several more minutes. Several more minutes, during which either one of my parents could decide to run out and change her mind about letting us go alone or making me wear a T-shirt. Somehow I don't think "pushing the boundaries of my experiences" means going to FabCon prom with my mothers. Again.

"Hold that door!" Jayla shouts, dropping my arm and sprinting the rest of the way. Thank god for battle-ready outfits. She slides in her arm just as it closes, and the door bounces back open. She grins as I stumble in after her, laughing hard. I lean against the rail to catch my breath and realize with a start that we're not alone.

Batman stands in the corner, head tilted, taking in the sight of us. Well, a smaller, teenage-looking version of Batman, anyway—in a white dress shirt, a skinny tie, and dark fitted jeans. Okay, fine, so it's basically just a dude in a mask. But it counts.

I can tell Jayla is probably about two seconds away from monologuing about the undue appreciation the comics industry shows for mediocre white boys and how this boy in a mask is case in point because he'll probably take prom king just for showing up. It's her favorite topic, and she's definitely *not* wrong—but it *would* make for an awkward elevator ride. I'm a little bit relieved when she just rolls her eyes at him and bustles to the opposite side of the elevator car, mumbling, "What's up, Office Batman?"

He bends down and picks up a feather I must have lost

while sprinting into the elevator, spinning it around in his long fingers. *Piano fingers,* I muse. I have a habit of reducing everyone down to the instrument they should play. Jayla would be a saxophone; my other best friend, Nikki, is a flute; my ex, Dakota, is an out-of-tune harpsichord. Vera is a—

"Lost one," Batman says, all quiet. And yeah, that mask and the scrape of his voice and the way he's sliding up his sleeves right now are kind of working for him. The idea of "pushing the boundaries" just got a lot more interesting.

"I guess I did." I smile and reach for it, but he just keeps twirling it, like he's in no hurry to give it back.

"She must be molting," Jayla deadpans. She pushes the button for the first floor, even though it's already glowing.

"Are you going to prom?" he asks.

Jayla widens her eyes, like *obviously, dude,* and nods.

"We are." I elbow Jayla. "Are you?"

"Nah." He reaches across and hits the button for the second floor, which is odd considering he had to have been the one who hit the button for the first floor to begin with. "I like your dress, though," he says, a little bit quiet, as the elevator doors ping open. He holds his hand out, offering me the feather.

"Keep it," I say, and a blush rises to my cheeks as he turns to leave.

CHAPTER TWO

Ridley

I BOLT AROUND the corner, shoving up my Batman mask and sliding down the wall before the elevator doors even shut. Okay, breathe in, hold it, breathe out. Repeat. This shouldn't be so hard. Wait. Do I hold it for one beat? Two? Three? Oh god, now it just feels like I'm drowning.

pullittogetherpullittogetherpullittogether

A cute girl dressed as my favorite comic character should not have this effect on me, but.

breathebreathebreathebreathebreathe

It used to be I could tell the difference between excitement and anxiety. It used to be I could handle crowds and small talk. It used to be a lot of things . . . but now it's not.

I take another gasping breath, replaying the moments in my head. The way her cheeks turned pink when she told me to keep the feather twisted me up in interesting, not terrible, ways. And yet.

And yet.

I dig my fingers into the carpet and stare up at the ceiling, trying to ground myself before this panic attack spins too far out of control, but seriously, fuck this. Fuck being seventeen and wired so wrong that a person smiling at you can spin you into heart failure.

A door clicks open and a couple—drunk and sloppy like the rest of the casino crowd—steps out. I slide my mask down and shove myself through the door to the stairwell across from me, a welcome escape from their questioning looks.

It's one flight down to the dance or eleven up to my room, but I start to climb anyway, wishing there was a delete button in my brain. I don't know why I opened my mouth at all. So yeah, I should go. To my room. And probably never come out. Because reasons. But I still have this feather and—

My phone buzzes in my pocket, and I pull it out, sighing when I see Gray's name pop up.

"Ridley, where are you?" she asks. It's nearly impossible to hear her over the background noise.

"In a stairwell," I say.

"For good reasons or bad reasons?"

"Are there good reasons?"

"Yes. Come to the ballroom and I'll tell you all about the time I made out with your favorite superhero in the stairwell at RICC."

"Never happened," I snort.

"Okay, fine, it was his stunt double. On the escalator. Still counts."

I laugh; I can't help it. Two seconds ago I couldn't breathe, and now I'm laughing. Gray is magic like that.

"Are you trying to make me meet you or run away faster?"

I ask, but I've already started trotting back down the stairs.

"Ha ha, baby bro," she says. "Seriously, get down here. I can only cover for you for so long."

I let out a long breath. "I'm on my way," I say before hanging up.

There aren't many things that could get me to change directions when my head is like this. In fact, there's only one—Grayson Nicole Everlasting, Gray to me, heir apparent to the family business, the golden child to my black sheep, and the best big sister I could ever ask for. Not that I'd admit that last part. She's got a big enough head as it is.

I hit the bottom of the stairs, and Gray texts again to make sure I'm coming, the buzzing phone equal parts accusation and encouragement. I drag the heavy door open, focusing on the pinch of the mask's elastic strap behind my ears and the prick of the feather in my hand to keep from freaking out even more. The sound of slot machines and the smell of cigarettes waft through the air, and I try not to cough.

My parents don't usually bring me along to this stuff, since I kind of suck at being social, something that seems to frustrate my dad on a cellular level. But once a year, FabCon comes around, and with The Geekery being its biggest sponsor, my dad insists our presence is required. So Mom and I fly in from the Seattle house and he drives over from Connecticut with Gray, and we all fake being a happy little family for seventy-two torturous hours.

I skirt around the edge of the casino floor on my way to the convention center, holding my breath, with a smile pasted on my face. Mom spent the whole plane ride reminding me to hold it together in front of her Very Important Friends and to not piss off my father, so that is THE GOAL. All caps. Because I would give anything for this fake family reunion to be real, for just once my dad's hand on my shoulder to not pinch.

I take a long, deep breath when I finally cross into the no-smoking area—god, I hate cigarettes—and come to a stop in the hallway outside of FabCon prom, undoubtedly the most ridiculous part of this whole weekend.

There's a giant banner on the wall with my family's logo under the words PROUDLY SPONSORED BY written in the biggest letters imaginable. I don't know whether to tear it down or high-five it. Everything my father does is big, bigger than big, like a superhero from one of his favorite books. You kind of have to respect it.

"Ridley!" my sister calls, leaning over the railing the bouncer put up. She's dressed like—I don't even know. Poison Ivy, I think, but with a masquerade mask, I guess. Not like I'm in any position to judge. What did that other girl call me? Office Batman? Cool, cool, cool.

"Get in here before Allison tells Dad you were late," she says, frantically waving me over. She's right, but I roll my eyes anyway.

Allison Silverlake is Dad's assistant, spy, and latest hookup. Like it's not even a secret; he literally moved her into the Connecticut house with him. When my mom heard the news, she just raised an eyebrow and said, "Really, Mark," mildly exasperated, like he had called to tell her he got a speeding ticket or forgot the milk or something. I assumed finding out your husband of twenty years was shacking up with his mistress in your old family home would warrant a bigger reaction, but nah. That's not how my supremely fucked-up family rolls.

I squeeze the feather tighter between my fingers and start to head inside, but the bouncer, a big burly guy with a shaved head, puts his leg out, blocking me from getting in. "You got a ticket, kid?"

I reach into my pocket to pull out my lanyard, which says THE GEEKERY STAFF, EVENT SPONSOR in big block letters, but before I can show him, my sister reaches across his leg and grabs my arm.

"He's with me, Jake."

The bouncer drops his leg with a big smile because Gray always has that effect on people. "You all have a good night," he calls after us.

"Doubtful," I grumble, which makes her punch me in the shoulder as she pulls me through the crowd. Everybody thinks Gray is this perfect lady, but for the record, she is not. I mean, around other people, sure, but I've wrestled her over a slice of pizza before and that girl leaves bruises.

"Hey, Bats," someone calls out, and I whip my head around just in time to see the girl in the peacock dress walk by with her friend.

I want to say hi back, but *hi* seems too simple now that she's upped the ante by assigning a nickname.

thinkthinkthinkthinkthink

Calling her Mora like the character seems so formal. But what do I say? *"Hey, bird girl"*? Nope. *"Hey, Peacock . . . Lady"*? Nah. *"Hey—"* But the moment's passed, and she's still walking, and the tightness is back in my chest, and my sister is holding my wrist, which helps, but it also probably looks like she's my date. I shake my hand free, even though the loss makes my heart rate spike back up.

"Who was that?" Gray asks, stepping behind a long table. She shoves an armful of T-shirts and glow sticks at me, all adorned with THE GEEKERY in big letters, as if she expects me to go through the crowd like a proper host and hand them out. I raise my eyebrows right as the music kicks up a notch, the DJ jumping around to try to get the crowd pumped up. I can't believe how many kids are here, 150 at least, and this room isn't even that big.

Gray flashes me an apologetic look. "You're probably not up to handing those out, right? You doing okay, though?"

"Well, I haven't jumped off any houses lately, so."

"Not funny," she says, taking everything back and pulling the feather loose along with it. Gray picks it up, examining it in the purple and blue lights. "What's this?"

"Nothing," I say, snatching it from her and smoothing it into a slightly wrinkled version of its former glory.

She taps her chin, narrowing her eyes. "This wouldn't have anything to do with a certain peacock that's strutting around tonight, would it?"

"No," I say, dropping into my seat.

"Okay, great. Because I think the way you were stroking that feather just now was weirding her out."

I shove my hands under the table and scan the crowd.

She ruffles my hair. "Relax, Ridley. I'm messing with you."

"Ha, good one," I deadpan.

"I'm just saying, if you're going to become lovebirds"—
she looks me up and down—"or lovebats, you need to step up
your game. As in, like, put the feather down and at least say
hi back when she talks to you."

"I'm not going to be love anything, with anyone, ever
again," I grumble.

"Ridley . . ."

"Don't you have shit to hand out? God forbid a single person doesn't have something with our company name on it."

"Don't be like that."

"Can we just get through this night so Allison tells Dad I
was here? Where is he, anyway?"

"You know him." She shrugs. "Always someone to
schmooze at our events."

"Right, so why don't you follow in his footsteps. You'll
be the delightful hostess, I'll watch the table, and we'll never
mention my personal life again."

Gray rolls her eyes. "She wouldn't have talked to you if
she wasn't at least a little bit curious."

"She didn't talk to me; she called me Bats."

"Same thing."

"Drop it, Gray," I say, because my leg is already bouncing
as fast as it can go, and if she keeps it up, it might bounce
right through the table.

"Fine." But then she scrunches up her nose, and oh no, I
know that look. I hate that look. It's the look she gets when
she thinks she's being clever.

She unties a balloon from the table, grabs a bunch of
free-soda coupons and glow sticks, and pushes herself out

into the crowd. And okay, maybe I was wrong. Maybe it was just her "time to get down to work" look. Maybe I can survive the next two hours in relative peace and then hightail it back up to my room without any more drama. Maybe I'll do such a good job that tomorrow I'll get invited to breakfast with my father . . . and maybe tomorrow pigs will fly.

I slouch in my chair. The bass line rumbles through my chest like an extra heartbeat, and I dig my fingers into my knees, reminding myself that I'm here and Gray's right over there and it's all okay. Someone comes to the table, and I shove some coupons and a glow stick at them, grateful for the distraction.

I spot my sister weaving through the crowd again. She looks over and gives me a little wave, and I know, I *know* whatever is coming next, I'm not going to like it. And shit, there she goes, right up to that girl in the feather dress, handing her the balloon and some coupons and leaning toward her ear.

Peacock girl—Peak, I decide, is the name I would have settled on if I'd thought of it when she first walked by— laughs and my heart twists. Peak and Gray talk for a bit, a few pointed looks cast in my direction. I slink lower in my seat, fiddling with a glow stick. I don't realize Gray's come back until she kicks my chair.

"Hey," she says, dropping into the seat beside me.

"What was that about?" I shout over the din of the music.

"I told her I was your sister."

"What?"

"I told her I was your sister," she shouts even louder.

"No, I heard you. I meant why."

"So she didn't think I was your date."

I tilt my head, glaring at her and swallowing hard. "What did you do?"

"Look." She points toward the middle of the dance floor. I can't see Peak anymore, but I see the yellow balloon bobbing along over the crowd like a latex buoy on an ocean of sweaty teens. "I just gave her the balloon so she'd be easier to spot. I thought it would make you feel better if she couldn't sneak up on you."

My anxiety kicks back up a few notches as Peak gets closer to the exit. "She's leaving, Gray." I shouldn't feel so disappointed, but I do.

dosomethingdosomethingdosomethingdosomething

Gray cranes her neck, leaning over the table to see better. "I don't think she is."

The balloon disappears, and now I'm standing up and leaning too. I watch Peak take a Sharpie from the bouncer and scribble something on it, and then she looks over at me and smiles.

I turn toward my sister, my eyes going wide. "What else did you say to her? Jesus, Gray, what did you do?"

"Okay, okay, I may have also mentioned that you could probably use a little encouragement." She scrunches up her shoulders. "Sorry?"

"I'm gonna kill you."

"Are you, though? Look."

I follow her gaze to where Peak stands. Over her head bobs the bright yellow balloon again . . . only now there's a crudely drawn bat in the center of it.

"What the hell is she doing?"

"Flashing you the Bat-Signal, dumbass. And it's friggin' cute." My sister laughs, giving me a shove. I stumble a little, my heart pounding in my chest, in my feet, in my tongue. The music isn't helping. Not at all.

"Go," my sister shouts behind me, and I do.

I do.

CHAPTER THREE

Jubilee

I FEEL RIDICULOUS holding this balloon, especially when it looks like he's desperate for an escape hatch, but there's less than twenty-four hours left at this con, and as much as I've been trying to "push my boundaries," I'm still con-crushless.

As a chronic overachiever, I will not be satisfied unless I check off every box on Jayla's list. As a chronic worrier, I don't want to leave any stone unturned on the off chance everyone's right and my music *can* be cured by a weekend of costumes, crushes, and tasting food I didn't even know existed before now.

For a second, Jayla was all "nope, no way, not this one, you can do way better than a skinny white kid in a crappy mask," but she got on board fast when his sister came over trying to talk him up. Jayla has a soft spot for awkward nerds, even if this one does happen to be a boy.

Plus, Bats is the only person in this entire place who's made my heart do a somersault. Also, bonus points to him for being bashful.

I pull at a little piece of my hair that came loose and wait for him to make his move. After an eternity, he comes over, practically destroying his lip with his teeth. The fact that he's so flighty somehow makes this whole interaction seem like more of an accomplishment than it probably should, but I like it.

I say hi, and he says something I can't hear over the music. I laugh and say, "What?"

He leans in even closer. "I said, 'Nice balloon.'"

And the way his breath brushes against my neck sends a little spark down to my toes. He smells like clean skin and soap and expensive deodorant that probably doesn't use half-naked women in its ads. He leans back, and I'm standing there slightly flushed over this good-smelling boy in a cheesy Batman mask. It's kind of ridiculous. I get a little dizzy off the whiteness of his teeth when he smiles, and all my plans go out the window, replaced by a song instead.

"Dance with me?" I say, or shout, really, over the music. He shakes his head, and I arch an eyebrow, surprised and a little confused. He stares down at his shoes, Checkerboard Old Skool Vans that look brand-new. He doesn't say anything else, and an awkwardness settles over us until I can't take it anymore.

"I'm gonna—" I say, gesturing vaguely in the direction I came from. He's worrying his lip again, and this isn't going how I expected, so it seems safer to just melt back into the crowd, preserving his piano fingers and stolen glances for my music and not having them spoiled by the reality of the boy behind them.

I turn and dance my way toward where I last saw Jayla. She was singing along with a group of girls on the edge of the stage, flexing her ability to build a squad from scratch in five seconds flat. She's not where I left her, though, and I stop quick to reorient myself in the crowd. Someone thumps against me and I nearly tip over, thanks to these damn shoes. I spin around to shout . . . but it's Bats standing sheepishly behind me. I crinkle my forehead. I'm usually a better judge of character than this, and now he's thrown me twice in the span of three minutes. He shrugs and flashes a shy smile behind his mask, a single dimple appearing and disappearing on his left cheek. It shouldn't work but it does.

There's a break in the music then, DJs switching out or something, and the room goes eerily quiet before bursting with conversations. Finally, we can hear each other. Sort of.

"Can we just—?" He gestures toward the exit, and I raise my eyebrows.

"Are you trying to get me alone?"

"Yes," he says, completely serious. "I hate crowds."

"If you hate crowds, why did you come to prom?" I ask, but then the music picks up again. People crowd all around us, jostling us with their dancing. He looks exceptionally uncomfortable. "Fine."

I nab the edge of his sleeve and pull him along behind me. He stiffens at first but relaxes into it when I shift our path over to the door. I let my fingers slip lower, smiling when we link our hands.

"No reentry," the bouncer says, lifting his foot up across the aisle, and okay, there goes my plan to come back and dance, I guess. I glance behind me and see Jayla, but she's talking and laughing with a group of cosplayers we met today. It'll be faster to just text her when I get out in the hall.

"Got it," I say, shifting past.

Bats drops my hand once we're out of the room. His kind of hovers for half a second, like he doesn't know what to do with it, before he shoves it into his pocket. I walk a little farther down the hall, but now we're almost to the lobby, which is nearly as busy and loud as where we just left.

"This way." He tilts his head toward a nearby hallway.

"I'm not going to your room," I say, because away from the music and the lights, it's becoming clear that—pushing the boundaries or not—this was not my best idea. Flirting in a relatively supervised crowded room is one thing; disappearing into a casino with a stranger in a mask is another.

"I'm not asking you to," he says. "There's this lounge thing around the corner. It's usually pretty empty."

Empty. Empty is a double-edged sword for any girl. I mean, on the one hand, it lowers the risk of my parents seeing me—let's be honest, if they walk by right now, I'm toast—but also, I don't know this guy. Like at all.

Maybe I'm just being paranoid or maybe this is what Jayla means when she says I'm afraid to take risks. Worse comes to worst, I could probably stab him with these shoes—which are killing my feet, by the way—plus there's pepper spray in my clutch. Mom doesn't let me leave home without it.

"One sec," I say, holding up a finger. I pull out my phone and fire off a text to Jayla, letting her know I left and who I'm with, and reminding her that his sister is running the merch table.

She writes back almost immediately: **OK, check in when you get where you're going so I know.**

"Ready?" I ask, sliding my phone back in my purse, and he nods, pushing off the wall he was leaning against, the one covered with a giant ad for The Geekery. I fight the urge to flip it off but can't manage to hold back the scowl.

"Everything okay?" Bats asks, following my gaze.

"Yeah, sorry, I know that's your boss or whatever. Gotta love our corporate overlords, right?" That's about as polite as I can be about our enemy number one.

It was bad enough when The Geekery was just famous for running indie shops out of business, but now that they're actively trying to take over comic lines like Vera's too—just, yikes. I didn't even know it was possible to hate something so much.

Plus, Vera and The Geekery's owner-slash-CEO, Mark Everlasting—by the way, could his name *be* any more pretentious?—have been trading barbs every chance they get since they paneled together a few cons ago. The moderator made some comment about them repping both sides of the industry and asked if they would ever collaborate. Mark said he would definitely be open to bringing her on board, and she responded by literally laughing in his face . . . which he deserved. I mean, if Vera is the Princess Leia of the comics scene, then he's Palpatine for sure. But yeah, her reaction went a little bit viral, and now their mutual dislike has ramped up to a full-on war.

"Come on," Bats says, pulling me away from the sign and leading me down the hallway.

CHAPTER FOUR

Ridley

THE LOUNGE AREA is nice and empty, which is good considering we're a peacock and apparently a middle-management bat. I found this place the other night when I was stress-pacing around the hotel and have been sporadically hiding out here ever since. Other than hotel employees or a few random stragglers, no one ever comes in.

I drop down into an oversized red velvet chair, and she sinks into the one beside me, kicking off her shoes and tucking her feet up underneath her. She's sort of half sitting on her knees thanks to the tightness of her dress, and I try not to stare at the way the slit on her thigh creeps up a little higher than it's meant to. I squeeze my eyes shut, trying not to be a creeper.

dontstaredontstaredontstaredont

My hands are all sweaty, which is the only reason I let go of hers in the first place, and I rub them on my jeans, trying to be discreet. I'm trying to be as casual and seem the least freaked out as possible, but.

"Are you going to take that off?" She flicks my mask, dragging my attention back to her face.

"I don't think so?" I say. I don't mean it as a question, and yet. She kind of makes a face, and a fresh round of self-consciousness washes over me. "I can, if you need me to."

"I don't know if I *need* you to—"

"Okay, great," I say, and she makes another kind-of-confused face that makes me feel like I missed something. And I probably have. I miss a lot when my head is spinning out with nerves like this.

"Are you ever going to answer me, though?"

I scrunch up my face; didn't I just?

"How'd you end up at the prom if you hate crowds so much?"

Oh. That. I shrug. I could tell her the truth, that it's my father's event and my deep-seated insecurity about my place in my family has left me desperate for approval and validation that never comes, but that seems too heavy to drop on someone whose only real conversation with me so far has been when I said "Nice balloon" and she said "What?"

Time to deflect.

"Why'd you leave if you love it so much?" I don't mean to be blunt, but I also really want to know.

"I wanted to talk to you more," she says like it's no big deal. Like she didn't just dump a shit ton of dopamine right into my brain, making it hard to think.

"Same," I lie, or half lie, really, because it seems like the right thing to say, but also because in this moment I can almost believe it's that simple.

dontfuckthisupdontfuckthisup

I shake my head a little, and she leans forward to catch my eye.

"Are you okay?"

My leg is bouncing again, the urge to run nearly overwhelming, but this is fine, I'm fine, I got this. But man, it would be nice if my bullshit could come off a little more low-key.

"Yeah," I say, but my voice sounds strange. She sets her hand on my knee, and I jerk it away, not because I want to, but because I have to. "I just get—I don't know. Sorry." I feel my cheeks heat furiously and pray my mask is hiding it.

"Hey," she says, and I snap my eyes to hers. I should have just gone to my room. I should have never tried to pull this off. I— "Did you know that peacocks are omnivores?" she asks, and that shuts my brain up real quick.

"Huh?"

"They're omnivores. Most people think they just eat seeds and vegetables and stuff, but they eat bugs and frogs and anything they can catch, really. And they roost in trees so that tigers don't get them while they sleep."

"Okay?" I sort of say-ask, narrowing my eyes.

"Did you also know that bats have belly buttons?"

"What are you talking about?" And it's possible I found the one person on this earth who's even weirder than I am, because what?

"They do; they have belly buttons because they're mammals, not birds. In fact, not only that, but they're the only mammals capable of powered flight. Pretty wild, eh?"

"They have belly buttons?" I ask, tilting my head. I have no idea what's happening right now, but the idea of bats flying around with little bat belly buttons is somehow both cute and disturbing.

"Yep," she says, and the smile is back, that goddamn smile. And that's when I realize my leg has stopped bouncing and I can breathe again. This weird-ass girl and her random facts just talked me down from the mother of all panic attacks. That's . . . new.

I take a long breath and catch her eye again. "Thanks," I mumble. "Like, a lot."

"For schooling you about bats and birds?" She ducks her head. "You're welcome, I guess."

"No, for—"

She waves me off. "My mom used to tell me random facts whenever I got nervous before recitals. We had a giant book of weird facts she'd cart around—worked like a charm every time."

"Recitals?"

"It's a long story. So, was it the dancing or the crowds?"

"Crowds." I wince. "But I also can't dance."

"Can't or don't?"

I shrug. "Is there a difference?"

"There's definitely a difference." She laughs and pulls her phone out of her tiny purse thing. "Hang on, I promised Jayla I'd tell her where we went. If I don't, she'll have the police swarming the place. So, if you're, like, a secret murderer or whatever and this was all a trap, you should probably just go now."

"I'm not," I say, trying hard not to overthink the fact that it's probably exactly what a secret murderer would say. "But I'm in awe that you essentially implemented a dead man's switch during our two-minute walk to this lounge. Very impressive."

"Yeah, well, I'm nothing if not resourceful." She smiles again, and it's a little bit contagious. "You have a dimple," she says, like it's something new and noteworthy.

"Nothing gets past you," I answer, and then bite the inside of my cheek. Was that rude? I was going for playful. Did she think it was rude? She probably did. I should stop talking. I should go.

"I like it," she says, and leans forward to poke her finger in it. I pull back, not because I don't like it. I just . . . wasn't expecting her to touch me.

"Sorry." She shoves her hands under her knees, and no, no, don't make that face. It was fine, maybe. I don't know. But nothing really comes out, so I just sort of shrug.

"You're fine," I say after too long because I'm awful at this. "It just caught me off guard."

"I find it hard to believe that you're ever off guard."

"I'm trying to be. Right now, anyway." I shake my head again. "I suck at meeting new people, sorry." Wow, nice, Ridley, nothing says flirting like dumping your social anxiety all over someone you just met.

"Same," she says, which seems fake, but okay. She waves her hand in front of me. "I'm digging this whole shy, stammering thing you have going on, if that helps you relax any."

I laugh; I can't help it. "You are definitely the first person who's ever said that."

"Well, it's true."

I narrow my eyes, looking for any hint that she's lying, and finding none. "I'm really glad you lost that feather."

"I'm really glad you picked it up." She leans forward and flicks the side of my mask again.

And I know she wants me to take it off. Hell, I even sort of want to take it off—like it's probably really fucking weird that I haven't—but it still feels safer in here. Like I'm watching it unfold somehow. Like maybe there's a chance I won't overanalyze every second of this conversation after it's over, because it happened to Office Batman instead of shithead Ridley. Also, I probably have those annoying red indents all over my face from wearing it all night, so.

We sit in silence for a second, just looking at each other—her through her feathers and me through my mask—but it doesn't feel weird. It feels . . . nice? Until she clears her throat and sits a little straighter, and I stare down at my shoes, willing my foot not to tap.

"How did you end up working for Satan's Comics with your sister tonight? Is it some kind of, like, sibling purgatory program or something?" she asks. "Did you do something really awful?"

"Satan's Comics?"

"Sorry, sorry, The Geekery." She rolls her eyes. " 'Satan's Comics' is just our little family nickname for it."

My stomach tenses. Right, she hates us, like everyone

31

else. Shit, even I do, and I own shares. Or will own shares someday. Maybe. If I'm in the will. Which I might not be, actually, but. "They aren't that bad, are they?"

"Oh my god." She frowns. "They've brainwashed you. Don't worry, I can help. Hurry, let's run away together. I'll introduce you to some real artists and a good comic shop, and we'll do our best to deprogram you before our evil overlords ever find out."

I do this snort-chuckle thing that I will definitely be cringing over for the rest of my life and shake my head. "Come on, they can't be as terrible as all that."

"You poor thing," she says, clutching her heart in mock horror. "Yes, they are. Do you know how many people they've put out of business? Not to mention the sort of events they promote." She makes a gagging face. "Plus, the way they go after Vera Flores now. I mean, come on."

Shit. Of course she would know about that—she's dressed as one of Vera's characters. She's probably as big a fan of hers as I am. If this girl finds out who my dad is, I'm totally screwed.

thinkthinkthinkthinkthink

"They do a lot of charity work," I point out, which sounds pathetic, but.

"Probably just for the PR," she says, which, fair. I should probably care that she's trash-talking my family's legacy, but the way she gets all animated and her eyes get all sparkly while she rants is a little bit addicting.

"Seriously, if you ever want to run away . . ." She laughs.

"Watch out, I might take you up on that," I say, the words just slipping out, and she smiles the kind of smile you can't fake, with the tip of her tongue sneaking out between her teeth. And I feel happy and sad at the same time and wish I was anyone else, because anyone else would be going in for the kiss right now, and I'm just sitting here staring.

Her phone dings. She reads a text message and frowns. "Shit. I have to go."

"You do?" I ask, trying to swallow the disappointment that's building like bile in my throat.

waitwaitwaitplease

Music starts playing—violins, maybe?—and it takes me a second to realize it's her ringtone. Which is surprising. I don't know what I expected, really, but I guess not classical music.

"Hello?" she says, wincing as she answers her phone. "Mom, I'm fine. . . . No. No! You do not have to come find me. Why are you even at the prom? . . . Uh-huh, sure, drink tickets, I completely believe that. I'm fi—okay, okay! Ten minutes? . . . Fine, five. Five. I'll be there. . . . Love you too. Bye."

"Everything okay?"

"Apparently, my mom showed up at the prom to 'give me drink tickets' and was pissed that I left without telling her, so now I have five minutes to make it to my room before I'm grounded for life."

I scratch the back of my neck, guilt turning it crimson. "I didn't mean to get you in trouble."

sorrysorrysorryyoucangopleasestay

"You didn't," she says, raising an eyebrow. "I knew what I

was doing when I left. This was basically an experiment anyway, so there was bound to be a learning curve."

"Experiment?"

whattheactualfuck

"Yeah, it's called 'stepping outside of my comfort zone.' You should try it." She pulls a pen out of her purse and scrawls some numbers up my arm. "Text me. Okay? I'm here all day tomorrow. I'll be working a booth, but maybe I can sneak out for lunch or something."

"Okay," I say, and then she leans forward and kisses me quick on the cheek before grabbing her shoes. I sit there stunned, my stomach doing a little flip as she runs off.

holyshitholyshitHOLYSHIT

CHAPTER FIVE

Jubilee

"GET UP," VERA says, flinging the curtains open wide so the sunlight slaps me in the face. I guess I'm still in trouble for yesterday. She's probably been hearing it all night since technically she's the one who went to bat for me. Still, this reversal of my parents' usual good cop/bad cop roles is slightly unsettling.

"I'm up, I'm up," I say, dropping my arm over my eyes. Jayla groans from the other bed. A quick glance at my phone tells me it's only eight a.m. "Why am I up, though?" I moan. The only time I willingly get up early on a Sunday is for string quartet . . . and this is not that.

"Because VIP hours start at eight thirty, and your mother and I decided that you will be helping us with that today, thanks to that stunt you pulled. God, Jubilee, what were you thinking? You know better than that. I trusted you to be where you said you were going to be."

Trust. Vera is huge on trust, and I definitely feel a little bit bad that she sees this as a violation of that . . . but also, come on. "I didn't go far, and Jayla knew where I was. I was being safe!" I push up onto my elbows. There are feathers and streaks of makeup on my pillow, and I don't even want to imagine what I look like right now.

Last night, I collapsed into my bed and fell asleep after spending an hour being lectured about everything, even though Jayla was still up watching *American Murderer*. We didn't even have time to dissect my speed date with Bats or the fact that—judging by the crown she came home with—she definitely won prom queen . . . and we probably won't until the car ride home either. Not if my parents keep this up all day.

"Safe? Safe is not wandering around a casino full of drunks by yourself late at night."

"I wasn't alone!"

"Oh, you think leaving with a strange boy makes it better?" Vera asks, turning to face me, and I realize my mistake too late. "Do you know how badly that could have gone for you last night? You just happily followed some rando out to a deserted hotel lounge! You could have been killed!"

"I said I was sorry." I groan, flipping the blankets back and storming into the bathroom. "What else do you want me to do? It was a bad decision. I get it!"

I slide the door shut and flip the shower on, hoping Vera will take the hint. A solitary feather still clings stubbornly to my eyelid, and it dangles in my line of vision with every blink. I pull it off and set to work wiping off the smeared green eye shadow, which is currently making me look like some kind of disco panda or something.

I step under the spray of the shower, trying to shove out the thoughts of how badly the night ended in favor of how well it began. Bats was so cute and nervous, and I've always had a weakness for dimples.

Jayla walks into the bathroom, letting out the steam and bringing a blast of cool air in with her. She flushes the toilet, scorching me under the water.

"Jayla!" I shriek.

"Sorry." She yawns. "Forgot."

I flick off the water and reach my hand out for a towel, which she tosses at me, and then she goes back to brushing her teeth. "Was it worth it?" she mumbles around her toothbrush.

I wrap the towel around myself and then grab a second one for my hair. "Was what worth it?"

"You and Office Batman."

"Maybe," I say, trying and failing to keep the grin off my face. Her forehead crinkles as I dart past her to get dressed.

"Oh my god." She spins around. "Another *boy?*" she teases. "That's two in a row, Jubi."

"I'm allowed to like boys," I remind her, tugging on my leggings.

"Technically, no one should be allowed to like boys," she says, grabbing her own clothes off a hanger and dropping them onto the bed. "But you do you."

"Stop it," I snort.

"Jubi, I love you and always will, but boys are gross. Don't come crying to me when he's all sweaty and smelly and just wants to talk about bacon and hot girls and Axe body spray."

"Okay, but that's like half of *our* conversations now."
I laugh.

"We do not talk about Axe body spray," she says, looking scandalized.

"But the rest—"

"It's different." She smirks.

And it is. Sorta. I mean, not the bacon thing. I'm pretty sure straights and queers have the same proclivity toward bacon. Probably. I can't say for sure, though. Neither of us are straight, technically. Jayla has a strict no-boys-allowed policy, and I'm . . . flexible on the topic. I haven't really put a label on it. I've only had one real boyfriend and I've never actually dated a girl, but I've had some pretty serious crushes, plus that one brief and glorious make-out session with Kai, Nikki's ridiculously hot nonbinary cousin. There are just certain things that make me turn my head, regardless of who they're attached to. Like, I'm endlessly fascinated by dimples and good hugs and people who can surprise me—which Bats did last night, repeatedly.

I'd be lying if I said I wasn't hoping to run into him today. But still, something nags at me that I can't quite put my finger on. I know Jayla was just joking about the two-boys-in-a-row thing, but a part of me is still wondering, *Is that okay?* I know I like more than just boys, but does it count if I haven't seriously dated anyone but?

CHAPTER SIX

Ridley

I KEEP HOPING she'll come by. That she'll run up to the booth and find me, with a big grin on her face. That the spark from last night will catch fire, burning down everything around us. That satellites will fall, wars will end, and life will become infinitely less shitty.

But it doesn't go like that.

In fact, I don't see Peak at all, just an endless stream of people asking if we're out of the con-exclusive Funko Pop. Which, yes, so stop.

I consider texting her anyway, cracking some joke about her just being in it for the Bat-Perks. I even pull my phone out of my pocket, my fingers curled tightly around it, her number burning up my arm where the ink stains my skin. It's right there, and she's right here, somewhere. I could try to find her or hit send on my phone or do anything to push down that first domino, but I don't.

Because it's pointless. Tonight, I'll be with my mom on

a plane back to our Seattle house, and . . . she'll be off to god knows where.

I hate Seattle. It's dreary and damp, and despite living there for years, I don't really know anybody. I had someone, a good friend, actually, okay, more like an almost boyfriend, but that . . . didn't work out. And Mom's never home, too busy running the West Coast offices, so I just sit in a house with too many windows, watching anime alone. It will never feel like home the way the Connecticut house did before my "incident," as my family calls it. The irony that I survived a backflip off the roof, only to lose my whole life anyway in the form of a cross-country "fresh start," is not lost on me.

Dad still lives in the old house, with Gray in an apartment nearby. They're only an hour or so away from this con, and every time I do this one, a part of me hopes we'll skip the hotel rooms and stay at home, or at least that he'll invite me back for dinner or something, but nope.

So yeah, it's pointless.

But also, maybe it isn't.

I let my mind wander, imagining what it would be like to get up and find Peak myself. To not cower in my dad's shadow, waiting for whatever happens next. I shove up my sleeve and jab her number into my phone, typing out a text message: **It was nice meeting you last night.**

Oh Jesus fuck. It was nice meeting her last night? Why did I go with that? I drop my phone onto the table in front of me and run my hands over my eyes.

stupidstupidstupidstupidstupidstupidstupid

My phone vibrates and my breath catches, the tiniest

bit of hope forcing its way into my chest. Maybe she liked my message. Maybe she's into awkward losers with anxiety issues. Maybe.

I flip it over only to see a text from my mother with my flight information. There's a forced apology saying that she'll be coming on a slightly later flight but she's arranged a car for me when I land in Seattle. It's fine. I mean, it's not, but it has to be. Yay, three-hour layover in a strange airport by myself.

I stare down at the screen for a few more seconds, waiting just in case. Allison crosses her arms and frowns at me from the other side of our giant corner booth. I flash her the most sarcastic smile I can muster. "I'm taking a break," I say.

"A break from what, staring at your phone?"

I scratch the side of my eye with my middle finger and walk away. My dad catches it and narrows his eyes—because of course this would all go down during the one moment he deigns to show up at the booth instead of schmoozing in the casino—and god, can I just not disappoint him for five seconds?

His jaw ticks as he walks toward me, and shit, this is going to be bad. This is going to be really bad. Dad's temper is never that great, but Dad's living-in-a-casino-and-partying-around-the-clock-for-three-days temper is next level. As in, last year he made half our teardown team cry because they parked to the right of the loading dock and he said to park on the left, so.

But right when he gets to me, right as he opens his mouth to let me know exactly how much of a fuckup I am . . .

one of his buddies walks up, and Dad's whole demeanor changes. His face softens and he looks welcoming, almost happy, as he clamps his hand onto the other man's shoulder and says, "Chuckie, where have you been hiding?" And off they go back out to the casino. To the casino *bars*, more accurately.

And okay, nice. Crisis averted, I guess? As long as I don't think too much about how he must not even care enough to yell. It's fine. It's whatever. It's not like today can get any shittier anyway. I have a long flight alone ahead of me, and Peak never texted me back or even came to see me—unless she did, and that's why she's not writing back, which sucks worse. And what right does Allison have to question me, anyway? I'm an Everlasting, at least by blood, and she's just my father's latest lay. So yeah, maybe I flip her off again, just once more, as I disappear into the mass of people around us.

For once, I think I have something better to do.

• • •

The crowd in the convention center is suffocating, all the jostling and the pushing, and there are so many crying kids because Sundays are always half-price family day. My breathing picks up, and I start mapping my escape routes, fighting my urge to run. But I'm a man on a mission right now: I'm gonna finally talk to my comics idol, Vera Flores.

I've been too chickenshit to ever approach her before, double so now that she's officially my dad's nemesis or whatever. But having a cute girl dressed as one of Vera's characters tell me I should try stepping out of my comfort zone kind of felt like a sign. And judging by the fact said girl didn't return my text, it clearly wasn't a sign that she and I were meant to be.

So maybe it meant this.

Peak said it was an *experiment*. Like going to meet Vera is an experiment, one that currently has me on the verge of hyperventilating on the showroom floor, but.

I squeeze my hands until my nails pinch into my palm, and then cut a corner toward Artist Alley. The booths are smaller there than over on the vendor side, more crammed together. It's where all the artists and writers sit, clamoring for attention and shouting things like "Hey, you like scary books?" There are a bunch of Marvel and DC dinosaurs all in a row, and a pile of indie artists across from them. I stop at a table with a giant squirrel banner, which, okay, weird, but I take a bookmark anyway.

I relax a little when I finally see it.

Her banner is large but unassuming. It's got the cast of *Fighting Flock* in an action pose and her name written across the top in block letters. I take a breath, hold it, and then exhale. I got this. I can walk up to her and tell her that she's amazing and that her newest comic about an immortal teenage superhero who just wants to stop, to rest, to be done, speaks to me on a level that no book ever has.

dontscrewthisup

Vera Flores—well, Vera Flores-Jones since her wedding a couple years ago—has been my favorite person on the scene for a long time, even before her newest book.

Everything she puts out is super diverse and often queer as fuck, which I guess is to be expected when the business is run by a gay Latinx, but still. She is the future personified, and I love her for it. And I'm intimidated by it. And technically, she's the enemy and my dad would kill me if he found out I was over here. Which is why I'm standing back and gnawing the shit out of my lip, watching her line move without me in it.

This should be easier, I think. As the kid whose parents own one of the biggest comic-store chains in the country, the son of "the man who helped make comics mainstream," I should be able to meet anyone, right? Like, I shouldn't be so goddamn freaked out right now. Sometimes, sometimes I can. I've eaten pizza with the guy who plays Captain America in the movies, brought water to the people who created Ms. Marvel, shown Stan Lee and his assistant where the bathroom is. So yeah, I should be able to. Except.

Except.

Vera Flores-Jones is different. She makes her own way and tells stories that actually say something, that actually *matter* to me. She's the self-made person that my dad pretends to be, and he'll always hate her for that, but I don't. I could never.

"Hey, kid, you okay?" someone asks. It's the artist across from Vera, and he looks a little worried.

"Yeah, great," I say. "I'm just in the middle of an existential crisis because I disappointed the one person whose approval I'm most desperate for, and I met a girl who won't text me back, and tonight I have to fly across the country by myself, and I'm spiraling into a deep depression, and my anxiety disorder is *not* helping with that. How are you?"

"Uh, good?" he says, and wow, yeah, I've got to get that whole trauma-dumping thing under control.

"Awesome," I say. "Well, I'm just gonna get back to it, then." The guy gives me a confused nod, and I inch closer to the edge of Vera's table to check out the prints she's selling. I linger as long as I can without making it weird, before slotting myself in line behind the others. I'm three people away and still torn on my print—a fish guy with some girl underwater or a creepy clown—when somebody gently pushes past me.

"Sorry, excuse me, sorry," she says, not even looking at me, and holy shit, it's Peak. Of course she'd be here; she's probably the biggest Vera Flores fan on the planet, based on her cosplay last night.

And I didn't even get to talk to her about it last night, since I was so busy freaking out. I bet she even has the original Kickstarter editions of the books like I do, I bet she's memorized half the comic scripts, I bet she knows it all. And I swear to god I will drop to one knee and beg her to leave with me right now if she'd only turn around and recognize me—even if she did cut in line.

Except Peak doesn't stop in front of the table when she gets to it; she goes behind it and hands Vera a bottle of Gatorade and a protein bar. It's almost my turn at the table, and I don't know what is happening, and now I can't decide whether to walk away or pray she looks up.

"Mom said to make sure you eat something. Do you want me to watch the table for a while so you can take a break?

I can tell people to come back later," Peak says like it's no big deal. Like she isn't sitting beside *the* Vera fucking Flores.

"No, baby, it's fine. We only have a couple hours left; tell her I'm good. I will take this, though, thanks." Vera nabs the protein bar and turns back to the man in front of her table. I shift so I'm slightly hidden behind him and try to discreetly observe Peak.

She sits at the table for a minute, messing with the Sharpies and restocking some of the prints while Vera talks to the fan in front of her. She asks Vera again if she's sure, and Vera waves her off with a good-natured shove, telling her to quit hovering and go back to the vendor booth in case they need help. I watch their easy interaction, a little confused. Is Peak a con volunteer? An intern of Vera's?

I cut out of the line to follow her. Yes, I am missing my big opportunity to talk to Vera, but what do they say about never meeting your idols? Plus, this is important. I'll never stop obsessing if I don't get to the bottom of the mystery. It's not that I'm being a stalker by following her; I just want to see where she's going.

dontbecreepydontbecreepydontbecreepy

Maybe it is stalkery. I don't know. What does it matter, anyway? I'll be on a plane in six hours and never see her again. I just want to know how she fits. The peacock dress probably would have won the prom cosplay contest if she hadn't ditched with me. And I had assumed she was just a fan. But now.

But now?

She waves at a couple other artists as she walks by, and okay, weird, how does she know them? They're big artists too, Vera's level or higher, and they're waving at her like they're old friends. She's got to be an intern or something. Vera probably introduced her. Wait. What if she's not an intern—what if she's an apprentice who draws similarly kick-ass comics? Be still, my heart. Maybe she's beautiful *and* nice *and* talented. That should be illegal. It's not fair to the rest of us drudges. But Jesus.

I trail behind her until she walks into another booth, and then I freeze.

shitshitshitshitshitshitshitshitshitfuckshit

It's Verona Comics, the shop and publishing line that Vera owns. It's not unusual for artists—especially ones as big as Vera—to have a table in Artist Alley with everybody else and another one for their shop or publisher itself. This one appears to be carrying their old comics and toys and promoting their line.

Peak hands some change back to the woman running it, who looks so familiar. It takes me a minute to place her, and I wouldn't if I wasn't obsessed with Vera, but the woman Peak's talking to is Lillian Jones. The same Lillian Jones who supplied Vera Flores with her new and improved hyphenated last name a few years ago. She gives Peak a kiss on the cheek and Peak smiles, dropping into a chair in the corner. When I glance from Lillian to Peak, I realize that they definitely have the exact same eyes and nose.

No. I cannot be texting Vera's stepdaughter. I cannot be flirting with her. There has to be some other explanation. Maybe she's just an intern after all. An intern that Lillian . . . kisses on the cheek?

"You looking for something in particular?" I jump at the voice. It's Peak's friend with the awesome Shuri cosplay. She's in leggings and a T-shirt now, though, and looks to be around my age. Does everyone work here?

I shake my head and mumble, "Just looking," and she goes off to help the next customer. I pretend to be checking out a rack of comics but pull out my phone and google Vera instead. There are tons of pictures of her and Lillian, but I have to scroll forever to find one of their whole family. Maybe Peak's an outcast like me, which shouldn't make me feel reassured, but it does.

But then I find it, an old wedding picture that Vera posted on the Verona blog a few years ago. And there's Peak, smiling, walking them both down the aisle. The logical explanation is that Peak is . . . Vera's stepdaughter. Shit.

And I happen to know that Vera's shop isn't all that far from my dad's house. Which means Peak might not be that far from my dad's house. Which means . . . absolutely nothing. Because I'm flying back to the other side of the country tonight.

fuckfuckfuckfuckfuck

I'm still squinting at the wedding picture so hard, it's blurry from my eyelashes, when a text message scrolls down across my screen.

I don't recognize the number, but the response is unmistakable: **Hey! How goes it in the Batcave?**

I flick my eyes up, glancing at Peak, who is now staring down at her phone. I shouldn't respond. I should blend back into the crowd and forget any of this ever happened. Forget about everything but going back to grab my duffel bag and getting as far away from her as possible because this can't happen. It couldn't before, but it definitely can't now.

I look down at my phone. I mean to slide it into my pocket, I swear I do, but instead I find myself firing off another text: **Glad to see you didn't get eaten by any tigers last night, Peak.**

And as I turn to leave, my stomach in knots, I can see that she's smiling.

CHAPTER SEVEN

Jubilee

"PUT YOUR PHONE down," Jayla practically growls, swiping it out of my hand. Her car swerves a little when she leans over, and I glance behind us with a guilty look.

"Careful," I say.

We're driving back home from the con, just me and her. My parents are driving in the store van right behind us, definitely ready to scream if we so much as go a mile over the speed limit, but still, it's like being in a tiny little freedom bubble for the next hour. But if they think we're goofing off in here at all, I'm going to be back in the van, suffocating under a pile of comics, while Jayla drives alone in her little Civic.

"You're a terrible copilot. Who are you texting, anyway?"

"Nobody," I say, trying to swallow down the smile threatening to break across my face.

"You're talking to that guy again, aren't you?"

My cheeks get all warm. I hate being obvious. "Maybe." I scoop my phone up off the floor. We've been texting nonstop since he sent that endearingly formal *It was nice meeting you* text. Who even does that? It was six thousand shades of cute.

"What do you guys even talk about? The fact that he decided to go to the biggest cosplay event of the weekend dressed as Office Batman? Or the fact that it's weird people want to cosplay as a maladjusted man who dresses in a bat suit at all?"

"Close."

She glances at me out of the corner of her eye, one perfectly arched eyebrow reflected in the rearview mirror. "Really?"

"Well, close in the sense that he just texted me a picture of a baby-bat nursery."

"I'm lost."

"It's a long story."

"Try me," she snorts.

"You kind of had to be there?"

"I was across the hall, so I basically was." She sighs, messing with her septum piercing until the ball is centered. "Just tell me."

"Well, we were talking about bats having belly buttons last night—"

"As one does." She laughs.

"And then today he found a picture of an actual bat belly button, which then devolved into this whole weird sky puppy conversation and—"

"Sky puppy?"

"He didn't make up the term or anything. A lot of people call them that."

"He calls bats 'sky puppies'?" She grimaces.

"What's wrong with that?"

"I don't know. Instead of getting to know you, he's sending you bat pictures. That's weird. That's a weird thing to do, Jubilee."

I didn't think it was weird; I thought it was cute. What does she expect? I've known him for like twenty-four hours; it's not that deep. I roll my eyes. "Oh, what, is he supposed to be sending me dick pics on day one?"

She bursts out laughing, and I cross my arms. "What's so funny?"

"Nothing," she says, struggling to catch her breath. "Just that there's a whole world between baby-bat memes and dick pics, you know? Maybe you could find someone more in the middle."

"I don't really want to find anyone; this is strictly for the good of my music," I huff. "And hey, you encouraged this when I told you what this weekend was about."

Jayla messes with her stereo, plugging in her phone and pushing play. Loud music starts thumping through the speakers, making the world vibrate in her rearview mirror. I glance behind me; I can't help it.

"Relax, they veered off to get gas ten minutes ago."

"Thank god."

"You're gonna ghost this guy, though, right? The whole point of con crushes is that you leave them at the con. It doesn't really work if you don't."

"Yeah, probably," I say. "Besides, he texted me earlier that he lives in Seattle and is flying back there tonight, so it's not like we could ever be a thing anyway."

Jayla glances at me. "I thought you didn't have time for . . . things."

"I don't," I say, fumbling with my phone. "I'm just saying, even if I did—"

"Right." But then she peeks at me again, her eyebrows furrowing. "I'm starting to think you actually *like* like this boy."

"I don't even know him." I'd want to, I think, if there were enough hours in the day and he didn't live on the complete opposite side of the country. But there aren't and he does, and I have a cello to get home to.

Jayla goes back to staring at the highway. "Mm-hmm."

"I don't," I say again, not sure if I'm trying to convince her or myself.

CHAPTER EIGHT

Ridley

THE CON FINALLY ended at five, and an hour later, we're barely halfway through teardown. Dad's crew is currently boxing merchandise and running hand trucks full of comics out to the vans as fast as they can, probably hoping to escape a repeat of last year. I'm mostly standing around, chewing on my lip, trying not to combust. I'm so keyed up, I can't take it, between Peak—who I absolutely shouldn't still be texting but yet compulsively am—and trying to convince myself I don't actually care that I'm about to fly to Seattle by myself while Gray and my dad get to stay here.

I grab a box of leftover glow sticks and carry it out with the guys to the loading dock. Grayson's driving me to the airport soon, but she's still making the rounds, hugging pretty much every single person she knows—i.e., every single person still here. Most of the smaller vendors and artists are already done with teardown, just mingling with friends before they hit the road. Vera is already gone, and Peak along with her, but we've been texting nonstop since she hit the road.

My flight's not for three more hours, and I try not to think about the fact that our house is only forty-five minutes from here the way Gray drives, and I could conceivably go see it quick before hitting the airport. Not that seeing it would make it easier to leave. It would just be nice to be asked. There are so many things I want to know too, like is my room still the same, is the tree fort still there, does anybody notice I'm not around?

I slide the box into the van, frowning at my own neediness, and turn around only to be met with the sight of my dad stalking toward me, Allison in tow. His eyes are bloodshot, his forehead is creased, his mouth open and ready to yell, and this is not what I meant by wanting to be noticed. There's no way to escape without making a scene, so I just brace myself and try to remember to breathe.

I'm outside, the sun is setting, it's cold but not unbearably so, my dad is going to scream at me, and it will be okay, even if it is not okay. Radical acceptance, my ex-therapist said, is the key to life. Meet life on its terms, even if the terms are totally fucked up. I thought it was bullshit then, and I still do, but.

"If it isn't the prodigal son. Back to help now that everything's over," Dad slurs. He's drunk, probably courtesy of his pal "Chuckie." Judging by the way he keeps rubbing at his nose, probably more than drunk too.

"Hi, Dad," I say, standing a little bit taller. Hopefully this will prevent him from also yelling at me for slouching.

"Where the hell have you been? Allison told me you didn't come back until the con was over."

Of course she ratted me out. Of course. I look at the

ground to the right of him, hoping this will end quicker if I don't make eye contact.

"Did you think it didn't matter? You flip her off and disappear, and you think that's fine? After you left the goddamn prom last night too? What do you think I bring you here for? You're a brand ambassador, Ridley. I bring you here to work."

"I thought—"

"Thought what?" He takes a step closer. "You're on my time here, and I expect you to do as you're told." Each word he says is punctuated by the stab of his finger against my chest, and I flinch away from the smell of the alcohol on his breath.

itsokayevenifitsnotokayitsokayevenifitsnotokay

But that's not quite true, is it? Not when your dad is slurring insults in your ear. And it shouldn't sting when he calls me useless, and it shouldn't crack me in places I'd never say. And I'm not crying—I'm not—I'm just staring at the ground near his shoe, studying it because I want to and not because I'm scared.

imnotscared

"Look at me when I'm talking to you," he says, and I shoot my eyes to his, taking it in—the disheveled hair, the crumpled clothes, his skin wrinkled in places I've never noticed before. I don't think he's stood this close to me since I was little.

And I shouldn't still hope he'll catch himself, apologize, and hug me. I shouldn't. And even Allison—Allison, who is nearly the same age as my sister—is tugging at his shoulders and telling him to quit it now, and the guys at the loading dock have all walked away, some shooting sad glances behind them. But he doesn't stop, and I'm just standing there, pressed against the van with wide eyes, nodding while he calls me a piece of shit, like *yes, sir, you're correct.*

itsfineitsfineitsfineitsfineitsfine

Even Allison's looking at me with pity now, and good, because this is all her fault, and I rub my eyes with the palms of my hands, every word he spits a sliver shooting straight to my heart and—

icant

I want it to stop; I need it to stop. My phone buzzes in my pocket, the sensation overwhelming against my leg, and I slide it out without thinking, because, god, if ever I needed a lifeline, it's now. I hope it's Gray, but I don't even care who it is. And I realize too late that it's the exact wrong thing to do.

"Pay attention when I'm speaking to you," my father shouts, banging his hand on the side of the van, and even Allison is freaking out now, saying she'll call security if he doesn't stop. Allison, who feeds me to the wolves every chance she gets, and oh, this is bad, this is bad, and his hand is still slamming against the van, and his spit is flying in my face as he screams at me about respect and duties and obligation and how I am falling so, so short of it all. He knocks the phone out of my hand, and it skitters across the ground, and there it goes, my link to the outside world, lost and cracked. I dig my nails into my hands and scrunch my eyes shut, and I wait and wait and pray he stops.

"Allison saw you at the Verona booth, Ridley. What were you doing?" And here comes the paranoia; I should have known.

"You followed me?" I ask, and Allison looks away.

"Come on, Mark," Allison says softly. "Let's go back inside."

"What were you doing?" he asks again. "What did you tell her?"

"Nothing, I swear," I say, my voice a near whisper.

"Don't lie to me, Ridley." He leans closer, panting harsh, furious breaths, and all I see is the smudge of white powder still stuck in the corner of his nose and the hate in his eyes, and Jesus Christ. Jesus Christ, okay.

tapouttapouttapout

"I think I have an in at Verona. I was checking it out," I croak, my voice sounding tinny and garbled. Or maybe it's just that my brain feels so far removed from this situation, which is both happening to me and not, which is both okay and not. And I feel cold, so fucking cold and heavy, like my blood turned to lead, and I just need to lie down.

Dad's mouth opens and shuts, and he leans back a little. Enough that I can kinda slump down, that I can suck in air that doesn't smell like booze and fear.

"What do you mean?"

"I don't know," I say, losing my nerve. I skitter to grab my phone, but he grabs my arm, not hard enough to bruise but hard enough to hurt, and I freeze.

"What do you mean, you have an in?"

dontdontdont

But it's every man for himself in times like these, and I won't go down with this ship. Except.

Except.

Her feather burns in my pocket, and I press my lips

together in a tight line, one last-ditch effort to keep the words inside. But it's not like I'll ever see her again anyway. And she'll probably stop texting me once she's back home and busy with her real life. So if it's her or me—

He loosens his grip on my arm, rubbing it up and down, then letting it go completely and dragging his hand through his hair. He looks confused, surprised, and while his eyes are still bloodshot, he looks a little bit more like the guy I knew way back when. The guy who didn't drink so much, the guy who took me golfing that one time when I was seven and commissioned my own Venom comic for my eighth birthday. I've had enough people tell me everything happens for a reason. Maybe this is the reason. Maybe this is the way back.

itsnot

It could be, though. I flick my eyes to Allison, who's being quiet now. And my dad, he doesn't *smile* smile, but his lips turn up in the corners while he waits. "What do you mean, Ridley?"

I link my fingers behind my neck, staring at the asphalt as I say it. "I met Vera's stepdaughter at the prom. That's who I left with. We've been texting, and—"

My dad grabs my shoulders. "Does she like you?"

I shrug.

"Ridley. Ridley!" he shouts, like I just handed him the Holy Grail. "Think of how much intel you can collect for us to help with acquisitions." And he pulls me into a hug. A hug. And I can't remember the last time I had one of these, especially from him. "I could kiss you." He laughs, letting me go. And I think, *You used to once, every night before bed. What changed?* But I don't say it. I know what changed. I couldn't take the pressure, and he couldn't take the disappointment. Maybe this time I could make him proud. Maybe this time it could be different.

I wish I didn't like the way he walked me back to our booth with his arm around me. Or the way he raised my arm up in the air when we walked up to Gray, like I was some kind of champion, even though I felt ashamed and unsteady on my feet.

I wish I could say that I pushed him away and left with my integrity intact.

That I got on the plane instead of going out to dinner with him for the first time in years.

That I didn't feel a swell of pride when he asked me to sit next to him, while Grayson ended up at the other side of the table, where she couldn't hear anything.

That I didn't tear up when he asked me to stay in Connecticut with him, at the old house, in my old room, and said that Mom would have my stuff shipped out when she got back home.

Or when he promised to buy me a new phone to replace the one he just trashed.

Or when he said he had a place for me in the business, finally—on the recon team.

I wish the voice telling me that this was *wrong, bad, very terrible* was louder, and the voice weeping *finally, always, please* was quieter.

I wish.

CHAPTER NINE

Jubilee

I DRAG MY bow across the strings, glancing once at the piles of books around me—Bach's cello suites right on top—before shutting my eyes with a smile. After a weekend away, tonight I play for myself—no plan, no audition—just me and my instrument and the sounds that we make. The fingers on my left hand press and arch and slide, sending the notes curling and curving through the air until a song takes form.

It's a cover of a song from one of my favorite bands. I was still working out the notes before I abandoned it to focus on my audition, but after a few days away, "embracing and absorbing life," I'm just happy to be back.

I've been playing cello seriously since the third grade. I don't think anybody expected me to stick with it, but the first time I made it groan and squeal under the power of my inexperienced fingers, I was hooked. I was creating sound. Other people were making sounds, sure, but it wasn't *this* sound; this squeal and shriek were mine and mine alone, and only for that second.

I loved it.

I think that's my favorite part of music, the impermanence of it. A book or a painting, when it's finished, it's done. People admire it, but it's become its final form—it is what it is. But music is never finished. Every piece changes when you play it; the note has heavier vibrato in this performance or draws out every rallentando in that one. People cover it and change it and sing it with their own voices or, in my case, transcribe it to cello.

Music is different. It's alive. It's an action and a reaction all at once.

Somewhere along the line, though, that impermanence, that change, has become a source of pain instead of pride. Playing has become less about the joy of it and more about getting it exactly right: holding the notes for precisely the right amount of time, calculating it for maximum impact. I've been chained to this chair practicing my audition repertoire for months, and now, nine weeks out, instead of making it better, apparently my calculations have only made it worse.

But tonight, I don't know, I feel like playing for the joy of it. If I can figure out how to shove this feeling into my audition, then I should be set. Better than set, even. I sink back into the music with a smile. Maybe this whole pushing-the-boundaries thing worked. I play harder, feeling my acceptance to the summer program get closer with every note. But I know to really do that, I need to be perfect. Consistently.

The summer program is open to kids from all over the world, and I can't help that tiny nagging voice that sometimes creeps up in my head and says, I know I'm good, but am I good *enough*? Maybe I'm getting ahead of myself—I haven't even been formally invited to audition yet. There's a whole first round where you have to apply and send in a résumé of all your musical experience and get recommendations before they even invite you to audition. I turned it all in a few weeks ago, and now I wait.

Even if I do make the cut, the board gives out exactly one scholarship in the high school program each summer—and I need to be the one to get it. I don't know how we'll ever afford it otherwise. I've even heard my parents worrying about that late at night. So yeah, consistently perfect, that's the goal.

I don't even notice my mom is in my room until she pokes me in the shoulder. I jump, my eyes flinging open, nearly dropping my bow.

"Sorry, hon," she says, tucking some of her hair behind her ear. It's wet; it must have started raining.

"It's okay." I set my cello in its stand and stretch my arms out while I flex my fingers. "You're home early."

"Late, actually," she says. "It's almost eight. You hungry? Vera's bringing home takeout."

I'm about to say no, but then I realize I definitely am. I glance at my phone; I've been playing for four hours, a full hour longer than my usual school-night practices. "Starving, apparently."

My mom pulls her hair back with a yawn and gives my shoulder a squeeze. I know the feeling; coming home from the con last night and diving into school today wasn't fun, but it was probably worse for her, sitting in a real estate office, praying someone will wander in needing to buy a house just so she can get paid.

"I'm gonna go change," my mom says. "I'll shout when Vera gets home."

I nod and sit on my bed. My cat, HP—short for Harry Potter, don't judge me, I was eight—jumps up and starts rubbing her head against me. I scratch under her chin for a second, pulling away when she stops purring and bites me. My phone lights up with another message, and I drop onto my pillow to check everything I've missed. Jayla and Nikki have both texted me about a dozen times—both separately and on our group chat—but it's Bats's message that I click on first.

I've considered asking his real name about a hundred times in the last twenty-four hours, but he never asked mine—he just calls me Peak—and I kind of like the mystery now. He's everyone and no one, ever evolving, a living thing, like music. He is a pleasant program that lives in my phone, and I'm happy to have him.

A close-up of a baby bat's face appears on my screen, along with the caption *hello*.

I send him back two crying-laughing emojis and a heart-eye one, and I wait, a smile etched on my face, when the three dots appear.

BATS: Where ya been, Peak?

ME: Around

BATS: . . .

ME: School and stuff

BATS: School is overrated.

I snort—if only he knew he was talking to someone ranked second in her class academically (screw you, Ivy Pasternek; I'm coming for your rank next year)—and try to find the perfect meme to send back. I grin when I see it. It's a tiny bat being held down with a single finger, and the caption says, *No, stop touching me! I am the night!* I press send with a little squeal and add **you, probably**.

I wait for those three dots to come back . . . but they don't. The smile starts to slide off my face, and I wonder if I somehow actually offended him. And then I twist my lips into a full-on frown. I meant to ghost him, I did, but then I started thinking— if one weekend away from cello land could help me climb out of my musical rut this much, then imagine what text-flirting until my audition could do. Jayla didn't exactly believe me when I told her my theory; her response was something like "for the music, sure, I believe that," but still.

My phone buzzes in my hand and I grin.

BATS: More than you know.

                                   ME: See, I'm onto you.

BATS: Let's hope not for both our sakes.

                                   ME: You're such a dork. ☺

CHAPTER TEN

Ridley

I CLICK THROUGH the website, tallying the missing assignments as I go. Eleven. Eleven assignments will get me back on track for graduating. Less than I thought, honestly, but more than I feel like doing. Keeping up with my high school work—online only now—was one of the requirements my mom set before agreeing to let me stay here. She must not have realized I was way behind before I even left.

Which means I probably have a *very* tiny window before she calls my dad to flip out on him about the missing assignments. Which would suck. I've been tallying the good days (the mental equivalent of a chalkboard saying *It has been __ days since the last incident*) and we're at five now.

Five is a good number, actually. I'll take it, especially when it comes to my dad, who hasn't been able to decide whether to kill me or ignore me for as long as I can remember, especially since the whole Chandler McNally thing last year. I shut my laptop and head downstairs, the steps of the old Victorian creaking in a way I sort of remember. I try not to be bitter about the fact that it's been so long I don't know where to step to avoid it. It's fine.

Gray's coming over tonight to help me strategize my plan to get in good at Verona. She was shocked when Dad informed his entire team that I had an in. She doesn't know that it's Peak. Mainly because I'm pretending it's not. I can keep her separate. This is easy, this is Compartmentalizing 101, and I'm a seventeen-year-old pro at this, so yeah.

Peak is Peak. She lives in my phone. She exists in the land of memes and magical one-off nights. It's nice, and it's mine. For once, I have something that is. Especially since Mom hasn't even bothered to send me more clothes and stuff like she swore she would. She's been *busy with work*, which is whatever. So yeah, Peak. Lives in my phone. Is my secret. Is her own separate thing.

If she happens to *also* give me enough dirt to make the entirely separate person called Jubilee Jones (compartmental-izing! yay!) like me enough to share some info my dad can use, then fine. What he does with that information has nothing to do with me. At least that's what I tell myself between stomachaches. It's just business. I can have my cake and eat it too. I don't feel guilty. I don't feel anything at all. Promise.

I open up the kitchen cabinet, huffing out a breath. I asked Dad to get Fruity Pebbles and Lucky Charms at the store, but he just restocked his PowerBars and protein shakes and talked to me about how important nutrition is if I want to bulk up. Considering I'm not trying to bulk up and that my entire being consists of a combination of sugary cereal and anxiety, this does me no good.

It's fine.

Then today he ordered me a pizza before he left, which I love, but he got pepperoni, which I absolutely hate. I like extra cheese. Peppers and onions in a pinch. Pepperoni over my dead body. I try to focus on the fact that he tried and not the fact that he got it wrong. Soon Gray will be here anyway, hopefully with some actually good food.

The door slams open as if on cue, and she comes flying in, nearly tipping the drink tray. Her arms are full of greasy bags; she's even got one in her mouth. I take the drinks and reach for the bag in her teeth. She growls before letting go, and I roll my eyes.

"Don't think you're getting any of those cheese fries just because you helped carry them," she says.

I laugh and bring it all into the living room, flicking on the TV and dropping onto the giant couch. I'm not totally sure if we're allowed to eat in here—I mean, Dad never does—but the way Gray follows me without hesitating says it's probably okay. I bet they do this kind of thing a lot.

I pretend that thought doesn't sting.

"How are you settling in?" she asks, pulling out various plastic containers full of more food than we can possibly eat. There are burgers and onion rings and chicken wings and regular fries and, yes, cheese fries, which Gray immediately slides out of my reach.

I huff and grab one of the burgers; it's about the size of my head and oozing BBQ sauce. "Everything's great."

"And Dad?" She shoves a cheese fry in her mouth.

"Is great too. He seems glad I'm here." Gray is the queen

of seeing what she wants to see, has been forever, so I know she won't catch the lie. The truth is, I still can't really tell what he thinks, and I spend most of the time staring at my phone, waiting for Peak to text.

Gray wipes her hands on a napkin, her mouth pinching in thought. "I know it's been . . . complicated between you guys, but I'm glad it's going good. This could be a chance for you guys to reconnect. It's been a long time."

She says it like that's normal, like being seventeen and still not having a connection with your dad is a regular thing. Maybe it is. I don't know. But I know that she and Dad—and she and Mom, for that matter—are practically best friends, so it seems a little bit like bullshit to me. My parents used to joke that Gray and I were so far apart in age that they had two "only children." But that always just felt like a nicer way of saying all they had was a daughter and the accident that came after her.

"Hey." She pulls a small box out of her bag and tosses it into my lap. "I'm really glad you're here."

I pick it up, my fingers tracing over the silver letters stamped into the side of the black box. "What's this?"

"Open it." She shrugs, taking another bite.

I pull the box apart, my forehead crinkling when I realize it's a watch. A very nice, very expensive watch, to be exact. "Gray . . ."

"Consider it a good-luck gift."

I run my hands over the silver face. "This is too much."

"Nah," she says, grabbing a chicken wing. "You deserve it. I'm proud of you for stepping up for this job. It could be a fresh start for you, for all of us, really. Besides, I never get to do stuff like this with you hiding out in Washington, so consider this me making up for lost time."

I bite my lip, my eyes feeling a little watery as I slide the watch onto my wrist and mess with the band.

"Okay, that's enough sappy shit for one night, though," Gray says. "Since this is your first time on a street team, I thought we'd talk strategy."

I want to roll my eyes at her, because it's a little bit insulting that she doesn't think I can hang out at a shitty comic store and watch what's going on without screwing it up . . . but she's probably right.

The street team is basically a euphemism anyway. Usually when you call people a street team, they're, like, out there promoting your brand, spreading the word and talking it up, that kind of thing. My dad's street team is the opposite. They're lurking quietly in the shadows of the industry, trying to tear stuff down or make it their own. Sure, some of it is innocent, but anything having to do with Vera Flores probably won't be. He doesn't want to re-create what she's doing; he wants to own her and everything she makes, and he wants revenge for making him look like a fool. Suddenly, I feel a little warm, a little out of my league, a little—

whatthefuckiswrongwithme

"Rid, you okay?" And I hate when she asks me that because I know what she's really asking: *Are you going to fall apart again?*

"Yeah, I'm great." I shove an onion ring in my mouth whole and chew with it open. Gray gags and throws a cheese fry at me, which sticks to my shirt. "And you said you wouldn't share," I say, biting into it with a flourish. She laughs, and it feels like a victory.

Crisis averted. For now.

"There's my annoying baby brother," she says, pulling files out of her bag.

I shouldn't preen at the sight of my name on a file. It should absolutely not make me feel this good. But Dad had his people put this together—specifically for me to read—and then made Gray carry it over, and that's probably the most thoughtful thing he's done for me in a long time. Which, shut up.

"All right, so the basics are all in here," she says, sliding the file over to me. "I know you've been a fan of Vera's work pretty much from the womb, much to Dad's dismay, but I think that will pay off here. You can use that awkward fan-boy energy to endear yourself to her. Just make sure her kid doesn't think you're using her to get to Vera."

"Even though technically I *am* using her to get to Vera," I blurt out, and shit, is that the sound of my conscience dying?

"You're okay with doing this, right?" Gray asks, her hand still pinning the file to the table so I can't open it.

"It's not a big deal," I lie. "I got it."

Gray looks at me for a second and then nods. "Okay, well, there's a lot of information in here. Study it, but don't memorize it. You don't want to accidentally say too much. Although you can probably pull that off better than most since you're such a Verona stan, but still, be aware of it."

"I got it, I got it. Read the file enough to have it down but not enough to come off as creepy."

"Right," she says, and she looks proud. "Generally, the people on the street team stop in and visit the store a couple times. Just grab some books, say you're new in town or whatever." She slides a paper out of the file. "Here's a list of titles to have them put on your pull list."

"I don't need a fake pull list." I cross my arms. It's insulting that they think I can't come up with one on my own. I've had a pull list—a list of comics the store preorders and holds for you—since I could talk. It used to consist completely of *DuckTales* and *Teen Titans*, but I'd like to think I've matured over the years.

"Ridley, come on, use the list. This is important. If you get Dad something he can use to make her sign on, you're going to be his hero."

His hero. That sounds nice. I would also settle for "person he vaguely likes."

I grab the paper out of her hand. "Let me see it." I scan it quickly; it's not bad—big enough to position me as someone the store wants to keep happy, but not so big that they get suspicious about where a kid like me would get all that money. There's a blend of indie stuff and titles from the big two, and . . . it isn't all that different from my actual list. I glance up at her. "How did you guys come up with these?"

"Dad brought in a bunch of market research people. They worked their magic and came up with a list that your average comic book consumer would have, I guess."

"Cool, cool, cool," I say, taking another bite of my burger

and frowning at the list because I am *not* average, not when it comes to picking books, and I resent the fact that some corporate suit developed some kind of algorithm that nearly figured me out. I've spent a lot of time curating my list, thank you very much.

"Anyway," Gray says, shooting me a weird look, "after that, just start hanging out around the shop more, work the daughter angle—which feels a little sleazy, not going to lie, but Dad said it was your idea, and I trust you."

"Yeah," I mumble into my burger.

She leans forward a little to catch my eye. "It was your idea, right, Ridley?"

"Yeah," I say, puffing out my chest. "Who else's could it have been?"

"Right." But it looks like she doesn't believe me. And now? Is now when she's going to look deeper? But then she goes back to eating and the look of concern slips away. "Enough work talk. How are things with Peak?"

And there it is, that little nagging feeling, subtle like having a piano dropped on my skull or stepping on a rusty nail.

imsuchanasshole

Deep breath. Compartmentalize. That's all.

"She's good," I say, which is true. She's been incredibly upbeat this whole week. It's a little unnerving.

"Just good?"

"What do you want me to say? She's great, I'm in love, we're going to get married?" I shake my head. "We text, Gray—that's it. She's funny, she's nice, but it's not like it's going anywhere."

"Why not?"

"Because it's not, Gray. Drop it."

I don't want to talk about her; Peak is mine, just for me, and even talking about it could dilute some of the magic. Or make things messier. I don't know. I'm compartmentalizing over here or whatever, and Gray needs to let me.

"Wow, okay." She crunches one of the boxes shut a little too hard. And oh no, I wanted tonight to be good.

"I'll let you pick any show you want if you drop it."

She freezes, looking at me out of the corner of her eye. "Even my werewolves?"

"Oh my god, Grayson, you are too old for that show."

"You're never too old for werewolves. That's a fact. Sorry, I don't make the rules."

"They're barely even werewolves! They're like Hollister models with five-o'clock shadows."

"Oh, so werewolves can't be hot? That's speciesist, Ridley. I'm disappointed."

"That's not what I said."

"Good—so you agree, then, werewolves are hot?"

"Oh my god," I groan, tossing her the remote.

"You'll watch it and you'll like it." She laughs. "Don't think I don't see the eyes you make at the alpha."

"Uh-huh," I say, trying to act like it's no big deal that she's joking about me crushing on a very hot, very male actor. She's the only person who didn't freak out about the "Chandler situation," as my parents refer to my brief and dramatic relationship with a state senator's son last year. I thought it was love; he thought it was something else—blackmail, mainly. It's whatever.

My mom yanked me from my private school when the pictures came to light, finally relenting and letting me attend classes online instead. She also immediately put me into counseling, which is hilarious because she didn't even do that after my dive off the roof at thirteen, the one that resulted in a broken leg, a sprained ankle, and too many bruises to count. To this day she insists I must have done it on a dare—even though I left a note.

So yeah, apparently liking girls *and* guys rates higher on the concern scale than . . . the other thing. I stopped going a couple months ago, though; I don't think my mom has even noticed.

I shift in my seat uncomfortably, but Gray has already started watching the show. I try to follow along, but I'm in a weird headspace now, so I mess with my phone to take my mind off things, relieved to see that Peak has texted me twice.

"Oh my god, why is this show so good?" Gray groans, actually groans, and I raise my eyebrows.

"Let's just agree to disagree on that," I snort. My phone buzzes again, and it's a picture of Peak's cat with its tongue sticking out a little. Only, Peak scribbled on the pic so it looks like the cat's wearing a Batman mask.

I smile and lean back in my seat. There are werewolves shoving people into high school lockers on my TV, and there's so much food, and my sister is smiling, and Peak is being cute, and for a second everything is not so bad. Given enough time, I could maybe get used to this.

CHAPTER ELEVEN

Jubilee

JAYLA SIGHS DRAMATICALLY and flips the page of her textbook. We're spending eighth period in the library for study hall, which means we have to be mostly quiet but can still talk a little. We have a history test in three days that we're both cramming for, though one of us is a bit more resentful about it. Jayla flips the page again, tapping her pencil until Nikki drops into the empty chair beside her and pulls it from her hand.

"Are you studying or trying to join Jubi in the music program?" Nikki asks a little too loud, which makes the librarian shush us. It also makes Ty Williams look up from the table next to us. She glances over to make sure he's looking and then pulls out her ponytail, letting her dark brown hair fall perfectly against her tan skin.

"Hey, Nikki," he says, sliding his chair back so he's closer to our table.

"Hey, Ty," she says, trying not to grin.

Jayla says Ty has been in not-so-secret love with Nikki

since the fourth grade and she's been in not-so-secret love with him right back, but since they both vaguely pretend otherwise, we just go along with it. Nikki flicks his hat off, and he makes a big show of scooping it up and dusting it off before shoving it back on his head.

"You're lucky you're cute, Hartley." And Nikki seems to swoon a little at the sound of her last name coming from his lips.

Jayla groans, ruining the moment. "This test is a third of our grade. How are you guys not freaking out?"

"It'll be fine." I sneak a peanut butter cup out of my bag and shove it into my mouth. "Relax."

"Easy for you to say—we can't all be musical prodigies destined to tour the world until we settle down to inherit publishing lines," Nikki says.

I shake my head. "If you think there's money in cellos or comics, you're nuts."

"Uh-huh, tell that to Marvel," Jayla says, casually holding up her Captain America folder and fanning herself with it.

I laugh as I flip to the next page of the study guide. "Verona Comics is hardly Marvel."

Sure, between Vera's freelance art jobs, the comic line she puts out, and the store, she does okay. Plus, my mom's real estate job has finally been picking up. But we're not Marvel level. We're not even Jayla level, where her parents can keep twenty dollars in a drawer for her at all times, replacing it whenever she takes it. We're just . . . okay. There's not really anything left over, but the bills are paid. Before Vera came along, though, we weren't on half as solid footing as we're starting to be on now. Like, there were a lot of postdated checks to my music teachers, and we pretty much lived off pasta and pancakes.

Nikki pulls out her notebook and starts studying too, and other than Ty asking to borrow a pencil—despite the fact that I saw him with one right before Nikki walked in—we settle into a comfortable silence while we read.

The bell doesn't work in the library; it's been broken since the end of last year. Even though I know the librarian will tell us when it's time to pack up, I grab my phone to check the time—and maybe my texts. But seriously, I have orchestra last period, and if I'm late, I'll spend the entire time dusting instruments instead of playing.

"Oh, you're pathetic," Jayla says, kicking my chair.

Nikki rests her head on my arm. "I think she's adorable."

"Who's adorable?" Ty asks, leaning back so far in his chair, he almost tips over. He flails around a little to regain his balance, and Nikki bites her lip to keep from giggling. "You know, forget it. I'm just gonna—" he says, pointing back at his homework sprawled all over the table in front of him.

"God, all you do is text with him now." Jayla slams her textbook shut, prompting another shushing from the librarian. "You barely even respond to my messages, but Bats friggin' texts you and the whole world stops."

I crinkle my forehead. "Why do I have to be texting you when you're one seat away?"

"I'm just saying, your response time has sucked since the con and it's annoying. You don't even know anything about this kid; he could be a catfish! You could be blowing me off for a catfish. I hope you're cool with that."

I roll my eyes. "How can he be a catfish when we've both met him?"

"I didn't meet him," she corrects. "I met his sister. At best, I glanced at him from across the hall."

"You shared an elevator with him," I say. "Plus, you thought his sister was cute."

"Irrelevant. It's been a week, and you still don't know his real name."

"So what? I know a lot of other stuff."

"Oh god." Nikki blushes. "I don't want to know."

I roll my eyes. "It's not even like that." And it's true—it's not like that at all, nothing even close to that.

"Then what is it like?" Jayla asks, arching an eyebrow.

I settle on "It's nice," which makes Nikki coo and get all dreamy-eyed again. "I like talking to him. He's funny."

"What if he's hideous under the mask? What if he's hiding some deep, dark secret?"

"I don't care," I snap. And I'm surprised by how true that feels, although I'm guessing by his absolute refusal to Face-Time that maybe there is something going on. Something he doesn't want to share.

Which is *fine*, because it's just harmless flirting, an attempt at getting the butterflies to last me through the audition. It's the texting equivalent of crossing my fingers or wishing on an eyelash—just a little extra insurance that may not make a difference but can't actually hurt. Jayla needs to relax.

"Are you coming to the soccer game tonight?" she asks,

changing the subject, and shit, I forgot about the game. I nod anyway, because unless I'm super sick, I always go when they play their rivals.

"I'll give you a ride after orchestra, then."

"Are you sure you want to wait?"

Jayla and Nikki both have early dismissal, and I don't. Jayla usually spends it getting in extra practice time, and Nikki usually walks home to check on her mom while she's waiting for us to finish up. I think it's awesome how dedicated Nikki is to her family, but Jayla says she wasn't like that before the accident.

I guess Nikki's dad does something in finance, and her mom used to be a pastry chef. They adopted her from Korea when she was two, and according to Nikki, they pretty much lived happily ever after until a drunk driver plowed through an intersection, hitting her mom's car and changing their lives forever. That was about a year before I moved here, though.

On her good days, her mom still bakes the most amazing desserts, which Nikki always brings in to share. On her bad days, Nikki says she can barely get out of bed. I can't imagine what it's like to have your whole life shift like that in the blink of an eye. It kind of makes me want to take this whole embrace-life thing a little more seriously.

"I can stay today; my dad is off," Nikki says, putting the cap back on her pen.

"You looking for something to do while you wait?" Ty shouts from the next table, but before she can respond, Mrs. Cavill, the librarian, is barking at him to quiet down and pack up.

"I'll see you guys in a little bit, then." I zip my book bag shut, and a picture of literally the cutest baby bat in all the world flashes across my phone screen.

"Gross," Jayla says, but I ignore her and text back a bunch of heart eyes.

As I walk into orchestra, I text my mom to let her know I'm going to the game, then click over to my conversation with Bats, ignoring the group chat with my string quartet. They think it's wild that I "waste my time" in a public school orchestra—their words, not mine—but I'll take any chance I can get to play.

"Phones off," Mrs. C says way too cheerfully. And even though I think that's a dumb rule, I hit the power button anyway. I suck in my lips and make a big show of dropping my phone into my bag. She's right; I have to focus. I have to get in the right headspace. I am infusing my music with passion. I am calculating exactly what it needs. I am exceeding expectations always. I am getting that scholarship.

CHAPTER TWELVE

BATS: Distract me. I'm begging you.

PEAK: What's wrong?

BATS: I just gotta get outta my head for a minute and I think we've exhausted every bat meme in existence.

PEAK: Want to talk about it?

BATS: No? Yes? I have to do something tomorrow. I can't tell if I'm dreading it or excited.

PEAK: I get it. I feel like that before some performances.

BATS: Are you going to finally tell me what you're performing? Or are we sticking with "a thing"?

PEAK: Two guesses.

BATS: Tap dancing?

PEAK: No. It's an instrument.

BATS: Okay, I got it.

PEAK: Yeah?

BATS: It's the kazoo. It's definitely the kazoo. I can tell. The moment I saw you in the elevator, I said there's a girl that knows how to blow.

PEAK: Yeah . . . um.

BATS: That . . . came out wrong.

PEAK: Right.

BATS: I didn't mean it like that. I swear.

PEAK: Moving on . . . Cello.

BATS: Cello?

PEAK: The thing I perform.

BATS: Are you good?

PEAK: Yes.

BATS: How good?

PEAK: Principal in the all-state orchestra good.

BATS: I have no idea what that means.

PEAK: It means I beat all the other cellists in the state.

BATS: Holy shit, Peak.
Send me something.

PEAK: What???

BATS: Do you ever record yourself playing?

PEAK: Mostly just for auditions.

BATS: Can I see?

PEAK: I'm totally going to regret this.
<u>**MVMT 1 Final Final For Real**</u>
It's not a video, but . . .

BATS: Wait. Was part of that the ringtone from prom?

PEAK: ☺ ☺ ☺ ☺ Maybe. You like it?

BATS: I fucking love it.

PEAK: It's Beethoven.

BATS: I have to go.

PEAK: You do?

BATS: I'm intimidated by your amazingness, so.

PEAK: You're a huge dork, you know that?

BATS: I do, actually? And I'm sorry, but it's a chronic condition. So yeah. Get in or get out on that front. Except please do not get out.

PEAK: Here I was worried you were luring me in with your awkward dorkiness, only to later prove yourself a dashing trust fund playboy or something. ☺

BATS: Dashing trust fund playboys can be dorks.

PEAK: Yeah?

BATS: I could be both.

PEAK: Sure.

BATS: I could!

PEAK: I said sure!

BATS: No you said "Sure." Totally different.

PEAK: You caught me.

BATS: ☺ ☺ ☺ ☺

CHAPTER THIRTEEN

Ridley

I JUST HAVE to pretend that I'm skateboarding to a random shop, in a random place, for a random reason. I just have to get a grip, stop digging my nails into my palm, will my heart rate to slow down, and act normal. I just have to be the complete opposite of everything I am.

It's fine.

I take a deep breath and focus on the sound of my skateboard on the concrete, the steady rhythm of the cracks on the sidewalk. I prefer to ride in the street, but the number of ghost bikes in this town tells me the drivers here are not especially observant. Sidewalks it is.

Skateboarding is a multipurpose hobby for me. One, it's practical—other than a couple lessons from my well-meaning aunt Mary in Michigan, no one ever bothered to teach me to drive. Two, it burns off a lot of nervous energy—well, normally it does, but nothing's touching that today. And three, skating is basically my art form. I can't draw, I can't play an instrument, but I can do an ollie impossible *and* a 360 hardflip, so my life isn't complete shit.

This morning was kind of decent, all things considered. Dad's been sort of trying, and even "sort of trying" is a massive effort for him. Like, when I was leaving, he handed me a pack of Pokémon cards and said, "Good luck today." Positive reinforcement is always thrilling, but I still haven't worked out if the cards were a nod to the old days, when he would have my nanny give them to me if I did well at school, or if he actually thinks I still like Pokémon. Both scenarios are equally likely, and to be honest, I don't even know which one I'd prefer.

I slow down about a block away from the comic shop and hop off, flipping my board up into my hand and then strapping it to my backpack. I'm kind of surprised by how sweaty I got, even in this cold March weather. This is not the first impression I want to make. I run my fingers over the watch Gray gave me; I could use a little good luck right now.

Shoving down the hood of my sweatshirt, I start to walk, trying hard not to think about what I'm really doing.

Peak texted me until I fell asleep last night, sending me music clips and keeping me distracted. How shitty it was to have her comforting me when I was freaking out about spying on her own shop is another thing I'm trying not to think about.

As is the fact that Vera is apparently a human lie-detector test obsessed with honesty, which I learned when Peak gave me the play-by-play of their argument about her leaving con prom.

Oh, and don't forget the fact that I'm starting to really like

Peak, and that I'm probably torpedoing that relationship for the faint chance of building one with my father. So yeah, no pressure today or anything. Nope, none at all.

Bells ring when I step in the shop, heavy gold things that dangle over the door. So much for quietly slipping in and observing undetected. Vera—*the* Vera Flores—pokes her head out of the back room. "Hey, kid, I'll be with you in just a second."

"You don't have to be," I say, and she crinkles her forehead. "I mean, I'm looking here at stuff. I'm new. I don't—I'm good. You can do whatever."

"Hey, Margot?" she says, and I didn't realize she was holding a phone until just now. "Let me call you back."

"Oh no you don't," I mutter, but she's already hung up.

"I'm Vera." She walks toward me, extending her hand. "Welcome to Verona Comics."

"Ridley." I return her firm shake with my own limp one, feeling a little bit like the walls are closing in.

pretendpretendpretendpretendpretendthisisfine

"Nice to meet you, Ridley. What can I do for you?"

"I said nothing." And wow, rude, holy shit, abort, abort, abort. "Sorry, I'm . . . I don't know. I'm just—I was skating by and I saw your shop, and I just thought I'd stop in. I want to set up a pull list, though, since I'm here." I reach into my pocket for the piece of paper, wrinkled and soft from my hands worrying it all night, where I copied the list of comics my dad sent.

Vera stifles a smile and takes the paper from my hand. "You were just skating by, huh?"

pretendpretendpretendpretendpretend

She goes behind the desk and turns on her computer. She's still smirking, and I don't know why. It's starting to stress me out more, if that's even possible.

"Do you always skate around with a list of comics you want to buy in your pocket?"

Oh.

thinkthinkthinkthinkthink

"Yes?"

shitshitshitshitshitshitshit

"You're my kinda kid, then, Ridley." She laughs.

Crisis averted? Maybe? I let out a deep breath and run my hand along the long boxes on the table beside me. This is fine. I am fine. I am standing across the room from my comics hero, but this is fine.

Fine, fine, fine.

Oh god, I'm freaking out. I take another deep breath and blow it out. Vera looks up from her computer, and I spin around fast and start flipping through the comics in front of me, trying to calm down. If I blow this . . . I can't. I can't blow this.

getagripgetagripgetagrip

"Fuck," I whisper, trying to keep my hands from trembling.

"What was that?" Vera asks from behind the counter.

"Uh . . . nothing. I just, yeah." And I apparently lose the ability to speak in front of this woman. Awesome.

She laughs again, but it sounds warm, not mean, and I relax infinitesimally. "Did you just move here?"

"Yeah, a couple days ago."

"Well, welcome to town, then." She comes around the corner. "Your pull list is all set. I can't sell you any of the new releases until tomorrow, but a couple of them just came out last week. Did you need those?"

"No, I'm good."

"Normally, I would require a deposit for a pull list this big, but you have an honest face, so I'm gonna let it slide."

"Oh, uh, thanks," I say, and try to ignore the way that makes my stomach hurt. Also, I should have expected this; we always take deposits for pull lists at our comic shops too. I look around a little bit, taking it all in. "I like your shop."

"Thanks." Vera smiles. "I made it myself."

"I know; that's awesome." Because she really did. I read through all her old blog posts last night in a last-ditch effort to be prepared, including the ones about her making her own shelves by hand and personally sliding every book in place.

"Just skatin' by, eh?"

"Something like that," I say, realizing what I just said. I have definitely screwed this up, and there's no coming back. She probably thinks I'm a total weirdo. I'm probably making her uncomfortable. I'm probably—

"Well, my door's always open, Ridley. Come anytime the light's on."

"Seriously?" I sputter, because I've spent this whole time making an ass of myself, and still, she seems somehow completely unfazed.

"Are you going to school here? I have a daughter about

your age. I'm sure she'd be willing to show you around and introduce you to people."

Peak. She's talking about Peak.

dontthrowupdontthrowup

"No, I don't think so."

Vera's eyebrows draw together, but then she makes a little humming sound. "Well, maybe you two will cross paths some other way, then. In the meantime, why don't you come back soon. I'm inking a new book, and I'll let you take a look."

My eyes get huge at the idea of seeing a Vera original *in process*. Holy shit. This is amazing. This is impossible. Be cool. Be cool. I take a deep breath. "Yeah, that'd be great. I'll stop back."

"You do that," she says with the warmest smile I've ever seen.

"I have to go now." I start walking backward toward the door. "But thanks. It was nice meeting you."

"Nice meeting you too," she says as I hit the door and make the bells ring again.

I shove it open and step onto the sidewalk. I did it. It might have been awkward and messed up, and I wasn't like a James Bond–level superspy or anything, but I went, and I did it, and I'm going to go back. And that feels like a win. It feels good.

And then my phone buzzes in my pocket, and it's Peak checking in, wishing me good luck with whatever it is that I have to do today. And my heart sinks to the concrete, because every win comes with a loss for me. Everything good is also bad. Plus one with my dad means minus one with Peak.

CHAPTER FOURTEEN

Jubilee

HE'S BEEN IN the store for nearly five minutes, and other than getting startled by the bells—which Vera says he does every time—and then looking to see if I noticed, which I did, he hasn't acknowledged me at all. Well, technically, he did that ridiculous grunt-slash-nod combo thing boys do when I said hello. Hardly counts.

Vera mentioned he'd be in soon to get his holds, but it's weird he came in today, since the new books aren't out until tomorrow. I guess he's just into perpetually being a week behind or something—but I'm trying not to judge. She said to keep an eye out for the mop-headed guy in a hoodie, that he looked about my age and seemed like he needed a friend. Then she gave me a look, like it's my job to welcome him to the fold or something. No, thanks, I have enough on my plate.

Speaking of enough on my plate, I glance at my phone—and nothing. Well, there are a few texts from Jayla and Nikki, plus the two violinists from my quartet blowing up our group chat over which performance of the Haydn Quartets is the best and the violist trying to get them to chill, but . . . none from Bats, which is weird. Normally we talk nonstop when I'm at the shop. It's practically what gets me through the shift. This afternoon—silence. Granted, normally I don't work on Tuesdays—Mrs. G had to reschedule our usual lesson because she has the flu—but still.

I glance back up at the new kid, who is still standing awkwardly near the entrance. He's fairly unremarkable as far as new kids go, and I would know—I've met about a trillion in the three years we've lived with Vera. I swear to god, she collects wayward kids the way some people collect baseball cards. They come in and out of the shop, barely buying anything, but she lets them hang around anyway—feeding them, talking to them, giving them a safe space to be. My mom calls them strays, but Vera doesn't like that. I asked her about it once, and she said someone did that for her too when she was young and needed it, and she's just paying it forward. Which is great, honestly, but I don't see why I need to be a part of the welcome wagon.

I grab another snack out of the candy bowl on the counter—I take the peanut butter cups, always; Vera can keep the Skittles—while still keeping an eye on the new kid. He's cute-ish, I guess, with his little lost expression on his face, and he's rocking some bright white Vans that I don't hate. I guess cute-ish boys in rad sneakers is a theme now for me or something, not that I'm complaining.

I looked at his pull list before he got here, even though I

felt guilty about it because Vera says that's like looking into someone's soul. It was pretty good, maybe a little clinical, a little trying too hard. Objectively, they're all good titles, but collectively it doesn't *feel* cohesive. Pull lists have a style usually, a vibe. Like, even if it's a mix of indie and mainstream, and most of them are, you'll see themes and patterns emerge. If somebody shuffled all the comics in the pull boxes together, I'd probably still be able to easily sort out which ones belonged to our regulars. But this kid is all over the map. His pull list has taste but no heart.

It's like the difference between my audition rep and the music I'd put on a recital program. My audition requirements are strict: two excerpts, a Bach suite, a romantic concerto, and a twentieth-century solo work. It's curated to show off my technique, my musicality, and my range across all different periods—but it doesn't flow. If it were up to me, I'd just play all the Beethoven sonatas and call it a day.

I lean against the counter and sigh. He's moved from the door finally, but he's been staring at the wire rack near the new-release wall for too long now. I don't even think he sees it. I mean, it's the kids' rack. How long can one person really spend looking at the newest *DuckTales* cover?

He glances up at me, startling when we make eye contact, and then goes back to looking at the rack. I feel a pang of pity; obviously, I'm freaking him out. Comics are getting pretty mainstream, but we still get a lot of quiet, quirky folks in here too. Like James, one of our regulars, who's fine with Vera but can't talk to me with his eyes open. As in, he literally keeps them shut the entire time. It's totally fine, and we actually have a lot of great conversations . . . but it does make cashing him out a bit of an adventure.

And Macy, who's so shy she just hands us pieces of paper with the titles she wants added and practically runs from the shop when we give them to her. It's just part of working here. Besides, I'm not exactly the poster child for being a well-adjusted social butterfly either. If I were, then maybe I wouldn't have essentially been assigned "live a little" as a homework assignment.

I lean over the counter so I'm closer to Mr. Glaring-at-*DuckTales*—but not too close—and clear my throat. "Hey, if you're looking for Vera, she'll be back in a few. She just had to do a delivery."

He finally looks up at me and then nearly knocks over a stack of comics sitting on top of the dollar bin. I had been meaning to bag and board them—no point now. He scrambles to catch them, crinkling some covers in the process. Better than the new releases, but still.

"Help," he says, and I tilt my head as the blush creeps up his neck. "I mean, can I help you?"

"Uh, I think that's supposed to be my line, right? Since I'm the one who works here?"

"Right." He smooths the cover of one of the comics. "I can pay for these."

"It's fine." I wave him off. "We end up donating half of them to the children's hospital anyway. It's not a big deal if they're a little bit wrinkled on the corners."

"Oh."

"I'm Jubilee," I say, trying to look friendly because this guy looks like he's about to lose it. "You're the new str— Ridley, right?"

His eyes widen in response, and for half a second, I swear I know him. He must have one of those faces.

"How . . . ?"

"Vera said you'd be in to pick up your books. I've got a few holds over here whenever you're ready, but if you need anything else, let me know."

He scratches the back of his neck and does this half-cough thing, like he's got something stuck in his throat. "Thanks." I catch him grimace as he turns to the rack in front of him.

"There are other racks, you know, unless you're super into talking ducks," I tease, smirking at the way his ears pink up.

"Yeah," he says, moving on to stare at the actual new-release wall instead.

I pull out his holds, checking to make sure they're all there. I glance over when I see him pick up a comic. It's not one on his list, but it is one of my favorites. He flips through, looking at it like he wants to marry it, and then slides it back into the rack with a frown.

"That's a good one," I say. "And you're at a great jumping-on point. They're coming back from hiatus, and the first volume just came out. You grab that and the one in your hand, and you're all caught up."

"I have all of them except this one. I've been reading it from the start."

I crinkle my forehead, flipping through his books in front of me. "Oh really? Is it supposed to be in your pile?"

"No." He shakes his head. "I can't—I don't have—it's a thing."

I pull back, surprised. "Your parents monitor your pull list or something?"

He looks down, and holy shit, if there's one thing I hate most in this world, it's parents policing content. I can't help but notice that it's the very queer comic that they don't let him have; meanwhile, his pull list is loaded up with all the violent ones. Typical.

"That's so wrong." I come from behind the counter and pull the comic out of the rack. "Here, it's yours."

"I can't."

"Seriously, I read it on break earlier. I'll just replace it with my copy. It's fine." I push it closer until he takes it.

"Thanks." The corner of his lips turns up, and I feel a little swell of pride.

His eyes catch on my Green Lantern ring, sterling silver with an actual emerald in it. A gift from my mom on my sixteenth birthday. I'm about to show it to him when he opens his mouth.

"Did your boyfriend give you that?"

Cue record scratch.

"My boyfriend?" I roll my eyes. "I work in a comic shop. I don't need to rely on a boy to give me merch. I guarantee you my pull list is bigger than yours, and it was even before I started working here."

He shakes his head. "I didn't mean . . . I wasn't implying—"

I raise my eyebrows and cross my arms. "Uh-huh."

"I swear. I have a sister that's way more into this stuff than I'll ever be. If she even thought I implied—which I didn't, by the way—but if she even thought I did, she would kick my ass. It came out wrong. I didn't mean anything by it."

"Oh really?" I snort. "You didn't mean to ask if it was from my boyfriend, even though that's literally exactly what you said?"

His eyes go wide. "I was just making conversation!"

"By implying that I could only have this ring if it came from a guy?"

He rubs his hand over his face and frowns. "Listen, I really, truly did not mean it that way. I'm sorry."

At least he looks properly ashamed. "Fine. How did you mean it, then?"

"What?"

"How did you mean it? If you weren't asking out of some last-ditch misogynistic gatekeeping, why else would you ask if it was from my boyfr—wait, were you trying to see if I *had* a boyfriend?"

"I—" He blushes again and starts flipping through the books in the dollar bin. "No."

I sigh. "I don't know if that makes it better or worse."

"What?"

"Why are you all such clichés?"

"Comics fans?"

I roll my eyes. "No, boys. News flash, it's not okay to hit on every random person you meet."

"I don't, I swear. You're the exception, not the rule.

And technically, I didn't hit on you. I just asked if you had a boyfriend."

"I'm going to find out who your sister is and tell her everything."

His mouth pops open, and I swear to god, the boy looks terrified.

"Okay, now I want to find her even more. She seems fabulous, and I think I'm already in love."

"Does that mean I should have asked if you had a girlfriend too?" He chuckles and scratches the back of his neck.

"Probably, yeah," I say. "Also, congrats on making it even more awkward by questioning not only my relationship status but also my sexual orientation all within five minutes of meeting me."

He groans and drops his head down. "Can we just start over? Or else I could go over there with *DuckTales* until Vera comes back. I'd totally understand. I was trying to be funny, but I made it uncomfortable. That is . . . kind of my superpower." He grimaces.

"Ugh, now I feel bad. *DuckTales?* Really?" I huff. "Okay, fine, you get one last chance to turn this all around: tell me what book you'd recommend. You do a good job, you can stay. You don't, there's the door, come back later." I'm just messing with him. Of course I wouldn't really kick him out, but it turns out he's adorable when he gets flustered.

He crinkles his eyebrows, a little mischief in his eye. "I thought your pull list was bigger than mine?"

"I'm completely positive that it is, but I still want to know what you'd recommend, because obviously the pull list you made here isn't accurate. And I can tell a lot about a dude by what he reads."

He bites the inside of his cheek, looking from me to the wall and back to me again. He walks over to the third row and slides a glossy superhero book from the shelf. Ms. Marvel stares back at me from the cover.

"Explain your reasoning." I love it, but I want to know why he picked it. If he even tries to pull the teen-girl card . . .

"Eisner *and* Hugo Award–winning writer, fantastic art, amazing plot, compelling main character. I don't believe for a second it's not already on your pull list, but if you want to keep messing with me, fine. That's my first pick, and yes, I would recommend it to you even if you were a guy."

"Your *first* pick?"

"Give me two seconds; we're not done yet." He walks around the comic shop, pulling various trades and single issues. I already own most of them, which should maybe not impress me, but it does. When he pulls my favorite comic, a super-obscure indie book you pretty much have to be deep into the scene to have even heard of, my heart beats a little faster. Did it just get hot in here, or . . . ?

He walks back with a little smile, tapping his finger on it. "This one is a little out-there, but give it a chance. It's worth it."

"I own it. I love it. I have a signed copy." His face lights up as the smile turns into a full-on grin that stretches across his face, and oh my god, he has a dimple.

"Yeah? Not many people have even heard of it."

"I told you my—"

"Pull list is bigger than mine. Yeah, yeah, got it. So? How'd I do?"

"Okay, I guess." I laugh. "But now you have to put it all away before Vera gets back, and I need to finish organizing the books for tomorrow. I'd hurry if I were you; she hates when the store's a mess."

The little bell over the door jingles, and both our heads whip toward the entrance. Ridley darts to put the books away, and I swear he's still grinning, but it's hard to tell from the way he's hunched over by the racks.

"Ridley! You're just in time," Vera says as she bustles by us with bags of takeout. "You like Chinese food, right?"

Tuesday-night Chinese in the back room is a weekly tradition. Vera barters with the owner of the Chinese restaurant next door. We keep him in comics, and he hooks us up with dinner every time my stepmom delivers them. Usually I'm rushing here from my lesson to get some before it's gone, so I'm pumped to have first dibs tonight.

"I should go," Ridley says, sliding the last comic back in its place.

"Nonsense, come eat," Vera insists, and this, *this* is why she picks up so many strays. Vera and her stellar business sense. I mean, people love when they come to get their holds and find out they weren't sorted yet because everybody was too busy eating takeout, or that their sticky note with new requests was used as a makeshift napkin. I roll my eyes and follow my stepmom anyway, because Chinese food.

Ridley hesitates until I raise my eyebrows, and then he follows. He trips over the little half step between the back room and the store and then squeezes his eyes shut when I giggle. Okay, fine, it's definitely cute how easily he gets embarrassed. And if I had any extra time to "push the boundaries," maybe I would spend a little of it finding new and clever ways to make him blush.

But I don't. I can barely keep up with the boy that lives in my phone. Who still hasn't texted me since this morning, by the way.

"So?" Vera says, pulling cans of soda and white take-out boxes from the greasy paper bags. "Did our guest pass inspection?"

Ridley watches as I wave my hand in a *so-so* gesture. "It was touch and go for a minute, but he did all right in the end."

Vera shakes her head before looking at Ridley. "Jubi doesn't always trust my judgment when it comes to kids hanging out here. If she's giving you the all clear, you must be doing something right. Now sit, eat."

I kick a chair toward him with my foot, and he looks up when it bangs into his shin. "Sit." I shove my fork into a pile of white rice. "Unless you want me to change my mind about you."

Vera laughs, reaching for the box of crab rangoon. I smack her hand. "Not until he sits. It's rude."

Ridley stares at me for a second, watching the exchange with this sort of confused expression, and then he grabs the chair and slides it back to the table, sitting stiffly upright. His knee bumps into mine, and I feel it bounce up and down a little.

"So," I say, trying to get him to relax, "what brings your family to Silver Hills?"

Ridley coughs, choking on his egg roll, and I slap him on the back. "Easy, slick." He's sweet in an awkward-puppy way. It's familiar, and strangely comforting.

"Um," he says finally, when the coughing has subsided. "I'm staying with my dad for a while, so."

"Oh, is he here in town?"

"Outside of it. In Claremont. He's got a house there."

"Wow, fancy. Too bad your dad is such a tightwad about your pull list. I hoped maybe it was just a money thing."

"Jubilee!" Vera scolds, knocking the rice over in the process. The little bell over the door jingles, saving me from dying of embarrassment.

"I'll get that." I start to stand up, but Vera pushes me back down into my seat.

"Relax, it's probably just Rutherford picking up his holds," she says, disappearing into the store.

Vera says that all the time when the bell rings, that it's probably just Rutherford. It's become a running joke. Rutherford rarely picks up his holds. He'll come in once a year or so, slam down a few grand, and take everything home. The rest of the time they just sit, wasting space and money.

I clean up the rice she dumped and put it on a napkin. "Are you going to start at Silver Hills too, then?"

"Silver Hills what?" he asks.

"Silver Hills High School? We technically cover Claremont, although most of the kids there go to private schools."

"Oh," he says, looking down. "No."

"Private school?"

"Probably not."

I tilt my head. "Wait. How old are you?"

"Seventeen."

"So did you graduate early or drop out or what?"

"I don't really know," he says, shrugging like it's no big deal.

I take a sip of my Sprite, marinating on that thought. "I didn't think that it was possible to not know."

"It's just, it's a long story—"

"I've been texting you nonstop!" Jayla practically shouts, sliding back the curtain and stepping into the room. "This is getting ridiculous. You can't just—" She glances at Ridley and down at where our knees meet. "Am I interrupting something?"

"What? No!" I say, scooting my chair over closer to Vera's, which means the only place for Jayla to squeeze in is right between me and Ridley. She grabs a chair and sits, looking him up and down.

"Favorite Robin?" she asks.

"Uh, what?"

I roll my eyes. "She does this with everyone, sorry. Jayla, can we skip it this time?"

She flicks her eyes to mine. "Did you make him give you book recommendations?"

I bite my lip. "Maybe, but—"

"If you got to test him, I get to test him," she says, and turns back to Ridley. "Favorite Robin?"

"I don't know. I guess Dick Grayson."

She stares at him for a second before shifting so she only faces me. "Anyway, I've been texting you. I want to go—"

"Jayla," I say, arching my eyebrows.

"Ugh, fine," she says, turning her chair back to the table. "But he said Grayson, Jubi. Dick Grayson. Out of all the Robins, he's the worst."

"Well, my sister's named after—"

"Don't worry about it. She's just a Jason Todd fan," I say, hoping that explains everything. It should. There have been so many Robins standing by Batman's side over the years, but the Jason Todd fandom and the Dick Grayson fandom are especially precious about their guys each being the best of the best.

"Everyone should be a Jason Todd fan," Jayla says. "But seriously, how is the new guy already invited to takeout night? Shouldn't there be more of a vetting period? I mean, the kid likes Dick Grayson." She whispers the last part with an exaggerated cringe.

"I should go," he says.

"No, she's just being obnoxious," I say, widening my eyes at her. "She means it with love."

"No, I mean it with mild trepidation," Jayla says.

"Liking Dick Grayson doesn't make him problematic, Jay!"

"It means he's got poor judgment."

"I'm just gonna go," he says, standing up.

I lean around her to grab his sleeve and yank him back down. "Eat. She's kidding."

"Mostly," Jayla says, giving him the evil eye before laughing. "I'm Jayla, by the way."

"Ridley." He blows out another breath, looking uncomfortable.

"Welcome to the family, I guess. Try not to suck, okay?"

"I—" Ridley starts, but Jayla's already turned back toward me.

"Come on, Jubi—if we hurry, there's still enough time to hit up the thrift store before it closes."

"I'll catch up with you, okay?" I give her my most pleading look. "I'm still eating."

She rolls her eyes and slides her chair out. "Fine. Stay here with the Grayson-lover."

We sit for a while after she leaves, eating our Chinese food in silence. I fight the urge to break it with a random fact, because that's a me-and-Bats thing, and it feels like cheating to do it here with Ridley. He'd probably think it was weird anyway.

"So, she's great," he says finally. And I burst out laughing because he sounds so genuine that I can't even tell if he's being sarcastic.

"Her heart's in the right place. She's just very protective of me and my moms."

"Moms?"

"Oh, come on, you had to have known. That doesn't bother you, does it?"

"Nope," he says, shoving his chopsticks into one of the boxes in front of him.

I pull out my phone and check my texts. The quartet chat is still going bananas—something about Shostakovich now—but still nothing from Bats.

"Got someone better to talk to?" he asks, ducking his head a little.

"Apparently not." I sigh. "But I do have to catch up with Jayla. She'll kill me if I don't."

"Can't have that."

"Right?" I stand up, grabbing my coat. "And just so you know, since you're so curious, I'm not seeing anybody."

He chokes on his rice as I walk out with a smirk. Score one for pushing the boundaries.

CHAPTER FIFTEEN

Ridley

I FLICK OFF the bathroom light and turn the water to its hottest setting. Gray calls them my "sadbaths." But I kind of hate that. It's too close to *Sabbath*, and if I'm going to worship something, it's not going to be at the altar of depression and soap scum.

But there's just something about hot water and scorched skin and a quiet dark room that's . . . soothing. I squeeze my eyes shut and pretend it's my worries swirling around the drain instead of cheap hotel shampoo. Dad still hasn't bothered to stock my bathroom, so I'm relying on shit I stole from the casino. But still, it's fine.

I can't label what I'm feeling right now, but my head's been spinning since yesterday when Peak gave me that book, shoved it into my hands like it was no big deal. Like I deserved it just because I wanted it. Wait, no, not Peak, Jubilee. Jubilee Jones. I'm trying so hard to keep them separate.

It's harder than I thought.

I lean my head against the wall. I thought it would feel

different to be back in this house. I don't know what I expected. Like I would be better somehow if the water beating down on me was from pipes that run underneath the floor I learned to walk on instead of the floor of a new-construction house with no history and heating problems. And yet.

And yet.

I just feel more alone. If this isn't my home and that isn't my home, do I even have one?

I finish up, wrap myself in a towel, and pad across the floor. I wriggle my toes appreciatively when the cool tile of the bathroom gives way to the plush carpet of the hallway, leaving damp footsteps in my wake.

My ex-therapist suggested I keep a running list of good things to look at when all seems lost. I think she wanted me to actually write it down, but I never did. It's more of a running tally in my head. I add *plush carpeting* to the list, right after *dewy spiderwebs*, but before *baristas of any gender wearing sparkly nail polish*.

I grab a pair of boxers out of the duffel bag by the nightstand, shaking them out like anybody's going to care they're wrinkled, and then I flop back onto the bed with my phone. The urge to text Peak is strong, but I don't know. I kind of just want to think more about Jubilee right now. And I know, I KNOW they're the same.

But compartmentalization and all that.

I slide the comic out from where I hid it under my pillow, frowning at the silly sentimentality. It's not like it means anything; she didn't even have to pay for it. She probably doesn't even remember giving it to me.

It's fine.

I try to call my mom—I tell myself it's not because I'm lonely, it's just to remind her to send my stuff—but she doesn't pick up either way. I text her the reminder instead, and she responds surprisingly fast: **Can't talk, out with friends, will call later.** I'm not holding my breath, though. She has called exactly once since I've been here, and only because she couldn't find the remote. It's whatever.

I start to call my sister next but then cancel it. She's in Boston; she even sent me a snap earlier of her making fishy faces in the aquarium there. Boston's not too far from here, an hour or two at most, but I have no idea why she's there.

I pull up her Instagram and click through, anything to keep my mind busy tonight, and ah yes, it's a charity event sponsored by The Geekery. Makes sense. There she is, smiling with a bunch of sick kids at the New England Aquarium. There she is, posing with Spider-Man in front of a sign that reads SWING INTO ACTION WITH THE GEEKERY CHARITIES. There she is with a glass of champagne, laughing. There she is, visiting a hospital with Captain America earlier that day. I can't decide if I feel better that she's close if I need her, or worse that she's this close and not here.

Regardless, it's not her fault. I'm not her responsibility. A new picture appears right before I click off, a selfie of her pointing at the penguins in the enclosure behind her with an overdramatic "wow" face. I'm just about to leave a comment about what a massive nerd she is when a text pops up on my phone.

PEAK: Bats!

I stare down at the words on my screen like a deer in the headlights. And oh shit. This feels wrong somehow. Like sharing crab rangoon changed everything, and now it's all different and confusing.

donttextbackdontdontdont

ME: Peak!

imgoingtohell

PEAK: Oh good, so you're not
dead in a ditch somewhere.
You really did just abandon me. ☺

And okay, even with the emoji at the end, the idea that she felt remotely abandoned, kidding or not, just sucks. It sucks even more because I was right in front of her yesterday and couldn't say anything. And I kind of hate that. I don't want her to feel like that ever.

ME: I didn't abandon you

PEAK: You haven't texted me in forever

ME: I was working.

Okay, it's not technically a lie, but.

PEAK: Likely story. 😉

Be cool, Ridley. Steer this away from work. It's too fucked up.

ME: Cross my heart.

PEAK: Still doing promo for Satan's Comics? 😜

ME: No, something new. Just started.

shitshitshitshitshit
This is the opposite of steering things away from work. This is making work a priority. This is literally going into more detail about it. What if she figures it out? What if she already has? What if she's just messing with me, dragging me along? What if this is a setup?
whatifwhatifwhatifwhatifwhatif

PEAK: Funnnnn. Hope your coworkers were nice.

ME: They were exceptional.

fuckfuckfuckfuckfuck
WHAT IS THE ACTUAL MATTER WITH ME?

PEAK: Exceptional, eh? Should I be jealous?

ME: I can't even begin to tell you
how not jealous you should be.
Wait . . . Jealous?

PEAK: Can't go having some hot coworker
stealing away my bat in shining armor.

ME: I don't have armor.

PEAK: Semantics. Bat in skinny jeans then.
Same difference.

ME: The difference between jeans
and armor is far greater than semantics.
I don't even know where to begin.

PEAK: Nice subject change. ☺

ME: . . . ?

PEAK: Listen, you've been texting
me nonstop for two weeks, and now
radio silence. There's definitely a hottie.

Should I tell her? Oh god, I should. I should tell her everything, come completely clean. This is too stressful. I'm sure my dad will get over it, right? I mean, probably? Never mind.

ME: Would you really care?

ohgodohgodohgodohgodohgod
Am I really asking her if she's jealous of herself? What is the matter with me? Seriously. WHAT. IS. THE. MATTER. WITH. ME?

PEAK: Nope.

Annnnnd ouch. Well, okay, then.

PEAK: I mean, I would have.
But then maybe I met someone too.
Turnabout being fair play and all.

My stomach sinks to my toes. Fuck him, whoever he is. They probably met at the thrift shop after she left yesterday. He was probably donating all his very nice clothing while combing the racks for "authentic pieces." He probably has a nice house and a family that loves him. He probably is handsome and well-adjusted and plays sports and has hipster glasses or something. His laundry is probably always clean and good smelling. He probably has more clothes than he can handle because his mother didn't promise to ship them to him and then forget, and I bet his teeth sparkle in the sunlight. He probably doesn't even know how great his life is. He's probably the exact opposite of me in every way. She's probably already in love. She's probably never going to text me again after this. This is probably her way of cutting things off, since she seems too nice to ghost someone.

And I know I have to respond, that it's weird that I haven't, but the words keeping dying in my fingers.

ME: I don't know what to say here.

PEAK: Really? That's it?

ME: I hope you guys are happy?
I don't know. What am I supposed
to do with that? Good for you.
Have fun. Etc. Etc. Etc.

And yeah, I'm pouting. And yeah, I know that's messed up. And yet. And yet.

PEAK: Oh god, I was just teasing you.

ME: So . . . There is no "hottie"?

PEAK: Well, I mean, there is? But he's just
some rando who hangs out at my mom's store.
N E V E R going to happen.

I bolt up in bed, choking on my spit when I read the words on the screen, my mind whipping around itself, alternating between *holy shit, she's talking about me* and *wait, did I just cockblock . . . myself?*

Oh god. Seriously, no. I have to tell her. This is so messed up.

But I can't. I can't screw this up. My father is counting on me, Gray is counting on me, and even worse, what if telling her means I lose her on both fronts? Not that I have her on both fronts, but I could? Maybe? If we keep talking and hanging out.

No.

But now the silence is stretching on too long, and I have to get a grip. I have to write back. I have to handle this. Compartmentalize. Don't cross the streams. Figure it out.

thinkthinkthinkthinkthinkthinkthinkthinkthink

ME: Lucky me.

PEAK: Lucky you. 😉

God, this girl. This girl. She makes me feel like my brain is electric, in a good way for once. And I don't know. Maybe other people have felt like this before, but I haven't. Not like this. I don't know how anyone could? How do you go to the store, how do you eat, how do you buy toilet paper and brush your teeth and do anything other than sit inside your head with this feeling? I thought I had this before with Chandler, but this, this is next-level stuff, and I don't even know what to do with it.

I don't even know.

• • •

A knocking sound pulls me from my sleep, and I jolt up in bed. Suddenly, I am seven years old and I overslept again, and maybe it's my dad coming to wake me up for school. But he never would, not even then, and I'm a decade past seven, so.

The knocking continues, and it's not a hard knock, not a Dad knock, and not my sister's either.

"Ridley?"

Shit. If there was anything that would make me crash hard after getting high on Peak—or Jubilee, I don't even know how to keep that sorted or separated anymore—it would be the she-devil on the other side of my door. Satan's Comics indeed.

"Ridley?" Allison calls again, still knocking.

I glance at the time; it's nearly midnight. "What?" I groan, yanking open my door. I'm standing in boxers and no doubt have pillow creases on my cheek.

"Huh, and your dad said you never slept." Based on the way she crinkles her nose when she glances over my shoulder, she appears to find my room lacking. It's not my fault that the only thing my dad kept in here after I moved to Seattle was my old twin bed.

She walks over to where my duffel bag sits open on the floor and nudges it with her foot. "Is this all you have still?" Her tone changes then, pity lacing her words.

I cross one arm across my chest, grabbing my shoulder hard so I don't say something I'll regret. Yes, it's all I have. Yes, it's all that's mine. Yes. Yes. Yes. It's fine.

Allison shifts her weight. "We expected your first report tonight. Your dad wanted me to check on it, since he's held up at the aquarium thing."

Oh. Right. I was supposed to do that before I went to bed.

Oops. And then the rest of what she said hits me, and okay, sure, it doesn't bother me that both he and Gray did the charity event and neither of them invited me. It's whatever.

Allison lifts up one of my shirts strewn across the floor, frowning. "If you won't send it out with the wash, you should at least have our girl steam the wrinkles out before you wear it again."

"You don't steam T-shirts, Allison," I say, ripping it out of her hand and tossing it on top of my bag.

"Well, at least put them in the dresser, then," she grumbles. "We're all stuck together for a while. Might as well make the most of it."

"A while?"

"At least till the end of the month," she says.

nononononononono

I thought I'd have more time. I thought it would be different. I thought—

"That's not enough time," I blurt out, because two and a half more weeks sounds like nothing at all.

"Not enough time?" She turns back toward me. "Enough time for what? We already know what they're doing. We just need you to find us a new angle to approach a deal, and your dad will take it from there."

I swallow hard, switching gears. "Why is he so obsessed with Vera Flores?"

"It's a pride thing. You wouldn't understand."

I roll my eyes at her insult. "Don't you feel shitty, though?"

"About what? It's not like we're trying to put them out of business. Ultimately, we're looking for a partnership."

"Yeah, like when he *partnered* with Trinity Comics?"

"He learned a lot from that misstep, Ridley."

"Misstep? That's one word for it."

More like *all-out disaster*. Trinity Comics had three of the most successful comic stores in the Northeast, indie but big indie, with some serious scene cred. Then they had the misfortune of meeting my father.

He offered to bring them in to do a joint business venture, to become affiliates and go from there. We were supposed to stay separate. They were going to be our indie leg. Only they still repped The Geekery brand. And, shocker, Dad got obsessive about it. Pretty soon, he was bringing down rules and regulations "from corporate," but who are we kidding? He *is* corporate.

Then they weren't so much affiliates as something else entirely. A mash-up. A corporate store with an indie front. Artists stopped coming for signings, customers stopped coming in to buy, prices went up to cover costs, inventory went down. It became this weird, sad chimera, leaving everybody unsatisfied on both sides.

Finally, after Dad ran their business into the ground, he bought them out at a teeny tiny fraction of what they were once worth. Dad rebranded them as The Geekery minimarts, selling mostly cheap merchandise and Funko Pops instead of comics. He even hired one of the old owners as the manager. Twenty-five years of comics history down the drain, and all they could do was watch.

The idea of him doing that to Vera . . .

"She'll never go for it. Ever."

"That's why we're counting on you to find a way for us to make an offer she can't refuse."

"You've been watching too much of *The Godfather*. Vera Flores is not a sellout."

"Grow up, Ridley. Everyone has a price."

"Whatever you say." I reach for my headphones, planning to tune her out completely, but then she says something I can't ignore.

"You did." She pulls my laptop off my desk and drops it onto the bed in front of me before slamming the door behind her. Fuck. She's actually right. Except.

Except.

Maybe I can still fix this. I open the report file on my computer and start filling it in, feeling lighter the more I write. And if it isn't *strictly* accurate, well, nobody has to know.

CHAPTER SIXTEEN

Jubilee

RIDLEY AND I are an hour deep into sorting and stocking books—he's been here so much this last week, I figure he's an honorary employee at this point anyway—when Jayla walks into the shop. She frowns when she sees him, and I sneak a glance at my phone and see she's been texting me this whole time. I dropped the ball. Again. I was working, though, sort of, so she can't really be mad.

I say *sort of* because, while I did help a customer, and we have gotten a bunch of stock out, we've mostly been talking. And laughing. And awkwardly bumping into each other accidentally on purpose. That's basically our MO here, and maybe, *possibly* the reason I've been picking up so many extra shifts.

I just like talking to him. Like today he was telling me all about how close he is with his sister, and I was telling him all about playing cello. I even almost told him about the audition but changed my mind at the last second. I'm weird about that. Superstitious. Like if I tell too many people, I won't be invited to the next round.

"Hey, Jay," I say, mustering up a big smile.

She glances at Ridley. "You work here now?"

"Just helping out."

Jayla hums and then checks the time. "My shift starts in a half hour, but I wanted to talk to you, Jubi. Alone?"

"Okay," I say, following her into the back room.

"You two sure are hanging out a lot," she says the second I'm behind the curtain.

"Is that what you dragged me back here to say?"

"No, I dragged you back here because I miss my best friend and you never answer my texts anymore."

My face falls. "I know—I'm sorry. I've just been busy. I've had to cram in practice around all these extra shifts. It doesn't leave a lot of time to—"

"Yeah, what's up with that? You never work extra shifts, because you don't get extra pay and it cuts into cello time."

"I'm just trying to help out more."

There's a shuffling sound on the other side of the curtain then, and I hear Ridley sliding comics into the rack right beside us.

"Yeah, seems like there's a lot of that going around lately."

I want to be mad, but I can see in her face that she's genuinely upset. And she's right; I haven't really been around lately. She's used to my hard-core musician schedule and constant studying, but this is different. Adding in Bats and Ridley lately has meant dropping the ball on other things, important things. And it's not cool.

"Listen, I'm out at eight tonight. Are you working till

nine still?" I ask, and she nods. "I'll ride my bike over when I'm done, and we can hang then. Okay?"

"What about cello?"

"I practiced before school. I knew I was meeting—I knew I was working late tonight. Seriously, I'll be there right after we close."

She smiles, but it looks forced. "Whatever you say, Jubi."

She pushes the curtain back, nearly tripping over Ridley on her way out. "Sorry, I have to go. I have to get to my actual job that pays me money to be there."

"We should all be so lucky," Ridley says, and I can't tell if that's a joke about us not paying him or something else. Jayla flashes him a look and then leaves. I slide the curtain into place, taking a second to regroup before stepping back out onto the floor.

• • •

"I don't know," I say, slouching in my favorite booth at the fro-yo shop. Jayla is supposed to be behind the counter, but she's commandeered the seat across from me to tackle her homework.

"Well, I can't answer you if I don't know all the variables!"

"Oh my god, fine, yes, they can get multiple flavors of yogurt and as many toppings as they want. Happy now?"

"Okay." Jayla sighs and flips the page over in her notebook. "Okay, this I can work with."

I laugh and slide out of my seat, going back behind the counter. Ten minutes to close means it's time to start wiping down the counters and pulling the toppings, and if she's too busy doing math homework, then I'm going to have to be the one to do it.

If the owner ever discovers that I help Jayla out sometimes, they will possibly kill me and definitely fire her. But it's March and it's dead here, which generally means that anybody wandering into this sad little fro-yo shop doesn't care who's doing the serving as long as the lights are on and the topping bar's filled.

There are fourteen flavors of frozen yogurt and seventeen toppings, and I suck at factorials, but Mr. Lucas is apparently giving extra credit to whoever can come up with the most complicated real-world math problem in his class. I guess figuring out how many combinations of yogurt and toppings exist counts as a "real-world" problem. I could be wrong, though; she's in a different math class than me.

I wipe down all the counters and hope Jayla doesn't go back to asking what I know she's dying to. I scrub the counter a little harder, frowning as I rub at a spot of hot fudge that probably dried on hours ago.

"So, real talk, what's the deal with you and the new kid?" she asks, glancing up from her notebook like she could hear my thoughts.

"No deal," I say, taking the tray of hot fudge and carrying it back to the fridge now that the lip is clean.

"Jubilee, come on. You're practically living at the shop now. And every time I walk in, you guys are making eyes at each other from across the store."

"We are not."

"You are! You're my best friend, and it's like you've fallen off the face of the earth."

"I'm not intentionally blowing you off, I swear." I wipe a few stray sprinkles off the counter and toss them in the garbage.

Jayla sighs. "You got like this with Dakota too. You crawl inside your little relationship bubble with your boyfriend, and it's like no one else matters."

"Ridley isn't my boyfriend."

"Are you sure? Because from the outside, it really seems like you both want him to be."

"We're friends," I say, sliding the lid over the maraschino cherries.

She puts the notebook down—I guess the factorials will have to wait—and comes over to help. Her pin-striped hat sits slightly askew on her curly black hair, and I resist the urge to fix it. "I don't think so," she says.

"And why's that?"

"Because I know you, and I know boys like him are your kryptonite."

"You were the one who said Mrs. G meant flirting and goofing off when she said to 'go find my passion' or whatever."

"No, actually, I said you had to try something new every day. And a con crush was *one* of them. And now you've warped it into, like, your main pastime and added in—I don't even know what to call it—a shop crush?" She pulls the pan of cherries out of my hands and starts walking back to the fridge. "You always fall for these tragic little antiheroes."

126

I huff, "Ridley isn't some tragic antihero. He's just a boy that likes the same comics as me. That's it."

"Is it?" she asks.

"I don't even have his number. It's a strictly in-shop relationship."

"And what about Office Batman?"

I roll my eyes. "Bats is on the other side of the country. There's nothing there with him either."

She drops her chin. "Jubi, you check your phone every five seconds to see if he texted you. That's not nothing."

"So what? Am I not allowed to have other friends? You've been texting Emily nonstop since you guys started hooking up!"

"No, you are, but Emily and I are different."

"How?"

"For one, I was actually looking for a relationship. And for two, I'm not ditching the whole rest of my life to fit her in."

"I'm not ditching my whole life."

"You are, though. You don't even know what's going on with Nikki or me or anyone."

I raise my arms up, utterly exasperated. "Then will you tell me what's up instead of wasting this whole night lecturing me?"

"I'm just worried about you."

"Why? Don't be."

"I don't know; I get a weird vibe from him sometimes. He shows up out of the blue, and now he's *always* around. Doesn't he have anything else to do?"

"I don't think he has anywhere to go or any money to go

there with. He made that comment to you about not having a job. I'm thinking of asking Vera if we can pay him. At least part-time." I can tell by the way she rolls her eyes she doesn't believe me.

"His watch could probably pay your mortgage for a year. Money is not the problem."

I tilt my head. "What watch?"

"That watch he wears all the time," she says. "He might walk in with a wrinkled Hulk shirt and jeans with holes in them, but that watch is straight off the yacht."

I bite the inside of my lip. I never noticed a watch, but then again, I wouldn't. Jayla's the one who spends her days buried in lookbooks and fashion magazines.

"It could be a hand-me-down," I say finally, and Jayla slams the lid on the strawberries hard enough to let me know exactly what she thinks about that hypothesis.

"That's this year's design. Nobody is handing down a ten-thousand-dollar watch they've barely even owned."

"Ten thousand?" I say, nearly choking on my gum. "It's gotta be a knockoff."

"It's not."

"How could you possibly be sure?"

"I know accessories," she says, and crap, she does. She really does. "The dude is hiding something."

"Come on." I groan. "He's not hiding anything, except maybe a rich uncle or something."

"Oh, you sweet summer child." Jayla laughs. "How about this, then: Do you know how much houses cost in Claremont?"

"What does it even matter?" I say, because I just want this conversation to end. "Even if he has money, it doesn't mean he can't love comics and hang out at the store."

"Look, you get three types of people hanging around at your mom's shop: the wannabe artists, the lookie-loo Vera Flores superfans, and the rare people who actually need her to, like, feed them or give them a job. Why is he acting like the third one when he's, at best, one of the first two or, at worst, something else entirely?"

"Like what?"

She shrugs. "You tell me."

"Maybe he's just lonely."

"Well, yeah," she snorts. "And obviously the dude's in love with you, but that still doesn't explain where he came from in the first place. Rich people don't slum it in our town just because they like comics. There's, like, three Geekerys on the other side of Claremont that are more his speed. And if he's not here for comics, and he hasn't been pitching his portfolio or gawking at your mom, then what is he doing here?"

"I love you, but you sound so paranoid." But even as I say it, I feel a tinge of concern. Jayla's planted a little seed of doubt, and it's unfurling across everything I thought I knew.

My phone buzzes and I pull it out, smiling when I see that it's Bats and texting back immediately. I don't even realize what I've done until I look up, coming face-to-face with Jayla's frown.

"Let me guess, Office Batman?"

I shove the phone into my pocket and go back to wiping down the counter. "Whatever."

"Yeah, well, just so you know," she says, wrapping up the last of the fruit, "if either of them hurts you, they die."

"They're friends," I say. "Though I *have* heard heartbreak is a good source of inspiration."

"Funny." She opens the cash drawer and shoves the day's take into a deposit bag, putting it into the safe's drop slot. She flicks the lights off. "So, Nikki and Ty have been hooking up."

"What?!" I shout. "Finally? Oh my god, this is amazing. Since when?"

"Since two days ago."

"Why didn't she text me?"

"We did; it's on the group chat. And she tried to tell you at lunch today, but you were too busy texting Bats."

And just like that, I feel like an ass. "Wow, I suck."

"Yeah, kinda."

"What else did I miss?"

"Nothing really, just, you know, Emily and me telling Coach that we're together because people wouldn't stop talking about it at practice."

"What?! When did that happen?"

"This afternoon. I texted you *and* called. That's what I came to talk to you about today, but then I saw Ridley and just—"

"How did it go?"

"About as well as you'd expect when a slightly conservative middle-aged man finds out that his two co-captains are together. We got a long, awkward lecture about making sure the team always comes first and no kissing on the field."

"Yikes," I say, feeling like crap. "I should've been there for you."

"Just promise you'll stop shutting us out, okay?"

"I promise. I'm sorry."

"Good." She smiles, and for the first time tonight, it seems real. "So dish, then."

"What?"

"You've got *two* boys in love with you. Are you telling me you don't need any girl time?"

And I know she doesn't mean it in any sort of way. I know by "girl time" she means "girl talk," but I can't help the knot that forms in my stomach. The "am I still queer if I date a guy?" knot. I hate it. It's a big part of why Dakota and I finally broke up too. I put up with a lot from him, too much, including the fact that he never understood something so fundamental about me. He actually once said, "How can you be bi if you're dating me?" Like dating him voided out every part of my queer identity or something.

"Let's just go," I say, because suddenly cold night air sounds incredible.

"What's wrong?" She locks the doors and follows me out to where our bikes are parked.

"Nothing."

"Yeah, that's not even remotely convincing."

"Is it weird that I like boys?" I ask, my breath coming out like fog in the night air.

"Well, I'm a lesbian. So yeah, I think it's weird anyone likes boys." She chuckles. "But like, in general, no, it's not weird that *you* like boys. Why?"

"Liking a guy doesn't make me straight."

"I know it doesn't." She looks legitimately horrified as we

131

get on our bikes and start to pedal home. "I don't care that you like boys. I just wish you had better taste in them."

"No, I know. I think I just needed to say that out loud." I take a deep breath. "Who I date doesn't change who I am."

"Right, and if anyone says different, they're going to have to deal with me. Personally. And I've been working out." She lets go of her handlebars and flexes her biceps.

I laugh. "Thank you for being so cool, even though I've sucked lately."

"It's my job as your best friend to both point out when you suck and tolerate a small amount of it, so you're good," she says. "But if I'm playing the supportive best friend role, then level with me—which of these two sad disasters you call crushes would you actually pick if you had to?"

"I have no idea," I say, shaking my head. "I feel this pull toward Bats, but he's on the other side of the country . . ."

"If Bats wanted you guys to date, like, hypothetically, if he wanted to be exclusive or whatever, would you do it?"

"I have no clue, because there's Ridley! And Ridley is right here, and also awesome."

Jayla laughs, pedaling faster. "So then what if Ridley asked you to stop talking to Bats? Would you be able to?"

"I really don't know." I spin the pedals backward and stare up at the moon. I wonder what Bats and Ridley are doing right now. I wonder if they're thinking of me. If they're wishing we could talk.

I wonder, if they had to choose, would they choose me?

CHAPTER SEVENTEEN

BATS: Hey, what are you up to?

> **PEAK:** Lying on my bedroom floor having an existential crisis.

BATS: Uh . . . I think that's my line?

> **PEAK:** Is there some kind of existential crisis timeshare we were supposed to negotiate ahead of time?

BATS: Yes.

> **PEAK:** I'm listening.

BATS: Wednesdays are reserved for my angst only, so.

> **PEAK:** LOL

BATS: Oh good, you're laughing.
Now I don't have to sue you for
infringing on my official angst day.

>   **PEAK:** What days do I get?

BATS: 1am to 5am on Sundays,
3:30pm to 5pm on Tuesdays,
Thursdays from 6am to 7am.

>   **PEAK:** Those are all times I'm
>   sleeping . . . except for Tuesday,
>   which is when I have a lesson?

BATS: Yeah, that was the whole plan.
Sleep through your suffering or channel
it into music.

>   **PEAK:** Why don't you do that?

BATS: Because I have no self-control
and am needy as shit. And yet for
some reason you like talking to me.

>   **PEAK:** Stoooooop.
>   You're not needy.

BATS: . . . Have you met me?

PEAK: Once for a second, but I was distracted. You were v cute and nervous, and I didn't hate that.

BATS: I was trying for manly and strong, but.

PEAK: Have you met you?

BATS: Once for a second, but I was very nervous.

PEAK: 😊

BATS: Did you want to talk about it?

PEAK: ?

BATS: Whatever's got you lying on the floor creeping on my angst allotment.

PEAK: Yeah, but I don't think you would understand.

BATS: I'll try not to take that personally. (I'm totally going to take it personally, though. So thanks. I'll be needing that angst allotment back to deal with it. It might even

135

creep into your Sunday hours tbh,
but you brought this on yourself.)

PEAK: Ha. Okay fine. Do you
ever feel like you're not enough
of something? Or you're too
much of something else?

BATS: Every day.

PEAK: What do you do about it?

BATS: Nothing healthy.

PEAK: Helpful.

BATS: 🙁

PEAK: No, seriously. What do you do?

BATS: Obsess over ways I could make
myself more. Or less. Until I'm completely
spun out and don't know which way is up.
It is not a method I would recommend.

PEAK: Yeah. Sounds shitty.

BATS: Astute observation.

PEAK: I wish you were here.

BATS: Me too . . .

PEAK: I should probably get some sleep. It's late. Plus I don't want to take up too much of your angst allotment. It sounds like you need it.

BATS: I appreciate that. But Peak?

PEAK: Yeah?

BATS: Whatever it is, you're definitely enough. Like, exactly the right amount. I guarantee it.

PEAK: ☺

CHAPTER EIGHTEEN

Ridley

"I DON'T KNOW what you want me to tell you," I say, squeezing my hand around my phone so hard it hurts. I need to calm down; I can't get this worked up. I have to be at Verona in a half hour. Jubilee is working there after school, and I promised her I'd meet her—

"Ridley!"

If my dad will let me off the phone, that is. "What? I gotta go!"

"You know how important this is. Quit screwing around. Remember you're here for a reason," he says.

"Right, I'm here to get you what you need and stay out of the way."

My dad's barely even been home lately, and Allison stays locked in her room. Last night I even made dinner for all of us—I was feeling guilty about the whole fake-report thing.

My dad didn't even take a plate, because he was "full from a dinner meeting," and Allison just grabbed some and took it up to her room. It's whatever. At least I don't feel guilty anymore. I honestly didn't think it was possible to like a house *less* than the Seattle house, and yet.

And yet.

"You know that's not true, Ridley," he says, his voice softening just enough that I almost fall for it. Almost.

"Which part?"

He sighs. "Why do you insist on making everything so difficult?"

"Guess I learned from the best," I say, staring at the road below my window.

"Ridley, please. I'm happy you're here. I enjoy spending time with you, but I need you to find me something I can use. We're so close." He sounds so desperate, I almost feel bad.

I want to tell him there isn't anything, because so far there mostly isn't, but I know there's a huge chance he'll send me back to Seattle for that. And I can't. This house might blow to live in, but Verona feels like coming home. I'm not giving that up.

"I'll keep looking," I lie.

"There's always something," Dad says, which is my biggest fear. What if I do find something? What then?

There's a little thump at my door, probably Allison listening in, and I hate her so much, even though our eyes are matching in desperation these days. "Dad, I have to go. I'm meeting Jubilee soon, and I'm skating there, so."

"Why isn't Allison driving you?" he asks, like it never occurred to him that I might walk everywhere or take my board. That maybe Allison and I aren't even talking, let alone close enough for me to ask for a ride.

"I just want to skate."

I click my phone off while my dad is still talking and slide on my hoodie. It's cold enough for a full winter jacket, but I didn't pack one and Mom hasn't bothered to send it. Dad calls back but I let it go to voicemail.

He's got the same reports I do, which conveniently leave off the fact that I know Peak only works there because Vera can't really afford more help, and instead basically say Vera Flores is a comics icon and we're lucky to be alive at the same time as her and this buying-in thing is nonsense because it's never happening. Never.

As long as I don't do anything to fuck this up.

• • •

Warm air and the jingle of bells greet me when I push open the door to Verona. I breathe in deep, soaking in the scent of comics old and new. And this, this feels like home.

"Hey, Rid." I follow the sound of Vera's voice to the back room, where I find her buried in papers.

"Hey, Vera," I say, propping my skateboard against the wall. "What's all that?"

"Financial reports. I hate this side of things," she groans. "You any good with math?" She shoves a pencil behind her ear and pushes the paper a little way in my direction with a hopeful look in her eyes. I can't decide if I should look at them or if I should look away. Probably both, simultaneously.

"I suck at math," I say. Avoidance. Good.

"It was worth a shot."

My eye catches on her laptop, which is open to yet another article about my dad. I wonder what fresh way he's insulted her now, but then I make out the headline: "If You Can't Beat 'Em, Join 'Em: Everlasting Inc. Announces New Indie Line, Geekery Ink."

Shit.

Vera looks up, studying me. "You follow this stuff?"

"A little." I shrug, trying to play it cool despite the fact that my insides are churning.

"He's a piece of work, eh?" Vera says. "Starting a new indie line after what he did to Trinity? Mark Everlasting, and everyone who works for him, should be shot into the sun."

"Yeah, totally." I swallow hard, trying to ignore the voice in my head screaming to come clean or run or melt into the floor until everyone forgets I ever existed.

Vera tilts her head. "You okay, kid?"

"Great, excellent, why wouldn't I be? No reason." Nice, Ridley, smooth.

Vera raises an eyebrow. "Well, Jubilee should be here any second; she just got held up at—" The sound of bells and laughter cut her off. "Speak of the devil."

I trot out to see Jubilee and Jayla walking in, arms linked and laughing. I feel like I'm intruding somehow, so I hang back, just sort of standing awkwardly near the curtain, caught between two places I probably shouldn't be.

Jayla notices me before Jubilee does, and she raises an eyebrow. "I don't bite, you know. You don't have to lurk in the shadows when you see me."

"No, I know, I was just helping Vera in the back, and then

I didn't want to interrupt," I lie. Well, half lie. "You guys seem happy."

"You can come be happy with us," Jubilee says, shoving her backpack behind the counter.

I glance at Jayla and then at Jubilee. "I don't want to—you guys seem—it's fine. I can go back and see if Vera needs help still."

whyamisoawkwardfuckfuckfuckfuckFUCK

"Ridley, it's fine, come hang," Jayla says, and she's smiling, but I can't tell if it's sincere or not. Probably not. Very few people really mean it when it's pointed in my direction. But I go anyway. I'm willing to pretend if she is.

Jubilee nudges my shoulder as I walk by, and I drop onto the stool next to her. Jayla stays on the other side of the counter, leaning on one arm. She's looking around the store like there are customers in it, but there aren't. I try not to worry about that.

"So Jayla here just broke the pacer record for the third year in a row," Jubilee says.

"Pacer record?"

"It's a fitness-test thing in gym, tests speed and agility, kind of a big deal," Jayla answers, polishing her nails on her shirt and giving me a big showy wink.

I laugh. "Well, congratulations on both your speed and agility, then."

"Thank you." She bows. "I would be remiss to not point out that Jubilee also got news this afternoon. She was officially offered an—" Jubilee shakes her head, though, and Jayla's smile drops.

"Offered a what?" I ask, doubly curious now that Jubilee doesn't seem to want to share. I'm probably being an asshole for asking, but.

"Nothing," she says. "Just a music thing. Don't worry about it."

I look at her for an extra beat, but she just grabs a peanut butter cup out of the candy jar and looks away. I know that's not all, but whatever it is, she obviously doesn't want to share it with me. I paste on a smile and pretend that doesn't smart.

"Awesome," I say. I hope I sound genuine.

"What about you?" Jayla asks.

"Me?"

"You got some great accomplishment you're hiding up your sleeve?"

My brain starts to scramble. Let's see, I wrote a believable fake report, I convinced my father I was still spying for him, I had the willpower not to look at Vera's financial reports, I've been drinking enough water, I haven't tried to jump off the roof, and I responded to every one of Gray's texts this week so that she didn't worry about me. And I can say exactly none of that out loud. Every single one makes me sound guilty or worse.

"Uh . . . I made dinner last night?" I say, but it comes out like a question. And then I rub my hands over my face because I just made myself sound even more pathetic in my attempt to make myself sound cool.

"A man who cooks, not bad," Jayla says, but I notice the way she's looking at Jubilee.

She's probably thinking, *Seriously? I broke a record and*

Jubilee did whatever big thing she doesn't want to talk about and all you did was boil some pasta?

shitshitshitshitshitshitshitshit

"What'd you make?" Jubilee asks, and I can barely hear her over the sound of my heart pounding. She looks sincere, but.

holdittogetherholdittogetherholdittogether

"Spaghetti, asparagus, and bread," I choke out, and they both look at me. "I need some air." I hop off the stool and go outside, the cold wind burning against my skin.

I hear the bells tinkle again a minute later as the door pushes open, and Jayla comes out with her backpack on. "You okay?" she asks.

"Just needed some air," I say again, embarrassment painting my neck crimson. I tilt my head enough to see her out of the corner of my eye. She's watching me, but she doesn't look annoyed or mean like I expected, more like curious. Open, maybe. I don't know.

"Yeah, well, I have to get to work." She twists the strap of her backpack. "But if you ever want to come over when Jubi's hanging out, it'd be fine."

I look up at her, startled. "Seriously?"

She shrugs. "I gotta jet, though, and I'm sure Jubi is eager for you to get back inside."

I nod, because this feels like an olive branch, a peace offering, a genuine smile. And I don't know what to do with that.

CHAPTER NINETEEN

Jubilee

"YOUR ENERGY IS much better," Mrs. Garavuso says as I wipe down my cello and set it back into its case. "Whatever you're doing, it's working. Your interpretation in the sarabande was the best I've heard from you yet." She smiles. "I think you're nearly there for your audition."

"Don't jinx me," I say, heading for the door. I have tons of homework tonight, and it's already late, but I know Jayla and Nikki are waiting for me downstairs. I've been working on being a better friend since Jayla called me out on it, and tonight we're celebrating a major win for their soccer team.

"It's not a jinx if it's true," Mrs. G calls after me as I bound down her front steps.

Jayla's car is in the driveway, and both girls wave at Mrs. G when I come out. I slide my cello into the back seat and dive in after it, shivering even from the two seconds it took to walk to the car.

"Hot cocoa," Nikki says, handing me a cup. It's from Stacks, my all-time favorite coffee shop for reasons too numerous to count, and I smile when I taste the cinnamon.

"Awww," I say. "You guys remembered!"

"Like we could ever forget the cinnamon and live to tell about it."

"No Emily tonight?" I ask.

"I wanted it to be just us," Jayla says, messing with the radio.

"And Emily had to babysit her brother," Nikki adds.

"The truth comes out." Now that their coach knows, Jayla and Emily have been seriously inseparable at school. Jayla even started a new group chat with her in it, even though we mostly still use the old one with just the three of us.

"So where are we headed?" I spin the cup in my hand, letting it warm my fingers.

"Bowling," Nikki sings.

"Bowling? Why?"

Jayla sighs and I can tell this is a conversation they've already had. "Nikki suggested rock climbing, but since we have another game tomorrow and you have your audition coming up, I thought we should do something with a lower risk of hand and foot injuries."

"Good plan." I laugh. It feels good to be sitting here with my best friends, not stressing about school or summer programs or nerdy boys that live in my phone or my stepmom's shop. It's exactly what I need.

"Plus, it's black-light night at Bowl-A-Rama," Nikki says, and I want to question why she has the bowling schedule memorized, but I also don't want to know.

It takes a while to get there; the bowling alley is halfway

across town and we hit every red light on the way. I'm kind of grateful, though. By the time we slide into the parking lot, I've completely finished my hot cocoa and part of my history homework.

Nikki and I put our coats down while Jayla pays and gets our shoes. There are not many benefits to us all wearing the same shoe size (7 across the board) except that it's easy to remember and our footwear choices triple in a pinch.

Jayla drops our shoes on the ground, and we sit on the little set of steps separating the lanes from the snack area to shove our feet inside.

"Ready to lose, ladies?" Nikki laughs, standing up to grab her ball.

"Yes," I answer at the same time Jayla says, "Never."

• • •

"So when is the big tournament?" I ask. We're perched on stools at the Bowl-A-Rama snack bar, trying to ignore the overwhelming smell of beer and shoe polish while chowing down on hot wings. My lips are burning, but it's totally worth it. Bowl-A-Rama wings are undeniably the best in town, and—seeing as how I generally avoid the bowling alley at all costs—also a rare treat.

"The weekend after your audition," Nikki says, twisting slowly back and forth on her spinny bar stool.

The date of my audition has been hanging over us since I got the official invite last week. It's thrilling and terrifying all at once, a bright red X on the calendar that hopefully marks the beginning of the rest of my life.

"Great, so all of us will be anxious little stress balls for the next month," Jayla says, but the smirk on her face tells me she doesn't really mind.

"I've got it in the bag," Nikki says. *"Anxious little stress ball is not in my vocabulary."*

"Easy for you to say. You have a whole additional year of high school soccer to earn scholarships and make a name for yourself." I sigh. "I only have, like, five weeks to nail my repertoire, or it's game over."

"You will," Jayla says, squeezing my wrist. "You've been working toward this forever. You're going to make it happen."

Nikki grabs another wing. "It's not the end of the world if it doesn't work out, anyway."

I snap my head toward her. "Why would you even say that!"

"Because it's true. You're putting waaaay too much pressure on getting into this summer program. It's not like there aren't other ones out there. And it's not like you won't get into college without it. *You* have a whole other year left too."

"But this is my *only* chance to study with Aleksander Ilyashev before my college audition. I need this. I didn't even schedule auditions for any other summer programs."

She shrugs. "Maybe you should have."

"What the hell, Nikki?" Jayla says. She twists around so fast, I swear to god if these stools weren't bolted to the floor, she would have spun hers right over.

"What?" Nikki asks. "I think she'll get in! I'm not saying

she won't. But she's putting too much pressure on herself. There are way more important things in life. Things can happen outside of her control, and she—"

"*She's* right here," I say, hating the way they're talking over me. It reminds me too much of Vera and my mom. Like they know better than I do where I should be and what I should be doing. They don't understand; I wouldn't be putting this much pressure on myself if I didn't have to, if I didn't *need* that scholarship.

"Sorry," Nikki says, wiping her fingers. "I just want you to relax a little. Wasn't that Mrs. G's whole point? And you don't *have* to do the summer program with Aleksander what's-his-name to get into that school, do you?"

"Ilyashev. And no, but it would really help. Can you imagine his feedback? The edge it would give me when I audition with him for their college program next winter?"

"I know. Winning the Empire Classic would really help me too, give me a leg up going into my final year. Do you know how many college scouts are at that tournament?"

"I can guess," I say, hating that she knows more about my thing than I know about hers.

"I'm just saying, don't let one moment define you. Because there are going to be a lot of moments still to come, no matter which way things shake out."

Nobody says anything after that; we just eat our wings and listen to the sound of balls crashing into pins and people cheering or swearing. When the conversation does pick back up, we switch gears to safer topics—complaining about school, talking about how great Emily is, and joking about how Nikki and Ty are finally together but still aren't being super public about it.

But Nikki's words keep buzzing in my head, and I wonder if she's right. It doesn't feel like she is, though. For the first time, it feels like maybe she just doesn't get it. Like, at all. And it's weird to feel like that about Nikki, and maybe a little about Jayla too.

CHAPTER TWENTY

PEAK: I feel like an absolute alien
around my friends lately.

                       BATS: Really? What happened?

PEAK: So I don't want to jinx it
but . . . I'm trying to get into a really
intense summer program that would
let me study cello with my literal idol.
And tonight Nikki said it "won't be the
end of the world" if I don't get in.

                                    BATS: And?

PEAK: I think I would die if that happened.

                       BATS: Do you mean that?
                       Peak, that's not okay.

PEAK: Not literally or anything.

                            BATS: Oh. Well, good.

PEAK: But I've been working toward
this for so long, and now the audition
is almost here and one of my best
friends in the whole world is just like
"oh, it's not a big deal." It is, though.
IT IS A VERY BIG DEAL.

BATS: Yeah, that would suck
to hear. Like they're minimizing
your dream or whatever.

PEAK: Exactly! I can't believe she said that.

BATS: I think some people don't
understand what it's like to be so
singularly driven. They're wired
differently. You can't really get
mad at that.

PEAK: Can't I get a little mad at that?

BATS: Okay, a little.

PEAK: There is so much riding on this
audition. Like I can't just get in. I have to
get that scholarship, you know? And I can't
have Nikki acting like it doesn't matter.
I can't have that in my head.

BATS: It matters. Of course it matters.
It's a ton of pressure to be under.

PEAK: God, you just get it.
How do you just get it?

BATS: I have no idea.
I never get anything.

PEAK: You get me.

BATS: I hope so.

PEAK: I'm so glad you
were in that elevator.

BATS: Me too.

CHAPTER TWENTY-ONE
Ridley

IT'S NEW-COMIC day, same as every Wednesday, and I've been helping Jubilee out with a rare surplus of customers. Vera has offered to add me to the payroll more than once, since I'm here so much, but I declined. She makes me wear a sign around my neck that says INTERN whenever she sees me, to shame me into accepting pay—which I never will. I've noticed she gets around it by buying me extra food and giving me books. It feels good in a bad way.

A man named Rutherford came in a few minutes ago and picked up his gigantic stash of books, which had Jubilee laughing for some reason. But now it's just us again, back to restocking, and she's acting all jumpy and nervous.

"Sorry," she says the third time she walks into me.

"It's fine." I steady her with my hands, so starved for touch that even this little bit of contact makes my head spin. She smiles and I fight the urge to kiss her.

While Peak and Bats seem to be making a habit of baring their souls to each other, Ridley and Jubilee are much more tentative. We are stolen smiles and the occasional head resting on my shoulder. Peak and Bats are . . . more. And the closer they get, the shittier I feel about everything—especially since she handed me exactly the in my dad's looking for when she told me about needing that scholarship. God, I hate money.

She sighs. "I just have a lot on my mind today."

"Is this about the audition?"

"The what?" she asks, her face scrunching up. "How do you know about that?"

I should have known this would happen. I've been juggling too many balls at once, and that's never been my strong point.

"How do you know about my audition?" A little divot forms between her eyebrows when she asks, and I wish I could shrink down like Ant-Man and hide in it until she's less angry, or until she forgets about me completely. Whichever happens first.

"You told me," I say, but suddenly I'm not so sure. Did she tell me? Or did she just tell Bats? She must have told us both. She had to have. It's like *the* most important thing about her. She definitely would have told Ridley too—told *me* too, I mean.

"I didn't." She crosses her arms. "Conservatory prep and audition are inner circle only."

I wince at the implication that I'm not inner circle. But, of course, I'm not. I'm just the rando at her mom's store.

"Are you sure?"

"They only let in eight cellists, and I don't need anyone finding out I applied if I don't make the cut. Inner. Circle," she says, flicking me in the shoulder. "I wouldn't have told you. It's not the kind of thing I would let slip."

And okay, it is supremely fucked up, but a part of me is jealous that she told Bats all about it but wouldn't *let it slip* to me. I know.

I know.

But the bigger issue at the moment is that I know something I shouldn't, and she's standing in front of me, waiting for an explanation that I don't have. Here we go.

shitshitshitshitshitshitshitshit

I exhale slowly, fumbling with the rack we were just restocking. Maybe if I just stare straight ahead, another customer will come in, and Jubilee will forget all about this conversation we're having.

"Well," she says again, "I know I didn't tell you."

I chew on my lip, trying to buy myself more time. "Vera must have mentioned it?"

"She wouldn't. She knows how superstitious I am. There are, like, seven people in this entire world who know I'm going for the summer program, and I want to know how you make eight."

I turn around and walk back behind the counter, my heart pounding in my ears.

"Just spill it. I can tell you have something to say. I've known something was up for a while."

"You have?" I ask, because if she knows already, then maybe it's gonna be fine. Maybe there's still hope.

maybemaybemaybemaybemaybe

"Yeah, like I know you're not really broke, so whatever

you're hiding about your secret rich background or whatever, just tell me. I don't care. What, is your father, like, on the board of the conservatory or something? Are you going to break it to me gently that you've already seen my application?"

I laugh, hoarse and hard, and I hate it. But I can't believe this is what she thinks about, that I have money and she doesn't care. How big of her. When the fuck has anybody cared that somebody has money? Like, when has that been a detractor? As long as I'm the right kind of rich, everybody's in love. Jesus, why does everybody care so much about money?

She's not entirely wrong, though. I know for a fact that one of my dad's especially smarmy drinking buddies is on the board of the conservatory. If Dad told him about this, he probably *could* arrange for her to get the scholarship or make sure she never got it, depending on how Vera reacted. Which is exactly why he can never find out.

I clench my hands and shove them in my pockets. I don't want to do this anymore. I can't.

"Ridley, what's wrong?"

I glance up and meet her eyes. She looks worried, and I don't want to be the one to make her look like that.

icantdothisicant

Maybe I can leave. Maybe I can get away. Go back to Seattle. She'd still have Bats. And maybe Bats is better than nothing. Maybe. I don't know. I can't think here. There are too many books and not enough space.

gogogogogogogogogogogogo

"I have to leave," I say, and dart out the door.

It's pouring outside, because of course it would pour when

I have to skate three miles home. I'd call for an Uber, but I left my phone inside. Oh well, I'll just order another one.

And I know as soon as I get back to my dad's house, I'm going to lock myself behind a door nobody can get through and sit alone until the plane ticket processes and the Uber comes, until I can be a million miles away, where I can just be the boy that Peak texts when it's convenient for her, where I won't mess up her life just by being around.

I close my eyes and try to forget that, for a second, her leg was pressed against mine. For a second, I made her laugh, and she lit up my brain like the Fourth of July. For a second, she smiled at me. For a second, those were real things that happened to me, to her, and to us, but now I can't breathe.

I can't breathe.

I crouch down, not even caring that I'm in the middle of the sidewalk in the pouring rain, and it feels like hours but could be minutes before I hear the bells over the door clang behind her and then go silent.

"Ridley!" she shouts, and she's holding my phone. "You forgot this." Oh god, she's holding my phone; she's holding Bats and she doesn't even know.

Jubilee stands under the awning. Waiting. She's not chasing me, I realize; this isn't the end of some epic romance movie. She just wants an explanation, deserves one, even. "Tell me," she says, her eyes vacillating between concern and annoyance. "Tell me what's going on."

I stand, and finally, just to blow up the entire world—just to good and blow it up because of who I am and what I am and how I don't deserve good things anyway—I turn back to her with a grin that turns to a sneer that turns to a grimace as I feel all the fight fall out of me. This will definitely get me sent back to Seattle. This will probably ruin everything. But screw it. She deserves the truth.

She does.

"Hey, Peak," I say, my voice cracking.

She takes a step back, pressing her hand to the door. Her head tilts like she's trying to see more of me than what's in front of her, and then she raises her hand to her lips.

"Bats?" she says, like she can't really believe it, and honestly, I barely can either.

"Yeah."

"What?" There's a little smile on her lips then, and I shouldn't smile back but I do.

She pulls out her own phone and fires off a text, her mouth dropping open when my phone lights up in her hand. I shut my eyes.

"How are you here?"

I shrug, because I can't tell her that. I can't drop another bomb on her, especially not if there's a single chance that we can get through this conversation without her hating me. I didn't think there was, but that smile—that smile.

"Wait, are you stalking me?" she asks, crossing her arms around herself.

I hate that I did this.

"No," I say too loud. "No," I say a little softer, shivering slightly because of the cold rain and the March air and the mean look from the girl that I like. Shit. I do. I really like her.

I gulp the air because I can't breathe, I can't get a deep enough breath, and the world starts to spin, and I'm 200 percent positive that I'm going to suffocate in this moment, that this is the end, and if it is, I can't even care.

ideserveit

"Ridley," she says. "Bats." And I look up, because I didn't think that was going to be a word that I heard from her ever again. "Did you know that a cat's nose print is unique like our fingerprints?"

"No?" I choke out. The world seems to spin a little slower as I look in her eyes, but I can't quite trust it.

"Swear to god."

She looks at me from under the awning, and it feels like I can maybe inhale just a little. "Who tested that theory?" I ask.

And when she laughs, it feels like breaking through the surface of the water.

"Somebody really brave." She smiles, but then it fades. "I need you to tell me what's going on."

"I don't—" I huff and then look at the ground, shaking my head. I have no idea where to start.

"Why didn't you say anything?" she asks, the hint of annoyance back in her voice. "I've been texting you this whole time. I even told you about . . . you."

"I know."

"Is this a game?" Her tone changes again. Gets harder somehow.

"No, it's not."

"Okay? Then why did you let me keep thinking you were two different people?"

"I'm an asshole," I say, raising my arms and then dropping them. "I don't know what else to say. I was scared."

"Scared of me?"

"No, of not being able to text with you anymore. And—"

"And what?"

"I can't." I shake my head. "But there are reasons, okay? And I will tell you, but I can't right now. I can't do this. I'll—I'll text you."

"Uh-uh, you don't get to run away. Not after this. This is unbelievably screwed up."

"I know. I know! But what if you—"

"What if I what?" she asks, taking a step forward so she's as far out as she can be under the awning without getting wet.

"I'm not good at talking to people. I'm not good at a lot of things. But when I'm texting Peak—you," I correct myself. "When I text you, I don't get freaked out. I can relax. I can be there for you or be funny. And if I do get overwhelmed, I can just put the phone down and come back later. I didn't want to lose that. And I didn't want to know."

"Know what?"

I take a deep breath and drop my head. The rain is soaking into my sweatshirt and digging at my skin. "I didn't want to know if you liked that version of me better than the real me." I'm shaking now, but I can't tell if it's from the cold.

"I like both," she says, and looking back at her almost feels good. I can almost forget that there are more secrets lurking behind this one, that this is only the harmless tip of the iceberg destined to sink us.

"Ridley," she says, holding out her hand. "Come out of the rain."

"No."

"Why?"

"Because there's more. And if you knew, you wouldn't want me under that awning with you."

"So tell me, then!"

"I can't!" I shout, staring at the bricks on the wall.

icanticanticanticant

"Ridley, I just found out that the two boys I can't stop thinking about are the exact same boy, and I don't ever have to choose, so get over here," she pleads. "Whatever else there is, we'll figure it out."

Oh god, I want to, but.

"No," I say, so quiet I don't know how she hears me over the rain.

"How come?"

"Because if we pretend this is all okay, when you find out the truth and stop talking to me—and you will—I'll lose my fucking mind." I don't know if it's the rain or tears, but my face is wet, so I wipe it with my sleeve and hope she doesn't see. My hair is slicked down flat against my forehead, the longer strands slipping in front of my eyes. It's like I'm looking at her through bars. Fitting.

She takes a step toward me, and then another. My mouth has gone dry, and my clothes are soaked, and she's getting closer and closer, until we're both standing in the pouring rain. She wraps me in a hug that I want to melt into more than anything, but I don't. I just stand, straight and rigid, and wait for her to stop. It's everything I ever wanted, and nothing I deserve.

"You're shaking." She puts her hand over mine, lacing our fingers together, and the rain dripping down her face somehow makes her look even more beautiful. "Come on, let's go back inside. We can talk more while you dry off."

I almost give in. I almost think that I could belong in a warm, brightly lit room full of books with a girl that didn't run away. I almost let myself believe that the worst is over, that this is fine. That she never has to learn more than she knows now. That I can have my cake and eat it too. That I can keep her in the dark about who my dad is and keep my dad in the dark about what I found out. That I can make it all work somehow. But she looks at me, relief in her eyes because I'm following her, and I stop. This is wrong.

This is really wrong.

"Peak, wait," I say, and she turns around.

"What?" she asks, looking a little nervous behind her smile. The divot reappears on her forehead, and I want to smooth it away.

"My full name . . ."

"Is Ridley McDonough. I know, you told me."

"McDonough is my mom's last name. I use it when . . . sometimes," I say, taking a deep breath.

"Okay?" And the divot is bigger, her face more worried.

"My legal name is Ridley Oliver Everlasting."

She tilts her head. I can tell she's trying to figure out

where she's heard it before. "Everlasting?" she asks, and then her eyes get wide. "Everlasting, like Everlasting Inc.? Like the family that owns The Geekery?"

I swallow hard and nod.

"Are you messing with me right now?"

"No." It's not a lie, but I wish it was. I wish they weren't my family. I wish—

"What was all this, then?" she shouts. "A trick?"

"No. No! Please don't think that." I take a step toward her, but she pulls back.

"I thought people were paranoid after the Trinity Comics thing. But you guys really do have plants. And that's what you are, right? A plant, a spy for your company?"

I nod again, not breaking eye contact. "But I'm not spying. I'm not really doing it. I swear."

"Screw you," she says, "whoever you are."

CHAPTER TWENTY-TWO

BATS: I'm sorry, for whatever it's worth.

CHAPTER TWENTY-THREE

Jubilee

"I'M GOING TO kill him," Jayla says, and her screen gets blurry and starts cutting out just as she's miming a stabbing motion, leaving her stuck with big eyes and her fist in the air.

Nikki giggles. "You're freezing up, Jay."

We're in a group hangout on Skype. I texted everybody, begging for an emergency meet-up, but Jayla's mom wouldn't let her go out, because she missed curfew last night—thanks, Emily—and Nikki's mom's new home aide didn't show, so she can't leave either. Skype it is.

"I'll tell you who's about to freeze up," Jayla's voice cuts through, sounding at times like a stuttering robot. "Ridley, when I drag him out of his cozy little mansion in Claremont and dump him into the ocean right on his prep-school ass."

"I don't think he actually went to prep school," I say, not that it matters.

"Well, he—" Jayla says, and then she gets all pixelated, her voice turning into a series of weird-sounding vowels as her internet crashes. Her brother is probably live-streaming his video games again. It always messes with her Wi-Fi.

"What?" Nikki asks, leaning closer to her screen like it will help her to hear better. It won't. I shove another peanut butter cup in my mouth as Jayla's screen goes black and then just says CONNECTING.

"We lost her," Nikki says, looking sad. But Jayla will log off and back on, and if we get lucky, we might get a few more minutes with her before she has to do it all over again. The coffee shop would have made this so much easier.

"She'll be back," I say, more for me than for her. I need Jayla to come back on. She's my grounded friend; Nikki is the romantic. If she's not back soon, in all likelihood Nikki will have me forgiving him and picking out wedding flowers within the next two hours. And the worst part is, I almost want to.

Not the wedding flowers, but the forgiving-him thing. I know what Jayla will say, that I always do this, that I stayed with Dakota too long and forgave way too much, that I only see the good in people and people take advantage of that. But I don't know. Is it so bad to always look for the good?

"What are you going to do?" Nikki asks, tucking herself into the warmest-looking fleece blanket I've ever seen.

"I have no idea."

"What do you want to do?"

"I want to text Bats and tell him I've had a shitty day and let him make me feel better and pretend like none of this is happening."

"The hell you are," Jayla says, her face popping back onto the screen. "Do not listen to Nikki's star-crossed lovers BS. He lied to you. That's it. Game over."

I sigh and grab another piece of candy.

"It does seem a little like fate, though?" Nikki says, her voice lilting up at the end like a question.

"Screw that." Jayla leans closer to the camera on her phone. "It's not fate to manipulate somebody into caring about you so that you can spy on them. It's creepy and abusive, and we're going to tell the whole world what an absolute piece of trash he is and blast The Geekery all over the internet."

"No," I say firmly, "we're not."

"Why are you protecting him?"

"I just don't want to make it this big public thing. I'm not protecting him."

"Except you are," Nikki says, and okay, when even Ms. Optimist is calling you out on something, it's time to take a step back.

"How are you not more pissed?" Jayla asks.

I rub my finger over a smudge on my keyboard, avoiding eye contact. "I was furious earlier, but now I'm mostly just sad."

And lonely. I really miss them. Him? Both of him? This is so messed up.

Jayla sighs. I can tell she doesn't like my answer.

"I get it," Nikki says. "You lost two people you really cared about today."

"Yeah," I say, trying to ignore the ache in my chest. "I'm still processing it or whatever."

"That's it. I'm sneaking out," Jayla says.

"Don't!" Nikki shrieks. "Your mom will end you."

"Look at her face!" Jayla gestures toward her camera, and I can only assume she means me. "Jubilee called an emergency meeting, and she's getting one."

"Don't," I echo. "Seriously, I'm fine. I'm gonna crash soon anyway; there's no point."

"Okay," she says. "Here's what we're doing. Tonight, you mope. Tomorrow, you get angry. Friday night, we come up with a plan."

"Are we still watching *Captain Marvel*?" Nikki asks, and Jayla and I both roll our eyes.

"Yes," Jayla says. "Obviously. I need to scope out the costumes for our next con."

"Good, because I'm dying to—"

But I don't hear what else she says as I click my laptop shut. I can't think about this anymore. It's time to do what I do whenever I can't figure something out. It's time to play.

The bow is steady in my hand as I slide it across the strings, sending a long mournful note out into the atmosphere before changing tempo, making it more hectic, more agitated. I play until my arms are aching and my bow is fraying and sweat is dotting my face.

And when I can't play anymore, I collapse on my bed and pray for dreamless sleep.

CHAPTER TWENTY-FOUR

Ridley

I SLINK LOWER, the cold porcelain biting at my skin as I settle against the back of the tub. I bend my knees and dip even lower as the water rises—first to my chest, then to my chin, then to my nose. Sadbath central, but who cares. Allison has been screaming at me about my reports, and I just—I just need it to be quiet.

It's almost peaceful floating here, the water enveloping me, making me feel safe in a way I don't anywhere else. Somewhere in the back of my head, I know I should get out, need to get out, that I can't float here forever.

But there are bad things waiting on the other side of the bathroom door. Like the fact that Peak hates me, like I knew she would. She didn't even respond to the half-assed text apology I sent—not that I expected her to—or to the three I sent after it either. At the moment, exploring alternatives to living with what I've done seems pretty appealing.

I even tried calling my mom, telling her I was feeling down, that being here wasn't what I thought it would be. But she was rushing out to meet some friends and told me the standard "Tough it out, Rid. Tomorrow is a new day." Which, I guess, but.

The steam rises from the water and disappears into the air. I wonder what it's like to be like that, to fit so perfectly in the universe that you can disappear in it. I just want to *fit*. Somewhere. Anywhere. I don't know. I almost did for a minute. It felt like it anyway; goofing off at Verona with Jubilee was the closest I ever felt to home.

I slide down, all the way down this time, my hair floating up as my head hits the bottom of the tub. The water drifts up my nose and in my ears; it's a little uncomfortable but not bad, and everything is so quiet, just a hint of splashing and the sound of my heartbeat pounding in my ears. Somehow even that seems watery and far away, like it's someone else's heart in someone else's body. And it must be—it has to be—because it feels like Peak's got mine in her fist in the next town over.

I plant my feet against the front of the tub and shove up, breaking through the surface with a gasp as water splashes everywhere. The air feels good against my too-hot skin as I crawl out, grabbing a towel and leaving little wet footprints in my wake. I'll clean it up later. Or I won't. I suppose either way it doesn't actually matter.

I pull on some sweats and grab my phone, scrolling through to my sister's name. I promised Gray I would always call in an emergency, and I think maybe this is one. I know she's in Boston again, visiting friends, and I shouldn't be bothering her. But still, this is me keeping a promise for once in my life.

"Hey, Ridley," she says, picking up on the second ring, and I can hear her smile through the phone. It's loud wherever she is, and I glance at the time. It's barely nine o'clock; she's probably still out to dinner or something. Gray's like that—she's the kind of person who'll have dinner at eight, the kind of person other people want to be around.

"Hi." I try to sound cheerful. I am so not her problem, and I feel bad for calling now.

"Shit, hang on a second?"

"It's okay," I say, because truly I don't want to fuck up her night. I wouldn't have called if she hadn't made me swear.

"Can you hear me?" she asks half a minute later. Wherever she is now, it's quiet.

"Yeah, but don't worry about it."

"Shut up, Ridley. What's going on?"

"Nothing," I lie. "I was just bored."

"You sure?" She hesitates, and I know what's coming. "Are you safe?"

I roll onto my back and drop one arm over my eyes. I hate when she asks if I'm safe. It makes me feel like I'm two years old. "I'm fine. Don't worry about it. I was just calling to say hi."

"I'd rather talk to you than anybody in that room, and you know it. Whatever it is you're trying not to tell me, spill, or I'm driving over right now to make you say it face-to-face."

I scoff. "Boston's like ninety minutes away."

"Sixty in a rush," she says, her voice firm and worried. "Don't test me."

"Peak is Vera Flores's stepdaughter," I blurt out, because

172

Peak has been the subject of probably 60 percent of my texts with Gray lately, and she'll get exactly how bad that is.

"Holy shit," she says, and then goes quiet for a second. "How is that possible?" I don't answer, and there's a sharp intake of breath on the other end of the line. "You knew when you agreed to do this, didn't you?"

I roll onto my side, blinking hard. "Yeah."

"I can't believe I didn't put this together. Ridley, this is really . . ." She trails off like she doesn't know what else to say.

"I screwed up. I know."

"Peak was your in this whole time? I thought you liked her."

"I do like her! I really like her! But Dad was so happy, and it just snowballed. All of a sudden, I was back in my old room, and he was taking me out to dinner and making small talk, and he's never been like that with me."

"Ridley—"

"You know that's true! You and I might have the same last name, but we don't have the same parents. They aren't there for me the way they are for you. And when he dangled a chance to come *home*—"

"That's not home, Ridley. It's just a house we used to live in."

"You don't understand." My eyes burn, because she doesn't. She really doesn't.

"I'm trying," she says. "But you can't keep this up. It's not healthy for you, and it's not fair to her."

"I know. I told her today that I was Bats."

"Oh god, what did she say?"

"She seemed happy at first."

"At first?" Her voice sounds hesitant, and I squeeze my eyes shut because if I don't, I'm going to start bawling.

"Yeah." I sniff. "And then I told her my real last name, and she slammed the door in my face."

She sighs, and I count to five before she speaks again. "Okay, walk me through it."

I shrug, even though she can't see me. "There's nothing really to walk through. I told her everything, and now she hates me."

"All of it?"

"Well, she guessed a lot of it herself, but yeah."

"Oh, Ridley."

"I just couldn't do it anymore," I say, dragging a hand through my still-wet hair. "I care about her too much to lie."

"Do you love her?" Gray asks, and there's no judgment there, just a question.

"I don't know."

"That's a hell of a reveal for 'I don't know.'"

"Yeah. So how do I fix it?"

Gray's quiet again, and for the first time, I wonder if maybe she doesn't have the answer, but that's impossible. Gray has had the solution to everything since I was born.

"Grand sweeping gesture?" she says finally. "It works in the movies."

"Are you being serious?"

"No. Don't actually do that. Just try to talk to her, if she'll let you. And try to rebuild her trust. And stop spying on her store."

"About that. I'm actually not. It turns out I suck at screwing people over. No wonder I'm the black sheep of the family."

"Wow, thanks."

"I didn't mean it like that," I say, even though I kind of did. "But yeah, I've been sending fake reports too. I'd never tell Dad, but I did find out one thing that—"

"Don't tell me about it either."

I stare down at my feet, the reality of the situation washing over me again, making everything seem impossible. I swallow hard. "What do I do if she won't talk to me?"

"Then you back off and give her space," she says softly. "Either she comes around on her own, or you chalk it up to a lesson learned."

"That's it? You're telling me to give up?"

"It's not giving up; it's respecting what she wants, which you should have done in the first place by being honest with her. I want this to work out for you so bad, but what you did was beyond reprehensible, even if I get the reasons why you did it. Just be prepared, okay? Sometimes you can't fix things once they're broken. If she doesn't want to talk, then you need to back off."

"Yeah." I swallow hard and don't mention the fact that Peak's already been ignoring my texts.

Gray sighs again, and I swear I feel that shit in my soul. "Maybe tearing it all down wasn't the worst thing. Nothing good would ever come from the lies. So either you sped up the inevitable, or you have the chance to build something that's actually solid."

"Yeah, maybe," I say, even though I don't really believe it.

"I'm glad you called, Rid. Let's do something this weekend. Pick a cool spot to eat. We'll see a movie and go out to dinner after."

"Sure," I say, pretending not to notice that she's giving me something concrete to look forward to, a goal to reach. She read a bunch of self-help-type books a few years back—once she figured out what a mess I was—and decided I would benefit from concrete goals and plans. She's been not so subtle about doing it ever since.

"All right, let me know how it goes. I expect a text every day with an update."

"Yes, Grayson," I say, rolling my eyes at her and her goals.

It does weirdly help, though.

I set the phone down and then think better of it, scrolling to the last song Peak sent me. I put it on a loop and stay awake as long as I can, listening. And when I do fall asleep, I dream about butterflies.

CHAPTER TWENTY-FIVE

Jubilee

"YOU HAVE TO tell your parents," Jayla says. Nikki sits beside her, nodding in agreement.

I'm on my side on my bed, hugging my pillow and watching them paint their nails, while Captain Marvel saves the world on my TV. Nikki is going with pink; Jayla has gone for a brilliant yellow. I shut my eyes and try to forget about the fact that I basically broke up with both of my boyfriends this week, simultaneously. Not that I even realized I thought of them that way until after it was over, when I missed them so much I felt like I was losing it. *Him*—I missed *him*. I still can't get used to Ridley and Bats being one.

"Well, actually, maybe she doesn't have to tell them, unless he was really spying," Nikki says, and even though I declared it a state of emergency on our call the other day, I really wish we could talk about anything but this now. "He said he wasn't."

I shift the pillow to cover my face as I roll over onto my back. I hate this. I hate that he lied to me this whole time, and

I hate that I miss him so much I could scream. I should dislike him, like, as a person, probably forever. But I don't.

I'm more annoyed that all the times I said I wished he were here, he could have been. I wish he'd told me sooner. I wish there was more than a span of like three breaths between him saying "Hey, Peak" and me saying "Screw you." It isn't fair.

"Obviously he's spying," Jayla says, rolling her eyes. "He's an Everlasting; that's what they do."

Everlasting. It doesn't sound like a bad name, pretty cool actually, except for the family attached to it. Why does he have to be an Everlasting? Maybe he could get emancipated. That's a thing, right?

"Well," Jayla says. "What are you going to do?"

"I have time to figure it out," I say, flipping the pillow back behind my head. "I doubt I'll see him again anyway."

Jayla drops her chin. "No, you definitely will. What day do they have you working?"

"Sunday."

"With Vera or alone?"

"Alone."

"He'll be there," Jayla snorts. "I'd put money on it."

"He probably took the first private jet out of here," I say, all nonchalant, pretending like that thought doesn't hurt.

"He'll show," she says, going back to painting her nails, which makes my traitor heart twist in ways it shouldn't.

"Is he still texting you?" Nikki asks.

"Nope," I say, popping the *p* and scratching my eyebrow with my thumb. "Just the ones right after, and then nothing."

I climb off the bed and go over to my nail polish, picking out a wild shade of teal. I realize too late it's the same one I wore to FabCon prom.

"Don't you think this whole thing was one giant setup?" Jayla asks. "It's too convenient to not have been."

"Jay." Nikki waves her hand back and forth like that will make it dry faster. "You seriously think he rode the elevator up and down all night hoping you guys would get on? Doubtful."

Jayla shoots Nikki a look. "Not that part, obviously, but everything after that."

"It was fate, face it," Nikki says, like that's a totally normal, rational belief.

"Fate, right, that must be it." Jayla laughs, flipping over her buzzing phone to read an incoming text. "Crap."

"What?"

"Sorry, Jubi, but we gotta go. My mom needs me to pick up my brother, and I have to drop Nikki off first."

"It's fine. I'm okay," I say, even though I was hoping they could sleep over. But they have a super-early away game tomorrow anyway, so it's probably for the best.

"You sure?" Nikki asks.

"It was just a con crush, right? Who even cares?" I try to play it off, but those words hurt coming out.

Jayla narrows her eyes like she doesn't quite believe me. "Right," she says. "This is why we ghost them. Trust me next time."

• • •

"Jubi?" my mom says, peeking her head into my room.

"Yeah?" It's been an hour since the girls left, and I've been staring at my phone ever since, debating whether texting Bats back would be the worst thing in the world. Half of me has decided it would be. The other half has decided it wouldn't.

"I think HP got out."

I bolt upright. "What?"

"I just opened a can of her food, and she didn't come. I was hoping she was locked in here with you."

I flip off the covers and shove my feet into my unicorn slippers. "Nope. Vera was carrying in a ton of canvases earlier. I bet she snuck out. I'll go find her." This is bad; HP is *not* an outdoor cat.

"If she doesn't come running, we'll get her in the morning, okay?"

"Sure," I say, but there is no way I'm leaving my cat outside all night. One, it's cold; two, she's mean; and three, she has the common sense of a bag of rocks. Not a great combination.

My mom gives me a quick kiss on the cheek and says good night, and then, armed with stale cat treats, I head out to the back deck. The few times she's gotten out, that's where she's ended up.

"Harry!" I call, and . . . nothing. "HP!" I try, a little louder.

I walk to the edge and lean over the railing, shaking the treats as loud as I can. "Here, kitty, kitty, kitty."

There's a rustling sound, followed by some angry cat

noises. Shit. This is bad. What if she's fighting with that neighborhood stray?

"Harry?" I call, darting down the steps. My slippers are going to be ruined, but screw it. Some things are more important in life.

The angry cat sounds are getting louder, but now they're accompanied by someone shouting, "Dammit, stop. Ow—what's the matter with you?"

And that voice, it's a poison and an antidote all at once.

I pick up the pace, and we round the corner at the same time, nearly running into one another. We both stop at the last second, staring at each other with matching shocked faces, while HP hisses and tears at his arms.

"Ridley?"

"Peak, I—"

But HP swats him in the face—claws out—before he can finish. She goes flying as he jerks back, and I scoop her up before she gets too far. She struggles for a second but then seems to realize it's me and goes limp. I'd like to think it's because she's happy to see me, but I know it's more likely because she knows scratching and biting me won't work. I have a very high pain tolerance when it comes to her.

"Did you kidnap my cat?" I ask, utterly incredulous.

"No!" he says, his eyes huge. "I heard you calling her, and she ran by. I didn't want her to get away, so I tried to grab her, but, you know."

"Wait here," I say, walking back toward the deck. I deposit Miss Harry Potter inside the house, tossing her a handful of

181

treats before walking back to the railing. Ridley has followed me, at least as far as the foot of the steps, his face illuminated by the motion-detecting light over the door. So much for following directions. I pull my hoodie tighter. "Why'd you come here tonight?"

"I missed you, and I couldn't take it anymore," he says.

I blink at his honesty, my breath escaping in a little huff.

He crosses his arms and then uncrosses them, opening and closing his mouth like he doesn't know what to say. "Peak," he says finally. "I majorly messed up; I know I did. But if you don't completely hate me yet, can we please talk? If you don't want to, I get it, and I'll go, but if you do—"

"How did you get my address?"

He looks down. "It was in the file my dad gave me about Vera."

"Right, of course. Every spy has a portfolio." I cross my arms. He's got a small plastic bag around his wrist; I didn't see it before in the chaos with HP. "What's in that? Are you here to bug my house? Maybe set up some spy cams?"

"Oh." He looks down like he forgot he even had it. "No—peanut butter cups. And Sprite. They're for you."

"Why?"

"You always pick the peanut butter cups out of the candy jar at the store, and Vera gets you Sprite from the Chinese food place, so I thought maybe they were your favorites." He drags a hand through his hair and then drops his head back. I almost don't hear his whispered F-bomb.

He's absolutely right—those are two of my favorite

things in the whole world, and when you combine them, it's next level. I can't believe he noticed, but it's really the F-bomb that seals the deal, or rather the little anguished exhale that follows it. It feels sincere in a way words never could, and I melt a little. Or maybe I'm just looking for a reason to forgive him. Probably a little of both.

"I know you probably can't forgive me," he says, his breath puffing out in the cold air. "But I wanted you to know that I never spied, and I never would. I made up all of the reports." He rubs at the cat scratch on his cheek, the little bag of Sprite and peanut butter cups smacking against his shoulder. "I like you too much to ever do that to you, which I know is messed up to say, because I shouldn't be spying on anyone regardless, but . . . Here, though—at least take these and I'll go." He walks closer to the rail and holds up the bag. "I just wanted you to know that."

"Why should I believe you?"

"You probably shouldn't, but it's the truth. I swear to you it's the truth. I have the reports, if you want to see them. I wouldn't . . . I wouldn't do that to you. You matter too much to me."

I should go back inside, go back to my room, hug my cat, and never talk to Ridley again. That's what Jayla would do. But he's standing here, looking wrecked, holding a bag of my favorite things, which I never told him about but he noticed anyway, telling me he didn't spy and wouldn't ever, and it's everything I've been wishing for since that day in the rain and more.

The motion light clicks off—we've been still for too long—and the moonlight is just enough to make this moment seem magical.

"Come here," I say, and I meant up the steps, but he jumps up and hangs from the railing instead, shoving his toes between the slats so we're face-to-face. The light clicks back on, and it's kind of perfect in a really strange way. I move my hand to pull him closer. He flinches, like I'd slap him, and my heart breaks. I would never.

"It would be so much easier if I hated you," I say when he finally dares to slide his hand against mine. His thumb is rubbing over the top of my fingers, and it feels so warm on this coldest of nights.

"Does that mean you don't?" he asks, and I don't miss the hope in his voice.

"It's actually annoying how much I don't hate you. I can't, not even a little bit, and I really tried."

He's trembling—from nerves or the cold, I don't know—as I cross those final inches and press my lips to his. It's nervous, tentative, but when his hand slides back to grip my neck, our breaths tangling like his fingers in my hair, we both smile.

CHAPTER TWENTY-SIX

Ridley

SHE LEANS FORWARD, resting her arm on the railing like she's manning a drive-through and not stitching my heart back together with every breath. She doesn't hate me, and I can't help but smile at that. It's not much really, not in the grand scheme of things, but it's a start. My toes are wedged under the railing, my free hand supporting nearly all my body weight, and this . . . does not feel great. But I'll dangle here all night if it means she'll kiss me again.

"Peak," I say, but that ends in a yelp when my hand starts to slip and I nearly lose my balance.

"Shhh." She giggles as she takes a step back and motions for me to follow her.

"Can I . . . ," I start, forgetting the words at the sound of her laugh. I clear my throat and try again. "Do you think we could go inside and talk a little?"

She nods and tiptoes back over to the sliding glass door. It's dark inside, but HP seems to be gone, or possibly just lying in wait somewhere in the shadows. I never did trust cats.

I climb over the railing, coming up behind her as she slips the door open. "Shhh," she says again as we step inside. "Take off your shoes."

"Jubi?" someone calls out, and I realize it's Vera. I have one shoe off and one shoe on and no idea what to do.

"Crap." Peak shoves me into the little alcove behind her table. I hop backward on one foot, nearly knocking over a rack of plants in the process.

"What's up, Vera?"

I hear feet pad across the linoleum to where Peak is standing. Three more steps and I'm busted. I hate sneaking around—it feels like more lying—but I also just really want to talk to Peak, so.

"How's HP?"

"Good, she came in without any trouble."

"I thought I heard her yowling out there."

"Oh, that. That was a stray."

"Okay," Vera says, but I can tell she doesn't totally believe her. Vera takes another step, leaning forward so I can see just a little of her head. I shove myself farther against the plants, wincing when they rustle.

"Um, Vera, if you and my mom aren't going to sleep after all, can I practice more?"

"It's not that I don't love it when you play . . . ," Vera says, heading back the way she came. She'd better love it. It's the most fantastic sound in existence.

"Right," Peak snorts.

"Good night, Jubi."

"Good night," Peak says, dragging out the last word.

I take a step forward, but she holds up her finger, standing completely still until Vera's door clicks shut down the hall.

I kick off my other shoe. I kind of love that they care enough to not wear their shoes inside. I always thought it was gross that we do, but my mom always says the housekeeper will clean the floors. Everything is someone else's problem in my family.

Peak slides the bag from my wrist after we dart into her room, slipping the door shut and locking it. She opens the bag of candy while I look around. Her room isn't a bad size, about half as big as mine but way more comfortable. Every square inch of her walls is covered with posters or pictures of her and her friends. A worn pink blanket covers her bed, but not like the trashed kind of worn—more like the soft and loved kind.

And then I see it. Peak's cello. And I can't breathe. It's like seeing the actual Mjolnir up close or something. Every word I had planned flies out of my head at the sight of her instrument.

"It's beautiful," I say, thinking of how those strings and that bow have gotten me through the roughest of nights since I came here.

"Well?" she asks, interrupting my thoughts.

I turn back to her, shoving my hands in my pockets and waiting to see if she says something else.

She raises her eyebrows. "That's it? Really?"

"There was a speech," I say, taking a step closer to her.

"There was?" she asks, not moving forward but not backing away either.

"It was a great speech," I say, desperately trying to remember it now that she's so close.

"Oh yeah?" And I think she's maybe getting a little annoyed again.

"I'm sorry." I hang my head. "Your lips seemed to have rewired my brain. I'm, uh, attempting a reboot."

She sighs and climbs into the center of her bed, taking the candy and soda with her. She grabs her pillow and hugs it tight to her chest. "I don't know what to do with you. Part of me is so amped that you're here and that you're Bats." I smile, but then her face falls, and I follow suit, trying to brace for whatever comes next. "The other part of me knows that this is extremely messed up. You were sent here as a spy, right? You completely lied to me this whole time?"

I swallow hard because accurate. Well, except the one thing. "Let me show you the reports. I never spied."

"Seeing *is* believing, I guess," she says, her voice flat.

For once, my anxiety making me overthink everything is useful. I pull off my backpack and unzip it, taking out the now-wrinkled papers I printed earlier. She looks them over. Her eyebrows draw together, but then rise as she lets out a breathy laugh.

"He actually believes this?"

"Yeah, why wouldn't he?"

"You make it sound like we're completely loaded and she's buried in offers."

I smirk. "It's a shame there's no room for my father to negotiate, considering how in demand she is, right? Best if he just backs off and cuts his losses."

"Smart." She tilts her head and smiles, but then her face gets serious again. "If I were to give you another chance—and I'm not saying I am, but if I did—would you screw it up?"

I take a deep breath—it feels like my soul is crawling up my throat—and shake my head. "Not if I could help it," I say, because we both know that's the best I can do.

"I need to know some more things before this can be okay."

"Anything," I say, because just the idea that a reality exists where we *could* be okay has me drunk on nerves and anticipation. This is all I ever wanted, Bats and Peak against the world, like two characters from Vera's books.

She scoots over on her bed, gesturing toward the empty spot. I sit on the very edge, not wanting to presume. I'm trying so hard to be still and quiet and patient and everything she would ever want, but my leg is bouncing a mile a minute, and I can't stop biting the skin around my thumbnail. I am fucking this up already.

She unwraps another peanut butter cup, eyeing me. "I still can't believe you're really an Everlasting."

"What, do you want to see my ID or something?" I joke.

"Kind of. Yeah."

"Seriously?"

"Show me."

I grab my wallet and slide out my Washington State ID. "I don't have a license; my mom never had time to teach me," I say, shame heating my cheeks because that's another normal-kid thing I never accomplished. "I went to visit my aunt Mary in Michigan once and she tried, but—"

"I don't have my license either; driving terrifies me," she says, snatching the ID from my hand. Her face falls as she stares down at it. "You're really an Everlasting."

I nod, wishing so hard my name was something I could peel off like dirty clothes and leave behind forever. I don't want it anymore, not if it means losing her.

"Did you know who I was at the dance?"

I shake my head.

"Are you lying?"

"No, I really didn't find out until later."

Her eyes burn into mine. "When you *did* find out who I was, why was your first reaction to sell me out?"

And that, that's a hard one. I rest my forehead in my hands, my knees—one still bouncing—propping up my elbows as I try to remember how to breathe. Her fingers graze my back, and I resist the urge to melt into them, scrunching my eyes tighter and shaking my head. I stand up and pace. This was a bad idea. I should go.

shitshitshitshitshitshitshitshit

"Did you know that dragonflies can zoom along at thirty-five miles per hour?"

"Peak, don't," I say, my voice shaking. I came here to make it better, but every time she tries to comfort me, I just feel a thousand times worse. "Why are you so nice?" I mean it in a bad way, but it comes out embarrassingly plaintive.

"I'm not that nice," she says.

I look at her and raise my eyebrows.

"I was planning to ghost you after the con."

"But you didn't."

"No, I didn't. I blame your dimple." She tosses me a peanut butter cup, which I miss and have to scoop off the carpet. There are still vacuum lines in some places, and it seems wrong to be tossing candy on it.

I take a step closer as she pops open the Sprite and sets it on the table beside her without even taking a sip. She reaches out her hand and pulls me down on the bed, so close our knees are touching, harsh denim against soft pajamas.

idontdeservethis

"Get out of your head, Ridley."

"How?"

"You can start by telling me everything I should know about you."

I huff out a laugh, dropping my head back and staring at the ceiling. "If I do that, then you'll definitely hate me."

"I might," she says. "But there's only one way to know. And I think I deserve to have all the information before I make up my mind."

My first instinct is to run, because nothing good will come of this. I've never shown anyone the truth of who I am, of what I am, of how much of a goddamn mess I am even on the best of days. But then I remember what Gray said, that it's not just my heart on the line. That I dragged her into this, and I owe her, so I take a deep breath and I start talking. I tell her about what happened at the end of the con, when she was already on her way home, and I hint about my relationship with my parents. And it's hard. When we were texting, I felt like I could tell her anything, but now I'm suffocating under the weight of her stare.

icantdothisicant

But she asked for everything. And this is a big part of everything, the biggest, maybe. I run my hands through my hair and try to choose my words carefully, which doesn't exactly work. But it's now or never.

"You have to understand how it was growing up. The only time my dad paid attention to me was when I fucked up—I was either invisible or getting yelled at, no in-between. And there was constant pressure from tutors and school and life, and Gray was so fucking *perfect* all the time, and I—I wasn't. Ever. I couldn't take it. Eventually I started thinking of exit strategies or whatever."

"Exit strategies?" she asks. "Like what? Running away?"

I look down, studying the little threads of her carpet. "A little more permanent than that, Peak." I hold my breath, waiting to see how she'll react. This is usually when people freak.

She just whispers "Jesus" and rubs her fingers over mine, wriggling them in until our hands are linked.

"Yeah, so, it's whatever," I say, feeling a little bit like throwing up. I'm a raw nerve, a full-body toothache, but she should know what she's getting into.

ishouldgoishould

She's still holding my hand tight, like she wants me to stay, and I can't figure out why.

"Do you still think like that? The exit-strategy thing," she asks.

I pull my hand back and bite my nail, trying to figure out what the right answer is. I said no more lies, and yet.

And yet.

"You don't have to answer—"

"I said I would tell you whatever you wanted to know." She opens her mouth to interrupt, but I just keep talking. "Sort of, I guess? It's different now; it's not urgent like it used to be. It's more like a habit, if that makes sense?" I glance at her face. "You know how some people go to movie theaters and have to find all the emergency exits, or they go out to eat and have to face the door no matter what, and half the time they don't even realize they're doing it?"

She nods, but kind of slowly, hesitant.

"That's how it is, just like a glitch in the comfort matrix or something. Something my brain tosses out there, and I'm like, 'Cool, thanks for the suggestion, but maybe we could just play a video game instead.' It's just crossed lines. It's fine." I'm downplaying it some, but whatever.

Peak crawls up behind me and wraps her arms around me hard, holding tight, like she's worried I'll float away if she lets go. I rub my cheek against her arm and sigh. "It's really not a big deal, so please don't worry. I shouldn't have said anything."

She doesn't answer me at first, just squeezes me tighter. I think for a half second that I'm going to cry, but this isn't the time, so I blink hard and open my eyes wide and try to suck the tears back into my eyeballs before she notices. She keeps hugging me, and I focus on the ceiling, which is full of brilliant green glowing stars, because it's easier than facing her.

I should feel relaxed, accepted, proud of myself for being

vulnerable, excited that I didn't scare her off. But I'm not. I'm antsy, freaked out, on edge, and the longer she doesn't talk, the worse it gets. My brain spins out in a thousand directions, each one worse than the last.

She's only being nice because she feels bad.

She wishes you would leave already.

She still hates you and can't figure out how to say it.

"I should probably go," I say, even though it kills me, even though I haven't told her half the things I'd planned to.

She slips down beside me and tilts my face toward hers, brushing some hair off my forehead. "You could stay."

Confusion etches lines across my forehead. "What?"

She takes a long, deep breath, watching me, appraising me, her eyes focused on mine. "I said you could stay. If you want."

I smile before I catch myself, and then my stomach sinks. I know what this is; this is Gray and concrete goals all over again. This is pity. I shake my head. "I'm fine, Peak, really. You don't have to babysit me."

"Good, because I'm not," she says, with just enough attitude that I sort of believe her.

"Why, then?"

She presses a kiss to my nose and pulls me closer. My heart is pounding, clawing at my skin to get to her. I wonder how she can stand it. "I like you, okay? That's why."

I bring my arm up around her, letting my fingers trail over her skin, trying to be cool, to be nonchalant, to act like my entire body isn't on fire right now. "I like you too."

CHAPTER TWENTY-SEVEN

Jubilee

MY PHONE IS buzzing somewhere in the background, and I chase the sound back to consciousness with a little sigh. I roll over, half expecting Ridley to still be there, warm and drowsy, with his arms tucked behind his head, just the way I left him. But there are only cold sheets.

We talked all night; he told me about his family, his sister, and about growing up in the shadow of The Geekery. We talked about the fake reports and his sister's reaction when he told her everything. We even talked a little about fate. He filled in all the blanks between Bats and Ridley, and somehow, around two a.m. or so, the two sides of him officially fused into one in my mind. And I really like it, maybe even more than like it, if I'm being honest.

There's a small part of me, though, a quiet part, that still feels weird about how everything went down, but I shake it off and grab my phone, smiling when I see that it's him telling me to

BATS: Wake up already!

               ME: You left!

BATS: I didn't want your moms
to see me! Now get up.

          ME: It's 8:30. On a Saturday.
          The only people up now are
          like athletes or masochists.

BATS: And people who have to work.

          ME: Of which we are none.

BATS: Also people who have dates. 😉

          ME: Oh my god. You are
          a massive dork. 😊

BATS: Meet me at Malywick Park
in an hour?

          ME: An hour?!

BATS: Too soon?

          ME: I'll be there in 20.

BATS: Come on then, Peak.
I'm already here.

ME: ☺

I wiggle into some jeans, yank a sweatshirt over my head, pull my hair back into a ponytail, and toss my gloves onto my bed so I don't forget them. It's nearly April, but even spring-time in New England isn't so forgiving.

I am ready to go—teeth brushed, mascara applied, winter headband acquired—within ten minutes. I fire off a text to Nikki, because if there's one person who will have my back in this, it is definitely her. It's a short text, three words only: **We made up.**

She doesn't write back right away; I don't expect her to. She'll probably be tied up at the game for the next few hours. That's what Saturdays are like around here. I usually spend them practicing cello, but every other overachieving kid in town is either at a game or rehearsing for a play.

But today, today is different. Today is . . . fate. Today is meant to be. Today, we're going to test-drive this tentative more-than-truce we started last night and see how it flies in the daytime.

I slip out of my bedroom, tiptoeing down the hallway, but Vera's sitting at the kitchen counter already, her coffee steaming in front of her. She puts down her phone and looks up at me, her eyes still bleary. "Jubilee? You're heading out early. You going to a game?"

"No." I'm tempted to fib, but Ridley said no more lies. "I'm meeting a friend in Malywick," I say, lingering in the doorway. I know if I actually set foot on the linoleum, she'll start peppering me with questions I'm not ready to answer.

Even though Ridley is ready to be 100 percent transparent with his life, I'm not so sure I'm ready to do the same with mine. And I don't think Vera would be so forgiving either; you can't even mention The Geekery without her blood pressure rising.

"This wouldn't be the same friend who climbed our deck railing last night instead of using the stairs, would it?"

"Uh," I say, my face heating.

"They left muddy footprints everywhere."

"Maybe it was a raccoon?" I wince.

"A raccoon with size-eleven Vans that they left parked by the sliding glass door all night?"

"Maybe it was a very courteous raccoon?"

"I won't tell your mother, as long as it never happens again. Don't make me regret this."

"Deal."

She leans back in her seat, crossing her arms. "Will you tell me who it was?"

"Not yet, okay?" I say. "But I will."

Whatever Ridley and I have still feels tentative. Like a sudden gust of air could break us. I don't want to let anyone in who isn't going to be on board until it has time to grow. Until I know they can't scare it off. At least until I figure out a way to put a positive spin on the fact that he's an Everlasting.

Vera nods; she's always been the easier one when it comes to stuff like this. "It's cold out."

I point to my head. "The headband covers my ears."

"Bring your coat."

"I'm wearing a sweatshirt."

"A coat, Jubilee," Vera says, and then sips her coffee with a satisfied smirk.

• • •

The walk to Malywick takes way too long. Halfway there I curse myself for not riding my bike . . . but I didn't know what else Ridley had planned, and I didn't want to be pushing it around all day.

I turn down Southside Drive, grinning when I see the familiar sight of trees winding into the air. The park sits basically in the center of town, around the remains of some old settlers' houses. In the summer, the place is filled with tourists and buskers. Music and laughter—and the occasional argument—mix with the scent of the waffle cones from the fro-yo shop nearby, where Jayla works. This time of year, it's deserted, peaceful even, a place to sit and reflect in privacy.

The perfect place to meet the very cute boy who's currently sitting on top of a picnic table, bouncing his knee.

Ridley's hoodie is pulled down so low over his eyes, I can't even see them. He looks small, folded up like that, a little stress ball in a slightly too big sweatshirt. He glances up when he hears me, pulling back his hood, his eyes widening to match his smile. His hands are tucked into his pockets, but he jumps down without losing his balance.

"You came," he says, like he can't believe it.

"You knew I was coming!"

"I wasn't sure." He chews on his lip.

"I said I couldn't wait."

"I know, but."

I poke his shoulder, making him look up at me. "But what?"

"I'm kind of still waiting for the other shoe to drop, I guess."

"Well, it's not going to." I notice his skateboard tucked into his backpack beside the table, one wheel rolling lazily in the wind. He's had his board at the shop before, but I've never really gotten to see him skate. "Did you skate here?"

"Yeah," he says, a little shy, like I'll think that's dorky or something. I don't. I love it.

"I always wanted to learn. Show me?"

He pulls his board out and carries it over to a flat area away from the cobblestones, then changes his mind and walks down farther to the parking lot. "Have you ever skated before?"

"Once," I say, "but it doesn't count."

"Why not?"

"Because it wasn't with you." I meant it to be funny, but it comes out sounding sincere.

He blushes at my answer, ducking his head as I step onto the board. "Do you want to learn, or do you just want me to pull you along?"

"Both." I laugh.

"Okay, get your feet comfortable. Move them so they're kind of like this," he says, demonstrating on the ground.

I do as I'm told, marveling at how much warmer it feels when someone you like is giving you skateboarding lessons, even in an empty parking lot on the last day of March.

"Okay, push off," he says, reaching his arms out. I give it a shove, locking my arms on his when I start to lose my balance. "I won't let you fall."

I look up, startled, and he's smiling when our eyes meet, one dimple visible under the cold sun. We practice a few more times, until I start to figure it out, using his arms less and less as my confidence grows.

"What do you think?" he asks. "Should we give it a go?"

"Absolutely," I say, a little too enthusiastically. He chuckles, and then it's my turn to look down, embarrassed. "I mean, yeah. I think I've got this."

He drops his arms, and I kick off. The board slides forward; I'm a little wobbly but I keep it going, gliding faster and faster, shoving forward as fast as I can. I try to find a rhythm in the sound of the wheels on the asphalt, try to turn it into music so it makes more sense.

"Yes!" he shouts behind me, and I turn my head, almost losing my balance when I see him raising his arms up in victory. I hop off, running forward a few steps so I don't fall over, before I turn the board around to face him.

He grins, and it bolsters my confidence so much that I shove off a little faster than I mean to, careening toward him at a rate I'm not entirely comfortable with. He seems to sense the change in mood and races toward me, reaching me right as the board nicks the curb and sends me flailing in the other direction. I'm lost in the air, landing hard on top of him.

I cough into his elbow as I push myself up. He takes a deep breath and grunts beneath me, like I knocked all the air out of him.

"Oops," I say, sitting up and trying to give him space. "In fairness, though, you did say you'd never let me fall."

He raises his eyebrows and opens his mouth but then sighs in mock defeat. "Historically, I'm not good at keeping promises, so."

"Hey." I grab his chin. "None of that."

"Fine, half credit for catching you?"

"Half credit seems fair." I scoot forward, giving him the tiniest kiss on his cheek, not sure what the rules are in the daylight.

I slide beside him, looking up at the sky. I'd swear it was a summer sky if I didn't know any better. And god, summer with Ridley sounds perfect. Except how does that work? How do we keep our families from finding out that long? How do I figure out how to—

"Can I get another one of those?" he asks, catching me off guard.

"Another what?" He taps his cheek, and I twist my lips, trying to hold in a laugh. "You're shameless."

I lean in to give him an overexaggerated kiss on the cheek, but he turns his head at the last second, pressing his lips to mine with an innocence that make me giggle. He shuts his eyes then, and I shut mine, and the kiss turns into something different.

"Sneaky," I say when we break apart, before diving back in for another quick kiss. A cold gust of air rushes by, and I hunch down a little in my jacket. I'm glad Vera made me bring it.

He grabs my hands, and god, I wish I hadn't forgotten my gloves on my bed—they've gone numb from the cold, and I would've really liked to feel this.

"You're frozen!" he yelps, jumping off the curb and pulling me up. "Come on, let's get you inside somewhere." He does this little step move, and his board flips right up into his hands.

"So, that was awesome." I've never known anyone who really knew how to skate. A couple of my friends have longboards, sure, but that's just to get around, not really for fun.

He crinkles his forehead. "All I did was pick it up."

"Pretty sure you just worked some kind of skater magic and it flew into your hand. Do you do any other tricks?"

"Tricks?"

"Like, can you jump on stuff and slide across it?"

"Yes." He laughs. "I can jump on stuff and slide across it." He says it in a way that tells me these moves have actual names, but not in a way that makes me feel bad for not knowing them.

I tuck my jacket tighter around me. "Show me."

"You're freezing."

"I can be cold for another minute or two. Show me."

"Yeah?" he asks, like he's shocked I want to know more about something that so clearly matters to him.

"Yeah," I say, dropping onto one of the long marble ledges that run the length of the park. "Show me what you got."

He slides his board forward and runs after it, picking up speed when he hops on and shoves off harder and faster than I ever could. His wheels tear across the asphalt, dipping and racing with every thrust of his foot as he jumps and flips the board in the air. If my ride was music, then his is a symphony, and I don't want it to stop.

I clap—I can't help it—and he spins the board around to face me with a whizzing sound. He shakes his head like I'm ridiculous and sends the board forward again, racing toward me.

I tuck my feet up to avoid a collision, but he just sticks his tongue out and lands a jump on the marble wall beside me, the middle of the board skidding down its length like he's surfing. He flips the board off and lands on it without missing a beat, turning wide in the direction of the steps to slide down the rail onto the sidewalk below.

I stand up. I can just barely see the top of his head over the wall. He skates around and back up, doing the flippy thing again before coming to a stop right in front of me. He's a little bit out of breath, his cheeks pink from exertion and the cold, and he looks at me through his hair, waiting.

I want to be cool. But I also want to totally fangirl. I settle on "That was friggin' amazing."

And his face breaks into a grin so wide and beautiful that I want to turn it into a song and play it forever. He flips the board back into his hand, grabbing it with one and then reaching out with his other. "Come on, let's get out of here."

"Where are we going?"

His face falls a little, and I can tell he's thinking hard. "We could get coffee?" It comes out like a question, like I might say no. "If you'd rather just go back to your place or whatever, I understand that too." He looks nervous, like a rejection now would be a rejection always.

"Coffee shop sounds good. I could go for some hot cocoa and scones."

"Deal," he says, but then he's wrinkling his forehead as he looks up at the sky.

"What's wrong?"

"I know I skated by a Dunkin' Donuts, but I can't remember how to get there now."

"Why do we need a Dunkin' Donuts?"

"Your cocoa." He shrugs. "We could get an Uber maybe. I mean, if you still want to—"

"Oh my god, Ridley," I say, my eyes going wide. "There's no way we're going to Dunkin' Donuts when Stacks exists."

"Stacks?"

"It's only the best coffee shop on the planet. They have the best cocoa in town—they're, like, known for it. Well, I think technically they're known for their espresso, but the cocoa! They import it from someplace, and it's like a million dollars a cup."

"A million dollars a cup, eh?" He laughs. "Wow."

"My treat, by the way. I owe you for my skate lesson."

"I can't let you spend a million dollars on me," he says in mock horror.

"Okay, fine, they're four dollars, but when you think about it."

"I mean, yeah, I get it. It's so close, how could you not round up?"

I wait for him to pull on his backpack and readjust the board under his arm, and then I grab on to his hand again and drag him along behind me. "I don't know how you've been here for weeks already and never heard of Stacks."

"I literally know no one here except for you and your moms, so."

"Wait for it, Ridley. I'm going to blow your mind today."

We walk in silence for a few more beats, and then I hear him say it, so quietly I almost miss it. "You already have."

CHAPTER TWENTY-EIGHT

Ridley

PEAK TAKES A seat while I get in line. The place is nice, a typical hipster coffee shop, and very busy. I insist on paying and order at the counter—two hot cocoas with cinnamon, exactly as Peak directed—and then drop into the seat across from her. "They said it would be up soon."

My knee is already bouncing. It was one thing when I had the skateboard to distract me, but it's another entirely to have only nerves and cocoa to get by with.

dontmessthisupdontmessthisupdont

"You're going to love it," she says, but her enthusiasm has waned a little. Like some of what we had was lost the moment our fingers disconnected. I bite the inside of my cheek and let the silence settle over us. Just getting her here seemed so impossible twenty-four hours ago, and now that she is here, I don't know what to do.

"Is this a place you hang out?" I ask, desperate to break the silence. She pulls her coat off, draping it over the back of her chair. Her giant chunky headband is still on, though, and it's kind of weirdly hot.

"Are you asking me if I come here often?" she asks, dropping her voice a few octaves at the end.

"Something like that."

She flicks a discarded straw wrapper back and forth between her fingers. "Pretty much. We're friends with the family who owns this place."

A waiter comes out of the kitchen and from behind the counter. Peak looks at him, her eyes going wide.

"Frankie!" she shouts, jumping up to pull the guy into a hug. He's huge, taller than my dad, and built like a linebacker. He's also carrying a tray with our hot cocoa on it, which he somehow has managed not to spill.

"JuJu!" he says, and he looks so happy I almost want to trip him. He's staring at not-quite-my-girlfriend-but-also-not-*not*-my-girlfriend like she's the best thing he's ever seen. Who is this guy? And then I know.

This is the other shoe, and it's ready to drop.

"Here, give me that." She reaches forward to take the tray, but he holds it back.

"It's hot, JuJu," he says, like his instinct is to protect her, to care for her, and how many nicknames does one girl get? One from everybody, probably.

The guy—Frankie, she said—lumbers closer to the table, and I slouch in my seat. He's not graceful; he just . . . is.

It's whatever. I'm not jealous.

He sets the tray down and then turns back, wrapping Peak in a hug so tight she coughs. "I'm so glad you're here!"

he says, his voice booming. Something tells me this one doesn't have a quiet setting.

"I didn't even know you were here!"

I slide my chair a little farther away, feeling like I'm intruding on something private.

ishouldgothiswasstupidishouldgoishould

"I got back late last night. I was actually going to head over to your place in a bit. I thought you'd still be sleeping!"

Peak shakes her head. "You got home yesterday, and your mom already put you to work? Where's Martha? We need to have a word."

"Nah, I was just hanging out with her in the kitchen, and I said I'd take this one out. I was hoping it might be you, with the whole cinnamon thing."

"I'm touched you remembered." Her voice is teasing, but the sentiment sounds true enough.

"JuJu, you've drilled that into my head for the last three years. How could I forget?"

I roll my eyes. Okay, so I've got three years of history to contend with here. Perfect.

"Oh my god," she says again, taking a step back to look at him. "I can't believe you're really here! I missed you, you jerk." She punches him in the arm. "Why haven't you been emailing me? I worry!"

"Do you know how hard it is to get sailor mail out from the boat?" He yawns and wipes at his face. "Sorry, jet lag. What are you doing later? You want to get a bite somewhere that's not here?"

And okay, even I have my limits. I clear my throat, and

both their heads snap toward me like they forgot I was here. It would be comical if I wasn't so pissed off.

"Oh. Oh god, I'm sorry, Ridley," Peak says.

I stare at her blankly, not sure what to say. *"It's okay"*? Because it isn't. But I don't want to be rude. Especially since I'm really in no position to be. I knew her forgiving me was too good to be true.

"Ridley, this is Frankie. Frankie, this is Ridley."

"I gathered that," I say, standing up to hold out my hand. I try to make it sound funny, like I'm laughing it off, but the way he squeezes my hand hard while he shakes it suggests that didn't come through.

"Nice to meet you," Frankie says, not dropping eye contact as he squeezes a little harder.

"Likewise." And okay, this handshake is going on way too long.

"Frank," Peak says, swatting his hand. "Don't be an asshole."

"Sorry, force of habit." He lets go of my hand and crosses his arms. It's amazing they can even meet across his pecs. I wonder if that's what Peak likes in a guy, someone all huge and beefy and loud. Someone the exact opposite of me. My heart rate picks up, and it gets a little harder to breathe.

runrunrunrunrunrun

Peak comes and stands by me, nudging my shoulder and lacing our fingers together. The panic inside goes from a boil to a simmer, and when she smiles at me, it drops down to barely anything at all. "Be nice, Frankie. This one's important."

I look at her when she says that, my eyes wide, but she's still looking at the beast across from us. His shoulders drop a little, not like he's disappointed, but as if he just completely relaxed. "Really?" he asks, tipping his head down while he looks at her. I expected something else, alpha male anger maybe, but instead, he looks kind of happy?

"Yeah," she says, giving my hand a gentle squeeze. "And I'd like it very much if you didn't scare him off."

"He couldn't," I say quietly, so only she can hear it, but the way Frankie laughs says otherwise.

"See?" Frankie says, raising his hands. "No harm done."

Peak rests her head on my shoulder. "Good."

"How do you two know each other?" I ask. I'm missing something. He's not a romantic rival, clearly, but he also seems like more than just a friendly neighborhood barista.

"My mom and her stepmom are best friends," Frankie says. "When Vera married JuJu's mom, she and I effectively became family."

"He's the big brother I never wanted and can't seem to get rid of." Peak laughs, and Frankie pretends to whack her on the head. I still feel that pang of jealousy, but now it's for a different reason. I'm homesick for a life I never had, where I had best friends and a loving family and bonds that don't break.

Peak seems to sense the shift in my mood and squeezes my hand again. "Ridley, Frankie just got back. He's in the navy."

"I was underway for a while," he says proudly, and I feel like I should know what that means. "How did you guys . . . ?" he trails off, gesturing between us.

"Ridley started hanging around Verona," she says, and I hate that she's covering for me. I just want to tell the truth, no more lies.

Frankie plants his hand over his forehead and pretends to swoon. "Love across the comic racks."

"We actually met—" I start to say, but then stop. Maybe Peak doesn't want people to know about our night at the con. Maybe she's not protecting me; maybe she's ashamed.

"At a prom at one of the cons we were at," she says, and I look up in confusion. "He had a Batman mask; I was dressed like a peacock."

"A peacock?"

"From *Fighting Flock*."

"It was a very intense outfit," I say before I catch myself. Peak blushes and Frankie shakes his head.

"Frankie?" a voice calls through the kitchen doors.

"I better get back there before my mom flips. But remember," he says, jabbing Peak in the chest, "don't do anything I would do."

I scrunch my forehead. "Isn't it 'wouldn't do'?"

"Trust me," Peak says. "He definitely means 'would.'"

Frankie snorts and gives me a fake stern look before pointing at his eyes and then pointing back at me. I give him a salute, and he shakes his head.

"That is not how you salute, my dude." He chuckles as he walks away.

Peak and I sit back down, and I slide a mug toward her. The air feels lighter, the mood happier, and she smiles when she takes a sip.

"Hey, so," I say, hesitating when she looks up at me. "Um, he's cool."

"Yeah, you guys would probably hit it off."

"He's not really my type," I say, and I don't mean it the way it comes out, but she tips her head toward me.

"Are guys sometimes your type?" she asks, like that's a normal question. Like it's fine.

I take a deep breath, deciding how best to answer. I've had this conversation enough times to know that admitting I'm bi doesn't always go well. Girls especially seem to be freaked out by it. Usually I just lie and try to pretend I'm straight or gay depending on the circumstances. It's less drama, even if it makes my stomach hurt and my chest feel like it's caving in all the time.

But. No more lying. Not to her.

She leans in closer. "You don't have to answer. But you don't have to not answer either."

I stare down at my cocoa. "I guess certain people are just my type?" I say it like it's a question, even though it's not.

"Same," she says.

"I figured from what you said that first day at the shop."

"Then why did you freak out when I asked about you?"

I spin my mug around in my hands. "I don't know. Bad past experiences, I guess."

"I almost don't want to ask, but—"

And my stomach drops, because here come the inevitable twenty questions: have you dated a guy, yes, did you bang him, yes, did he bang you, no, but he could have, are you sure this isn't a pit stop to gay town, also yes, are you sure you like girls, yes, have you dated a girl, yes, did you bang her, no, but I wanted to.

"—you don't already have someone, do you?"

Wait, huh? I snap my eyes up. "What?"

"We aren't going through all this drama just to find out you have somebody waiting for you back in Seattle, right? I don't want to just be an extended con crush."

The relief washes over me, and I laugh. I can't help it. "No, there is no one and nothing for me in Seattle anymore."

"What's so funny?"

"I thought you were going to ask me something else."

"Like what?"

"Girls don't always take it well when they find out I'm bi."

"Well, this girl doesn't care."

"Because you're also bi?"

"I'm still working out the whole label side of things," she says, kind of wincing in a really adorable way, before taking a sip from her mug. "I say bi or pan sometimes, but I don't know if it feels right. I've never dated a girl, but I've had serious crushes and almost girlfriends. And then last summer I did hook up a little with Nikki's cousin who's nonbinary. I guess I just like who I like."

"That's okay," I say, in case she feels weird, because she shouldn't. And also because I really don't want to hear any more about who she's hooked up with.

"It doesn't always feel okay, though," she says. "Like you and my mom are bi, and Vera calls herself gay, and Jayla's a lesbian, and Nikki is straight, and I'm just—"

"Jubilee," I say.

"Yeah." She takes another sip. "It doesn't feel like enough."

"It is."

"Can I ask you something else?"

"I told you, you can ask anything."

"You're seventeen, right? That's what you said in your texts."

"Mm-hmm," I say, not sure where she's going with this.

"How come you don't go to school?" And ah, okay, that's a fair question, but not one I really want to answer.

"I do. I go to an online one, but I'm way behind."

"Why don't you go to an actual school, I mean. How'd you get out of that? Teach me your ways, O wise one." She smiles. "Do you know how much more cello time I'd have if I didn't have to sit in school all day?"

"Nah, trust me, if you're doing good where you are, you don't want to follow my lead on this. But it *is* an actual school, like, it's still hard and a lot of work, but I get what you mean. I've been to pretty much every kind of school out there, but none of them worked out."

"How come?"

And here we go. I did not envision having this talk in the middle of a coffee shop with her military BFF watching from the back room, but. "Because it turns out that formal education and being crazy don't mix."

"You're not crazy."

"I told you last night—"

"That doesn't mean you're crazy. Stop it."

"I can literally give you the numbers of multiple doctors who will tell you otherwise."

"Stop saying *crazy*," she says, and she looks legitimately annoyed. We sit in silence for a minute, and I wait for her next question. I've learned already there will always be a next question with her. And I don't even mind.

"Do you have a diagnosis, then, or whatever? How does that work?"

I snort. "I don't have a diagnosis, Peak. I have a laundry list."

"Well, I don't care."

"Why not?"

"It's not a deal breaker."

"It probably should be."

"Don't say that."

"It . . . can complicate things."

"It doesn't matter to me, honestly. I'm glad we're here," she says, and I look up, startled. How can that be true? I think this is the first time in the history of my life that anyone has been glad I'm anywhere.

"Why?" I ask before I can stop myself.

"I just am," Peak says, smiling strong enough that I know she means it. She takes another gulp of her drink, and I want to kiss her so bad, to know what the chocolate tastes like against her skin, but I don't. I duck my head and shift in my seat and try really hard to think about anything else.

"Hey." She reaches her hand out and tips my chin back up. It feels like something. It feels important. "We're going to figure this out."

I swallow hard. "What does that mean?"

"It means my feelings haven't changed."

"You still want me to fuck off, then?" I say, just to break the tension.

She laughs. "No, my feelings after that. Or before that. Or before and after that, actually. Have yours?"

"No." I grab the seat of her chair and slide it closer to mine until our legs are slotted together. And this time, when she laughs, I go in for the kiss.

CHAPTER TWENTY-NINE

Jubilee

"YOU'RE JUST GOING to completely let him off the hook? So this is Dakota 2.0, then, another person stomping all over you while you stand there saying thanks?"

I slam my locker door, and Jayla's frowning face is waiting behind it. "It's not like that."

She starts walking to biology, and I follow behind. It's my least favorite subject but usually my most favorite class because it's the only one the three of us have together. I've been dreading it all day.

Yesterday, Jayla came into the store while I was working, took one look at Ridley helping me stack, and walked right out. She wouldn't answer my texts last night and didn't even come to lunch today. I saw her eating with Emily in the courtyard.

"Then what is it like?"

Nikki walks up, linking arms with each of us with a look that says she's deliberately ignoring the tension. "What are we talking about?"

"Jubilee and Ridley made up."

"I know. I totally called it, by the way." Nikki grins, fluttering her eyelashes and spinning around in a circle while clutching her chest.

"I can't believe you told Nikki first." Jayla rolls her eyes as Nikki sweeps herself dramatically down the hall. "Actually, I can."

"I love that you look out for me, I do, but this isn't like the last time."

She raises her eyebrows. "Jubi, come on."

"Hey," I say, because now she's taking it too far.

"Am I supposed to act happy that you're sleeping with the enemy?"

"He's not the enemy."

"Are you sure?"

"I am, actually," I say, pushing past her and walking into the room, but Jayla matches my pace. "I know what I'm doing."

"Do you?" Jayla asks, sliding into her seat beside me at the lab table. "Because from here it seems like you're totally wrapped up in another kid who's just taking advantage of you. It's like you're genetically programmed not to see when people are bad for you."

"That's not Ridley," I say, more firmly this time. "You don't understand."

"Help me understand, then," she says, pulling out her notebook. Nikki settles into the table behind us, leaning forward to hear my response.

"It's not my place to tell you," I say, but I know it's not

helping my case. "Look, he's not spying, and he had a reason for not coming clean."

Jayla uncaps her pen, shaking her head. "I'm sure. Just like Dakota had a good reason for hooking up with another girl while you were at your cello lesson."

"That's not fair. This isn't the same thing at all."

"You stayed with him for another month after that happened, Jubi!" she says just as the bell rings. Mr. Lillis is, thankfully, late as usual.

"She has a point," Nikki adds, biting her eraser, and I shoot her an incredulous look.

"Well," I say, turning back to Jayla, "you and Elissa were a total train wreck, and I still stood by you for all of it."

"Elissa didn't lie to me."

"No, she just lied to everyone else about you, so she didn't have to come out. And then you turned around and started seeing Emily even though you had to keep it a secret from your coach at first, so pot, meet kettle."

"It's not the same thing," Jayla says.

"It's exactly the same thing!"

"That's actually also a good point," Nikki chimes in again, and this time we both look at her. I would laugh if I wasn't so ridiculously frustrated right now.

"Will you just trust me?"

"No."

"Why?"

"Because I'm worried. Your summer-program audition is at the end of the month, and you don't even mention it anymore! You're barely ever around, and when you are, it's just been Ridley this and Bats that, and how perfect they are, and now we hate them, and now we like them again. It's annoying! Are you doing *anything* besides worrying about this boy?"

"Okay, that's probably the best point so far," Nikki says. "You really don't ever talk about music anymore."

"Forgive me for trying to get out and live a little—like everybody wanted me to do. And now that I'm doing it . . ." I grip my pencil so hard I nearly snap it. "I've got it under control, but thanks for your votes of confidence."

"Fine," Jayla says. "But I don't know how you see this all playing out. Eventually, your parents are going to find out, and then what? Did you even see the guest post your stepmom wrote on ComicsAlliance last week about how corporations are destroying this industry? She name-dropped Mark Everlasting and The Geekery specifically, saying they were this totally insidious force, not even realizing they were *already in her store!*"

"I don't care about our families' stupid fight!"

Mr. Lillis walks in the door then with a huge stack of books from the library, and oh god, not another research project, but at least it spares me from having to reply. I pour myself into the lesson, desperate to tamp down everything Jayla's stirred up in me. Maybe I haven't been practicing as much, or maybe I just found a better cello-life balance. And maybe I don't know how this will all come together yet, or what's going to happen, but I do know I love being around him, and that his arms feel warmer than any arms I've ever felt in the history of arms.

When the bell rings, I bolt from my desk before Jayla and

Nikki can stand up, running to the music room even though it's not my period. I need to play; I need to make music; I need to be in control for once. Mrs. Carmine nods when she sees me cut into a practice room and then turns back to the students gathering for their rehearsal.

I play so long that I miss my next class, but it's gym and Mrs. C will definitely write me a note to get out of it anyway, especially with the audition coming so soon. My phone vibrates on the music stand—it's a text from Ridley—and I finish the Bach, smiling the rest of the way through.

• • •

I'm currently propped up against Ridley, using him as a half pillow/half desk, doing my lit homework while he scrolls through his phone and plays with my hair. Now that my parents know we're together or whatever, they let him come over a lot—provided we keep the door open. It's perfect, or it would be if I could stop obsessing over my fight with Jayla and the bigger problem of Ridley's last name. I sigh and turn the page, and he gives my hair a little tug.

"You could just call her, you know?"

I roll to my side to look at him. "She should be the one calling me, right? She's the one who's pissed for no reason."

"It sounds more like she's just worried about you, which is kind of nice? And she's right about the long-term thing."

My stomach drops. "What do you mean?"

"I mean, how is this going to work? I'm tired of lying already. You know we have to tell Vera, and who knows how that will go."

I bolt up. "My parents will flip; you know how they feel about your family. They probably won't even let me hang out with you anymore, and they definitely won't let you in the store."

"It'd be okay," he says, running his hand up my arm. "We'd make it work. As long as I have you, I don't care."

"Ridley, think. If they don't let you in the store, and your dad finds out, he's going to send you back to Seattle. And then what? I have to stay here. You'd be out there alone, and . . ."

His face falls. "Shit, I wasn't thinking about Seattle."

"Yeah, shit. You can't go back there."

He shoves off the bed and starts pacing around my room. I try to pull him back down, but he shifts his arm away and bites his thumbnail, squeezing his eyes shut. "I'm so fucked."

"You're not. You're *not*," I say, trying to calm him down. "We'll figure it out."

"How?" He raises his arms and drops them before dragging his hands over his face. "I almost lost you because of lies, and now the only way to be with you is to lie even more? I am so sick of pretending to be something I'm not. I've been doing it my whole life!"

"Ridley," I say, and this time he lets me pull him down. He sits at the edge of my bed, shaking his head. "This is different. We're just buying ourselves some time. It's just temporary."

He shoves his fist against his thigh, hanging his head before looking back up at me. "You promise?"

I smooth out his hands and pull them into my lap. "In a couple months, it'll be fine. We can tell my parents the truth, and it'll be okay. And if it's not, it won't matter, because I'll be in Boston for the summer program, and you'll be eighteen and your dad can't make you go anywhere. We'll have the whole summer together. And by the time we get back, everything will have blown over. It'll work out."

He looks down at where our hands meet. "If you say so."

"It's the only way," I say, because I've thought through ten thousand options already, and this is the only one that didn't seem doomed from the start. My phone buzzes then, an incoming call.

"You should get that."

So I do, because I think he needs some space. It's Jayla calling to talk about what happened. She says it's coming from a place of love—and I know it is, but still—and we talk until we both feel better, until things are as resolved as they can be. She reluctantly agrees to support me and Ridley, even though it kills her, and I promise to go to her away game on Saturday and cheer the loudest.

And when I hang up, feeling better than I have all day, I realize that Ridley left.

CHAPTER THIRTY

PEAK: Can this week be over?
I feel like it's lasted foreverrrrrrrr.

> **BATS:** Technically, after
> today it's the weekend, so.

PEAK: Still too long. Make it go faster.
I can't believe I won't see you until Sunday
because of "mandatory family time." 🙄
Beam me up or whatever.

> **BATS:** Wait, is there a portal?
> Because if you've found a portal
> through time and space and have
> been holding out on me, I'm going
> to be pissed. And family time
> sounds nice.

PEAK: Family time is only nice when
they don't say "no outside visitors allowed."

Otherwise it's like being in jail with two overly affectionate wardens. And no, no portal here. I was hoping you had one, Dr. Strange.

> BATS: Then we're screwed.

PEAK: Damn.

> BATS: Hey, you're the one going to the away game after your parole tomorrow instead of coming here, not me.

PEAK: I promised Jayla! And you could come. I invited you!

> BATS: No, I'm good on that.

PEAK: Come on, it'd be so fun.

> BATS: Jayla hates me.

PEAK: She does not. She likes you.

> BATS: Liar.

PEAK: Come onnnnnnn.

BATS: I miss you, but no.

PEAK: Please?

BATS: No.

PEAK: *pouts forever*

CHAPTER THIRTY-ONE

Ridley

"I DON'T PAY you to not write the reports," Dad says, dropping down into a seat at the kitchen table, where I'm slurping up Frosted Flakes. Technically, this is the first time we've had breakfast together. In my life, probably, but definitely since I got here.

I'd give anything to already be skating over to Peak's house, but after her "family only" time last night, she's spending the day at Jayla and Nikki's away game, leaving me to fend for myself. I'm trying hard not to bother her, but trying not to text her just makes me want to text her more.

"Are you even listening to me?" he asks, the corner of his eye twitching.

I tug my hoodie lower over my head, shoveling in another bite of cereal. "There wasn't anything to put in it this week."

That's technically true, only because I didn't have the energy to make up any new lies to cover for the whole conservatory thing, so I just . . . didn't. I know I have to keep it up. I know I gave Peak my word, but I'm so exhausted. I've been lying for so long now, and to so many different people, I'm starting to doubt I even know the truth anymore.

"You barely even pay me anyway," I say, because I'm a masochist. Because I'm pouting. Because I just want to see Peak.

My father leans forward, jabbing his finger at me. "I pay for this house, I pay for this food, I pay for your ridiculous online classes. Everything you have, I pay for. And for what?"

"Cuz you're my dad?"

He leans back in his chair, glaring at me. I chew the inside of my lip. My brain—hopelessly hopeful as it can sometimes be about this family—thinks for half a second that maybe those words meant something to him, that maybe he's going to apologize and say it's great having me around. Follow it up with a "hey, kid, let's toss the ball around or get ice cream" or anything else those sitcom dads do.

He does not.

He's abandoned even the slightest performance of fatherly pride lately. I think I'd take him misremembering everything about me like he did in the beginning over the cold indifference that's settled back between us.

I stare down at my cereal until he slides his chair across the tile floor. "I should send you back to your mother."

And then he's gone.

I carry my bowl to the sink and pour the rest down the drain. I'm not hungry anymore.

• • •

I tried not to text her. I really did. I don't want to mess up her life or pull her from her friends or get in the way, but everything hurts, and I just don't want to be alone.

I should send you back.

I've been hyperventilating since he said that. I can't go back. I won't. I can't go from all of this to sitting alone again in that giant fucking house. My father left with Allison for the weekend right after our argument. I called Gray first—but she's on the West Coast with Mom—and then finally texted Peak. I've been pacing ever since.

I wasn't even sure she would actually come, but here she is, smiling on my doorstep, holding two hot cocoas and a bag of what I can only assume is some kind of breakfast food. I look behind her and wave to Vera, who was nice enough to give her a ride. I smile when she waves back, trying to do my best impression of someone holding it together. Inside, I feel like broken glass. She backs out of the driveway with a little honk, and I usher Peak into the house.

"Are you safe?" Gray asked when I called her.

Yes. Now.

I take everything from Peak, setting the drinks on the table, and she pulls her coat off, hanging it on one of the hooks near the door. She looks around, taking in the house— it's a lot, I know, too much—before looking at me, really looking at me, and sighing.

"I hate your father," she says, coming closer and running her hands through my hair.

"I don't," I say, shutting my eyes.

"That's more than half the problem."

It's barely scratching the surface, actually, but it's probably best not to say that out loud.

"I don't want to go."

"You're not." She takes the bag from my hand. "Can you eat? I brought bagels and butter and cream cheese. It always settles my stomach when I'm nerved up before a big performance or something. I thought it might—"

Her words cut off in a whoosh when I pull her into a hug and hold on too tight, shaking my head. The bag crinkles between us until it falls to the floor, a stray bagel rolling out, and I bury my forehead into her shoulder, breathing her in, letting her hold me together.

"Let's go lie down for a while," she says, and I nod against her neck before leading her up the stairs, the bagels abandoned on the floor where she dropped them.

I perch on my bed, watching her catalog the contents of my room. It only takes a minute; there's not much. My mom never got around to sending most of the things I asked for, and I threw out half of what she did send because of bad memories.

"Where's all your stuff?"

I shrug, suddenly feeling a little embarrassed. "I travel light," I say, because that's easier than explaining that nothing really feels like mine.

She glances in the empty closet, the doors wide open. "Really light, I guess."

I reach over the side of the bed and rummage through

my duffel bag, searching underneath the wrinkled clothes and the boxer briefs and about a dozen Sharpies that I somehow collected, until I feel the pointy plastic of the mask and curl my fingers around it.

"Still have this, though," I say, holding it up.

She takes a step closer, pulling the Batman mask out of my hand and running her fingers over it. "Awww, Bats."

"And this," I say as she watches me snap the back of the case off my phone and pull out her feather. It's a little wrinkled, sure, but still hanging in there.

"You kept that this whole time?"

She says it like it's been an eternity instead of a month and a half. It kind of does feel like that with everything we've been through, and are going through, and hopefully will keep going through, together.

"Is that weird?" I ask, twirling the feather. Because maybe holding on to it is a little stalkery or whatever, but it feels right.

"No, I think it's sweet," she says. "But—"

"But what?"

"But if you get to keep my feather, then I should get to keep the mask. Fair is fair."

I glance at the mask, wishing the idea of giving it away didn't come with such heavy regret.

"It was a joke," she says, trying to hand it back, but we both know it wasn't.

"No, no, keep it." I push it back toward her. "I want you to have it."

"You look like I broke all your crayons," she says, studying my face, "and then ran over your puppy."

"No, it's just—it's good memories. But maybe I don't need it anymore."

"Why?"

"Because you're here."

She smiles at me, genuine but cautious. She's smart to be like that—I know she is—but I wish that she wasn't. Because that's the truth under the lie. She can say it's going to be okay as much as she wants, but one phone call and my dad could have me on a flight back to Seattle. One slip-up and Vera could learn everything and keep us apart.

"I am," she says. It feels like she means more, but I don't want to think about real life for now. I just want to get lost in this girl, in this moment, and forget everything else.

I pull her closer, resting my forehead against her chest and running my arms up and down her sides. She laces her fingers through my hair, humming a song I don't know, and for a second, I let myself believe it's enough.

CHAPTER THIRTY-TWO

RIDLEY: I'm fucking everything up.

> GRAYSON: It sounds like you're doing the best you can with everything going on.

RIDLEY: I still think we should tell Vera.

> GRAYSON: Is it just that you feel bad, or?

RIDLEY: I feel bad all the time, Gray, so no. It's that it feels WRONG.

> GRAYSON: I hate when you say shit like that. It makes me want to like wrap you up in bubble wrap and feed you soup.

RIDLEY: Wtf?

> GRAYSON: I don't know, it just does. But yeah, there's no good answer here.

RIDLEY: But is there a right one?

GRAYSON: I just want you to be happy.

RIDLEY: Yeah about that . . . ☹

GRAYSON: Okay, aside from all the drama with Dad and Verona, how are things with you and Peak?

RIDLEY: All her friends hate me, and her parents think I'm someone else. So good, I guess?

GRAYSON: Oh my god, Ridley. Why can't your life be easy?

RIDLEY: . . . right?

GRAYSON: Well, winning over her friends should be easy enough. Just go be your charming self.

RIDLEY: So funny.

GRAYSON: I'm being serious. Go hang out with them. Show them you're worth the trouble.

RIDLEY: I'm not though.

        GRAYSON: Ridley, don't make
        me come over there.

RIDLEY: That threat works better when
we're on the same side of the country.

        GRAYSON: I can be wheels up
        in an hour. Do not test me.

RIDLEY: Fine, fine, I'll hang out with them.
If only to spare some poor flight attendant
from having to deal with you.

CHAPTER THIRTY-THREE

Jubilee

I'M SITTING ON the bleachers, watching Jayla and Nikki wrap up soccer practice. They were running drills, but now they're scrimmaging and somehow they ended up on opposite teams, which means I don't even know who to cheer for. Yay, sports! It's their first outdoor practice, and it's unusually warm for April. The sunshine feels nice, relaxing even—or it would be if I wasn't sharing a bleacher with electricity personified.

Ridley sits beside me stiffly, the opposite of relaxed. He's chewing on his lip and bouncing his knee, which he's taken to doing whenever we leave the safety of our rooms or the store. I was shocked when he agreed to join me cheering on the girls today.

I slide our fingers together, wishing I could send him some serenity by osmosis or whatever, and he lets out a shaky breath. "Are you sure it's okay that I'm here?"

"Definitely," I say, and hope it's reassuring. I'm positive it's okay; they basically insisted on it. Even Nikki said it was time to break out of the relationship bubble, and she's all about romance. Not that this is romance lately—it's more like he's falling apart, and I'm putting him back together, and in between we kiss and I do homework. It's a lot . . . but I don't mind. And it's partially my fault for insisting he keep up the charade.

The scrimmage finally ends, 6–4 Jayla's team, and I head down to the edge of the field with Ridley. Jayla is leading a meeting, bringing the whole team back together and fulfilling her co-captain duties. Ridley shifts nervously beside me; we're supposed to be hanging out with everybody after this.

"Should we just go home?" I ask him.

"No," he says, a little too quick, and then squeezes my hand.

Nikki and Jayla grab their gear and jog over to us. Jayla's rubbing her side where she took an elbow at the end of the last half, but she's still smiling. "What's up, Batboy?"

Ridley nods but doesn't say anything. Nikki holds out her hand, and Ridley looks at it for a moment before shaking it, like he isn't sure exactly what to do. "I'm Nikki," she says, all out of breath.

"Nice to meet you," he says, so quietly that I squeeze his hand again. "I'm Ridley."

"I know," Nikki says.

"Right."

Jayla tilts her head but swallows whatever snarky thing she was about to say. I'll have to remember to thank her later.

"What's the plan now?" I ask.

Jayla picks up a giant mesh bag full of soccer balls. "I was thinking we'd head back to my house, hit the showers, get a pizza, and hang out, unless you guys want to actually go do something."

I glance at Ridley, not sure exactly how much socializing he's up for. "We could go back to your place for a little while and go from there." I told them I wanted this to be like a quick first visit to ease him in, but I guess they aren't going to let me get away with that.

"I'm gonna help Coach pack everything up," Jayla says, tossing me her keys. "You want to go meet me at the car?"

"I'll help Coach too," Nikki says, but not until Jayla elbows her.

The girls run off, and we head over to the parking lot, where I hit the unlock button over and over again until I finally hear the beep and find her car.

"Am I that obviously freaked out?"

"What? No," I say. I turn the car on long enough to put the windows down, and then pull Ridley into the back seat with me.

"They pretty blatantly just gave us time alone, so."

I nestle in, leaning my head on his shoulder. "This isn't a test, you know."

"I know," he says, but it doesn't sound like he believes me, and there goes his knee again.

I put my hand on it to stop it. "They just want to get to know you a little."

"Why again?"

"Because you're important to me." I chuckle. He's made me say this three times already today.

"I will never get tired of hearing that."

"Good, I hope you don't."

He leans in and kisses me . . . at the exact moment when Jayla and Nikki yank open their doors and drop into the front seats.

"Okay, lovebirds," Jayla says, "keep it PG back there or I'll split you up. If there are any suspicious stains, my dad is *not* gonna believe I didn't put them there."

"Oh my god, Jayla," I say, kicking the back of her seat.

"I'm just sayin'."

CHAPTER THIRTY-FOUR

Ridley

JAYLA'S HOUSE IS nice. It's big, not as big as my dad's, but more importantly, it's warm. Lived-in. A family stays here. A tiny dog greets us at the door, a teacup Yorkie named Cooper, Jayla says, and he continues hopping up and down around us as she leads us downstairs to a finished basement. This is obviously the hangout spot; couches and beanbag chairs take up most of the floor space, with an occasional text-book littering the floor. There's a giant TV against one wall, with every gaming system you could imagine underneath.

I wander around while everyone argues about pizza top-pings and Nikki and Jayla fight over who gets the shower first, just taking it all in. Cooper follows me, sniffing at my pants. There are pictures everywhere: tiny Jayla missing her front teeth, middle-school Jayla in what looks to be some kind of play, all the way up to co-captain-of-the-soccer-team Jayla. Professional portraits of the whole family line the walls, probably done because they wanted them, not because they needed them for a press release. But it's the candid photos that really get me: Jayla and her brother, the kids and the puppy, Jayla racing her brother on a bike, Jayla—

"Hey, whatcha doing?" Peak asks, and I jump, lost in my own head.

"Oh, just . . ." I trail off, waving my hand around at all the pictures.

"Yeah, my mom is basically the paparazzi when it comes to me and my brother," Jayla says, walking by. "Embarrassing."

"It's cool," I say, and she looks at me like I just said the sky was green.

"Right, well, I'm gonna go hit the shower, so make yourselves at home. But not as at home as you did when Kai was here." Jayla narrows her eyes at Peak before disappearing up the stairs.

"What's that about?" I quirk up the side of my mouth with the dimple. I know how much she likes it, so maybe it will distract her from the super-invasive question I have no right to ask but also really fucking need the answer to. I know she said she hooked up with them; I just didn't think she meant like *hooked up* hooked up. It's fine.

This is fine.

"Jubilee got a little frisky down here once, and, um, they weren't discreet," Nikki pipes up.

I look back at Peak, who has turned bright red. "Shut up, Nikki!"

"Hey, he asked! And it's a thousand times worse for me than it ever could be for Ridley, because it was with *my* cousin."

I grab Peak's hand and try to give her a reassuring smile. "I did ask."

242

She huffs and rolls her eyes, tugging me over to the couch. "She didn't have to answer you." Part of me, the part of me that's . . . less good than I want to be . . . wonders if this is the couch where she—

"Bats," she says, and that word will always, always work. "Stop overthinking things." She ruffles my hair and settles in while Nikki flips through the channels.

Cooper trots up a set of tiny dog stairs at the other end of the enormous couch and curls up in Peak's lap with a big yawn.

"You guys are adorable," Nikki says before settling on some cheesy movie on cable.

I clear my throat to respond, but take too long, so everybody goes back to watching TV. It's fine.

pullittogether

We're just past the meet-cute and elbows deep into a commercial break when Jayla comes back in the room. She shoots me a look that kind of freaks me out, but I focus on the warmth of Peak's body pressed into mine and how steady her breathing is. Peak makes everything seem more . . . manageable.

"Your turn," Jayla says, scooting Nikki out of the chair and dropping into it in her place. She's wearing threadbare pajama pants with little llamas on them that say DRAMA LLAMA and a bright pink sweatshirt that hurts to look at. I admire how she doesn't give a shit about making a good impression on me.

She pours some lotion in her hands, rubbing it into her skin while glaring at the TV. "Did Nikki pick this?"

243

"Yeah, it's cute," Peak says, sitting forward a little. Cooper seems to take issue with the new position and jumps down off the couch with his nose in the air.

Jayla rolls her eyes and changes the channel to a cartoon. "Hey, Jubi, do you mind running him out for me? I'd do it, but I'm in my PJs," she says. "If Coop has an accident on this carpet, my mom will flip."

"Seriously?" Peak says. "Since when do you care? You've gone to school in your pajamas."

"Please, Jubi."

Peak glances back at me, looking worried. "Come with me?"

"He's fine," Jayla says. "I don't bite. You'll only be gone a second. I'm sure he can handle it."

"Do you mind?" she asks, and I don't miss the hope in her voice. It feels a little bit like my sister asking me if I'm safe, and it makes me bristle.

"It's fine. Walk the dog." I expected this, to be honest. Although, to be fair, I definitely did *not* expect the lecture would come from someone in drama-llama pants. And yet.

And yet.

Peak looks at me once more, and then a whine from Cooper seems to seal the deal. She hops up and slips his leash off the hook on the wall, clipping it onto him and stepping out the sliding glass door on the other side of the room.

"We don't have a fenced yard," Jayla says, like that matters. I feel like she would have found another way to send Peak outside even if they did.

I lean forward, resting my elbows on my knees, which I'm trying so hard not to bounce.

becoolbecoolbecoolbecoolbecool

"Is this where you give me the whole 'if you hurt her, I'll kill you' speech?"

She sets down the lotion and looks at me, really looks at me, and I squirm a little in my seat. "No."

"No?"

"No, I'm not going to give you the speech, because it doesn't matter."

"What do you mean?"

"It doesn't matter what I say. You're still going to hurt her." I start to protest, but she shakes her head. "It's not a knock against you. Everybody hurts everybody, even if they don't mean to. Especially if they don't mean to."

"Then why is she outside?"

She narrows her eyes. "I just hope you know what you're doing."

"I have no idea what I'm doing," I snort. "But I'm trying."

Her eyes flick down to my bouncing knee and then back to my face. "How messed up are you, exactly? Like very or just moderately?"

"Very," I say. I should be offended, but I'm not. I'm sure Jubilee has told her things; I'm glad she has someone to talk to.

Jayla nods, like she expected that answer. Peak said there wasn't a test, but there is, there always is.

"For whatever reason, Jubi is convinced that you're worth the drama. If she thinks you're this special, I doubt you totally suck. I'd like it if we didn't hate being around each other, for Jubi's sake. That's all I wanted to say."

My ears get warm, and I stare down at my socks, wiggling my toes to distract myself. "Thanks?" I am profoundly uncomfortable now.

"I don't want to hug it out or anything, so don't look so excited. And this lying-to-Vera stuff . . . I know how she feels about your family, but—"

But then Peak bursts through the door, the dog rushing in and jumping up on me with damp paws. "Oh. Everything's okay?" She sounds surprised. I hate that.

I run my hand through Cooper's fur as he wiggles in my lap. "Yeah, we're just watching TV. What'd you expect?"

"I . . . don't know," she says, looking at Jayla and then back at me.

"All right." Jayla grabs her phone. "Pizza?"

"Yeah, definitely," I say. "I'm starving."

Peak waits for Jayla to go hunt down a menu and then squats in front of me. "You sure you're good?"

"Great," I say, kissing her forehead until she all-out grins. Another lie.

CHAPTER THIRTY-FIVE

PEAK: Are you ever going to
tell me what Jayla said to you
while I was out with Coop?

BATS: No, probably not.

PEAK: Rude.

BATS: I like your friends.

PEAK: I'm jealous. I want to meet yours!

BATS: So, you want to meet yourself?

PEAK: Ha ha. Funny. No, I want to
meet your friends back in Seattle.

BATS: Awkward.

PEAK: ?

BATS: 😖

PEAK: You're so dramatic.

BATS: Yes. But you like it.

PEAK: Only very occasionally.

BATS: I'll take it!

PEAK: Seriously though,
tell me about them?

BATS: There's not much to tell.
I didn't have a lot of friends before
I left here, and I had even fewer in
Seattle. I wasn't ever in the same
school long enough. There were kids
who used me to get into Geekery
events, a few random hookups . . .
That's about it.

PEAK: Wasn't there anyone important?

BATS: One. But in retrospect, I don't
know if I'd say important. I thought
he was at the time, but now . . . ?

PEAK: Oooh, tell me everything.

BATS: Not much to tell. Rich boy
with daddy issues. Trying to forget.

PEAK: I meant tell me about
the other kid ☺

BATS: So funny, Peak. So funny.

PEAK: What happened?

BATS: Someone is always more
into it than the other person.

PEAK: I'm sorry.

BATS: How do you know
it wasn't him!

PEAK: I've met you?

BATS: ☉

PEAK: Am I wrong though?

BATS: Not telling.

PEAK: Uh-huh.

> **BATS:** I'm trying to be
> mysterious. Is it working?

PEAK: Nope.

> **BATS:** Fine, it was me.

PEAK: I know.

> **BATS:** You're a very rude person,
> Peak. You're lucky I like you.

PEAK: I am.

> **BATS:** A rude person?
> Or lucky I like you.

PEAK: Not telling.
I'm trying to be mysterious.

> **BATS:** It's working.

CHAPTER THIRTY-SIX

Ridley

I DON'T MEAN to overhear. I'm not even trying to eavesdrop, I swear. It's just that the store is so small, and Vera talks so loud, and with all the windows shut because of another cold snap, there's not even the sound of traffic to drown it out.

Which is why I'm awkwardly reorganizing the comics in the dollar bin and trying not to listen to Vera yelling at Peak for hanging out with me too much. She's shouting that it's distracting her from school, that she got a C-plus on a test for the first time in her life, that she never sees her other friends anymore, and that she doesn't spend enough time with her family. I hate knowing I'm a part of that. I hate that I'm dulling her shine—that instead of her pulling me up, I'm dragging her down—and now she's lying to her family the way I've been lying to mine.

Which, speaking of, her parents apparently also want to meet my parents, which can't happen for very obvious reasons, the biggest being that the second she sees my dad, she'll know exactly who he is, and who I am by default, and how I ended up in her shop. She's been grumbling about my dad more lately too—especially since he responded to her latest op-ed by going on a ten-tweet rant about the dangers of idolizing indie shops to the point where we ignore the "evolving landscape of our industry." Yesterday, Vera even made a joke that my dad probably has a whole team working on a plan to "evolve her right out of his way." Which made me feel like shit, because it's true.

I should tell her the truth, or I should go. Or maybe both.

Jubilee raises her voice at Vera then, shouting that she's going to college in a year, that this is her life, that there's more to it than textbooks. I want to go and break it up; I don't want them to fight because of me. I shouldn't even still be here, and I know it. We've been on borrowed time ever since I sent that first text.

And it's always the wrong thing, no matter what I do. It's lies on top of lies on top of lies, all of it, and god, Vera is the mom I wish I had, and Jubilee is the person I've always dreamed of meeting, but this is all a house of cards, trembling on a foundation made of sand, and I can't breathe.

I can't breathe, and Vera is still yelling at Jubilee about a missed lesson, how they don't have money to waste on lessons she can't be bothered to show up for, and about everything else that used to matter in her life, and should still, but doesn't because of me, and.

icanticanticanticanticanticanticant

The whole thing started because Peak asked her mom if she could cut out early to grab some dinner with me and

Frankie. And I told her not to; I knew this was coming. I told her Vera wasn't my biggest fan anymore. That she was giving me the look, the same one Jayla gives me when she thinks I can't see her, the look that says I'm ruining Peak's life. And you know what? I get it. I do.

If I had a kid, I wouldn't want them hanging around someone like me either, but that doesn't make it not hurt. That doesn't make my stomach not churn deep down, doesn't make it not grow from a spark to a full-fledged panic attack, so that by the time Peak storms out of the back room, I'm already outside, gasping for cold air with my back pressed hard against the bricks and my head between my knees.

"Ridley." She crouches down next to me, and I squeeze my eyes shut tighter. She combs her hand through my hair more gently than I deserve. "Want to hear something cool?"

I give her the tiniest nod, forcing my eyes open.

"Did you know that if you measured all the blood in a newborn, it would only equal about one cup?" she asks, her eyebrows raised as if I'm going to challenge her. I'm not. Mostly, I just want to know who decided to measure blood volume by baby. But then I start thinking of, like, freshly squeezed babies and all this other weird stuff, which kind of freaks me out more, and I put my head back down.

"Okay, wait," she says. "That was a bad one." She laces her fingers through mine, squeezing tight. "Let me think . . . um . . . did you know you're less likely to get bitten by a shark if you blow bubbles in its face?"

I sniffle hard and wipe at my nose, hating the way the cold makes it run, while I let my brain catch up to what she just said. "Wait," I say, my voice rasping out. "What kind of bubble mix can you use underwater?"

She wrinkles her forehead, and I drop my chin, realizing too late she doesn't mean the soap kind you buy in the store. "I . . . see my error now."

"Yeah, seriously." She laughs and sits down next to me. "Feel a little better?"

"Not really."

"It was just a panic attack. It's over."

I shake my head. "I shouldn't be the reason you're fighting with Vera."

"You're not!" She reaches for me again, but I slide back up the wall and shove my hands in my pockets.

"I heard you guys."

"She's just freaking out like she does every time she gets stressed. It's not even about us. She just put a new title on Kickstarter, and it way overfunded, and she's going nuts about distribution channels and finding a new offset printer. That's it. I promise. She always takes it out on everybody around her. Mom and I generally try to avoid her when she first launches for this exact reason."

"I just don't want to be the thing that stands between you and the rest of your life."

"You give yourself way too much credit."

I feel like I've stepped into some kind of a trap here, and I don't know how to get out of it. Because the truth is, I think her life would be better, easier, if I left, that it's the right thing to do—not just for her, but for her family *and* mine.

But I'm selfish.

"Seriously, Ridley," she says, dusting off her backside as she stands up. "If you think I'd give up my dreams for a relationship, you're out of your mind. I love you, but I love myself way more."

And my jaw drops, and I kind of huff out a breath, because we've never said it out loud before. Never, but that's what this is, isn't it? Love?

My sister used to say all the time, "You can't love anybody else until you love yourself," and I believed that for a little while. It made everything seem so much bleaker and more hopeless, but then I met Peak, and the thing is . . . I love her. I do.

And it has nothing to do with me loving myself, because I don't even know where to start with that. But she makes me want to be here, to kiss that spot behind her ear that makes her breath catch, to hear her laugh when I fall off my skateboard, to see the faces she makes when she's lost in her music. She makes me see possibilities that I didn't know existed. Like the capacity to love and be loved was not a thing that was on my radar before.

"What are you thinking about right now?" she asks.

"I'm thinking that you're pretty fucking amazing."

"It's true." She laughs, and the sound settles across my brain, calming me in ways even her endless facts never could.

"And that I love you too."

She grins and kisses me, because we said it. We finally said it. I wish it was all we had to say. I wish the biggest obstacle was "I like you—do you like me back?" But.

"And that I can't lie to your family about who I am

anymore, and you shouldn't be lying to protect me," I say, and she frowns.

Because that's the thing. Thinking about love is one thing, but saying it out loud comes with responsibility—the responsibility to do right by the other person, no matter what. And doing right isn't turning them into the person you're so desperately trying not to be yourself. We have to tell the truth now, to her parents and mine. We have to believe that our love could survive it. There's not a future any other way.

"Come on, let's walk," she says. We fall into an easy silence, our footsteps striking in perfect rhythm.

"Where are we going?"

"I told Frankie to grab pizza with us before I realized things were going to get so heavy. He's waiting at the shop across the street."

I shrug. "I think I'm just gonna head home. Allison's visiting her parents in New York, and my dad's not back from his work conference until tomorrow. Maybe you can come by later, if there's time?" And this is not how I thought things would go after my first declaration of love.

"I'd rather you come with me." She takes a half step away, and even though our arms are still linked, now we're walking off rhythm.

"I can't." Just thinking of walking into the pizza place with all the noise and smells is setting me on edge.

"Because of Vera or because of your little freak-out?"

And it feels like someone just shoved toothpicks under my nails and ripped out my heart. I can handle everybody else acting like I'm crazy, but not her.

I drop her arm, blinking hard. "Don't say it like that."

She hesitates before pulling her hands into her coat sleeves. "Sorry, I didn't—"

I walk a little faster, leaving her a few steps behind, and then hop on my board. "Tell Frankie I said hi."

"Ridley," she says, but I push off faster and don't stick around. I can't.

• • •

I'm lying in the tub, water only up to my chin this time because I'm being safer, more careful. The room is dark, another of my sadbaths, and it's not that I'm even depressed—well, not more than usual—it's just that I want to not think for a minute. I want my brain to be quiet. I want to sit in the dark and float and not worry about anything else.

Except now someone is ringing the doorbell, and it's so goddamn loud I could cry.

I towel off and throw on some shorts, and whoever it is has taken to knocking now too. I grumble down the stairs. Maybe it's Peak. I don't know. That would be nice. She didn't text, but.

I enter the alarm code and pull open the door, ready to apologize for torpedoing her perfectly good night. Except it's not Peak; it's Frankie, which is . . . weird.

"Took you long enough. Now invite me in," he says, holding up a pizza box.

"I'm gonna just grab a shirt," I say slowly, pointing upstairs. "What are you doing here?"

"JuJu was freaking out about everything that happened

tonight. I sent her home and told her I'd check up on you."

"Yeah, well, I don't need a babysitter, so." But my traitor stomach growls at the smell of food.

"Get your shirt," Frankie says, pushing past me. "Your kitchen this way?" He walks off, not even waiting for me to reply.

I make my way back downstairs a few minutes later, my damp skin sticking to the hoodie I found under my bed. He's already sitting at the table, the pizza box open in front of him. He's not even using a plate, but he did seem to find the good linen napkins. "Eat," he says, without looking up.

I grab a slice and sit down. "You didn't have to do this."

"Actually, I did," he says, pausing his chewing long enough to look at me. "For one, I would never hear the end of it if I didn't, and for two, I wanted an excuse to eat another pizza. It's more for my benefit than yours."

"Thanks."

"Listen. JuJu's really worried about you, you know. If you need someone to talk to, I'm all ears."

I take another bite of pizza, considering the offer. It has been a while since I dumped my shit on a stranger, and that was my primary coping method before meeting Peak, so.

"You'll just tell her whatever I say."

"Maybe." He shrugs. "Maybe not. Depends on what it is and if I think it's her business."

"How do you decide if it's her business or not?"

"I'll know when you say it."

And yeah, I probably shouldn't tell him anything, but

once I open my mouth, I can't stop. Peak has helped me so much, but one person can't carry it all. Not all the time.

So yeah, I tell him everything. I tell him how Peak and I met at the con. I tell him why I'm really in town. He stops me there and asks a lot of questions. I don't miss the way his hands curl into fists when I talk about my dad's plan for Verona Comics. And then I tell him how I want to come clean, even though she doesn't, because how much of a fresh start can I really get when I still have to report to my father every Tuesday and Thursday, just like the rest of his spies do, even if I *am* feeding him useless info.

And that's what I'm most bitter about, I realize—that I'm not even special. I don't even get to tell him directly, even when he's home. I just send my reports to the marketing email, just like all the other people he has working for him. There are probably twenty other people just the same as me, vying for his approval via form emails. And maybe I paw at my eyes while I'm talking, but I'm not sad, I'm upset, and it's just that sometimes my brain can't tell the difference.

And I tell him what even Peak doesn't know, that my dad has a good friend on the board of the conservatory that could complicate everything. If he ever found out, my dad would have all the ammunition he needed, and Vera would have every motivation in the world to go along with it. Frankie rubs his temples when I explain that part, and I know, *I know*, but I couldn't keep it to myself any longer.

When the words finally stop, when there's nothing else to confess, I feel ten pounds lighter and completely exhausted, like I could sleep for a year and still never wake up.

"Hey," Frankie says when he's sure that I'm finished. "Listen, I've found myself in some tough jams over the last couple years, and all I know is that if your gut is telling you something is wrong, it probably is."

"You think I should tell Vera, then?" I ask, leaning back in my chair and tucking my hands behind my head. "That's what you would do?"

Frankie blows out a breath so hard his cheeks puff out. "I don't know, kid. I really don't. I can see JuJu's point. You're not doing it anymore, it won't change anything, so why does Vera really need to know right now? Especially with the risk of you getting shipped off to the left coast. But I see your point too. You're holding in a big secret, and you're looking for a little redemption. And if Vera found out from someone else, it would be way worse."

"Yeah," I say, swallowing hard. "So what do I do?"

"I think you follow your gut."

"Okay. Next question: How can I tell if it's my gut talking or my myriad of anxiety disorders?"

Frankie chuckles. "Is there that much of a difference?"

I laugh too, and it's a bitter sort of laugh. Because I don't know. I sincerely do not know.

CHAPTER THIRTY-SEVEN

Jubilee

"COME ON." HE grins, holding his phone out. "Let me record it!"

"Why are you so obsessed with me?" I laugh, covering up my face, but I don't really mind.

It's just that Ridley's been taking so many videos lately. He says it's because he doesn't want to forget anything, but I'm worried it's something else. I can't shake the feeling that he thinks we're less than permanent now, which I guess, yeah, at almost seventeen and almost eighteen that's realistic or whatever, but it feels like he just got here and now he's getting ready to go.

"Because I love you," he says, and his words come so easily, even though his eyes are like storms.

"I love you too."

He backs up until he hits the bed and sits down to get the widest shot possible.

And it's hard to think straight with him looking at me like this—his lips slightly parted, his eyes sort of sleepy and inviting. This feels more intimate, fully clothed and twelve feet across the room, than it did a few nights ago, when our kissing got a little extra handsy.

I blush and look down, and then I glare at my open door. My mom has been pointedly walking down the hallway every fifteen minutes or so, being completely non-stealthy about checking in on us. It turns out that time Vera took me to his house alone was not officially Mom sanctioned, and the "two yeses or one no" rule has officially been reimplemented for all decision-making as a result. Same with the "open door at all times" rule, and the "Ridley can only stay until seven on school nights" rule.

"Play me that song for your audition. The one you're always talking about."

"The Bach? It's not a song. It's a suite and it's like a half hour long." I laugh.

"Then just play the first part."

"Why?" I don't want to think about that now. I don't want to think about the fact that even if everything goes right, I'm going to be spending the summer almost two hours away in a program so intense I'll be lucky to have time to text. And he'll be . . . I don't even know, on the other side of the country possibly. Or hiding in my dorm if I'm lucky.

Ridley cocks his head. "You need to practice. I'm happy to just be in the background."

"What if I don't want you just in the background?"

"I don't want to be a distraction. *Don't* let me be one."

"You're not," I say, because I want it so badly to be true.

"Come on." He sighs, hitting record on his phone. "Will you please play the Bach? I don't have it yet."

That's because I still haven't perfected it, I think but don't say. He's right; I really could use the extra practice. Even Mrs. G made a comment along the lines of "Okay, that's enough living life now, dear" at my last lesson, but I don't want him stressing about it. He stresses about too much as it is.

"What about our mutual improvement plan?" I smirk. "Don't you have more homework?"

And that's another rule, my mom's "mutual improvement plan." It was part of the deal to have him over on school nights *at all.* We both have to do our homework either here or at the shop, and she checks it now like I'm back in elementary school. You get one C-plus and—

"I'll do it after."

"Fiiiiine," I whine, but I've already turned to the page.

I pick up my bow and take a deep breath, looking right at him before I start. Just seeing him so expectant and calm settles the nerves inside me. He makes me feel like I can do anything.

He gives me a little nod that simultaneously melts my heart and steels my spine, and I slide the bow across my strings. For the first time, I don't miss a single note.

For the first time, it's perfect.

CHAPTER THIRTY-EIGHT
Ridley

I CAN TELL right away that Vera is pissed. I don't even know why I stopped by the shop today, other than I just needed to get out of my dad's way and had nowhere else to go. He's been working from home more and more—the number of days he stays home directly proportional to the amount he drinks.

I've been doing a decent job of avoiding Vera lately. Every time she's nice to me, it feels like a knife twisting in my belly. But it's Friday morning, which means Peak's in school, and it's just Vera and me in the shop. Peak and I have plans to hang out later—a quick hot cocoa, and then it's back to her house for homework and practice.

Which has actually been working, by the way. I'm three assignments ahead now, and my GPA is, well, passing. Peak is practicing more too. My phone is so full I have to keep deleting apps to make room for new recordings. I feel . . . not good exactly, but like the possibility of good. Like I've been tied in knots my whole life, and then Peak came along and undid one, and now I want to untangle all the rest of them.

I texted Frankie, which is a new thing that I definitely don't mind, and he said it's called hope.

But when Vera looks at me the way she's looking at me now, like she has something to say but doesn't know how to say it, all that hope goes right out the window. Because there's a storm brewing outside the little bubble Peak and I have made for ourselves, and there's only so long we can ignore it.

Vera opens her mouth a few times but then just sighs and hovers nearby while I pretend to reorganize the new-release rack. I count the times she clears her throat, and after the third time, I push up from where I'm crouching, because I'm almost positive I want to have this conversation standing up. "Vera, whatever it is, just say it."

She looks at me all surprised, like she thought she was being subtle or something. Which, maybe she was, but seventeen years of suffering through anxiety attacks while trying to act normal has gifted me with the ability to be oddly in tune with people. Also, it's possible she wasn't being subtle at all.

"It's nothing," she says, "none of my business." But I can tell she's not done, so I stand there, waiting, with my heart rattling around in my chest like a panicked bird.

"Actually," she says, shutting her laptop. "You know what? No, I'm sorry, but it is my business."

"Okay."

"What's your story?" Vera asks, narrowing her eyes, and I swear the floor drops right out from under me. "You're a sweet kid, but you came out of nowhere, and you don't seem to have parents, and you've got my daughter all—"

I knew this moment would come. But the words are dying in my throat, or I am, because I don't know what to do. I promised Peak one thing, but my gut says another, and I've been turning it over and over and over, because either way, I'm betraying someone. I need to sit down.

shitshitshitshitshitshitshitshitshitshitshitshit

"Ridley? Are you okay?"

"Mm-hmm," I force out, because if I open my mouth right now, I don't know what will come out: hysterical laughter, maybe, or vomit. I look at the window, praying for a customer to walk up or park out front, for anything to save me, for the world to intervene and get me out of this, but there's nothing.

"Did you know that a single cloud can weigh over a million pounds?"

I look at Vera, so shocked that I sort of see through the haze of panic and pull in a deep breath.

"Um, shit," Vera says, opening her laptop up. "That's the only one I remember."

"What?" I croak out. Where is Peak? I wish Peak were here. Why does school exist?

"Dammit. Hang on, the Wi-Fi's being slow again. Just . . . just take a deep breath. I'm almost there."

"I—I'm fine," I grumble out, and I feel tired, so tired, so I walk over to a pile of comics and kneel down beside it, hoping that it looks like I'm sorting through them, when really I'm using them for support.

"Bingo! It's up. Let's see, fun facts, fun facts, fuuuuuun facts."

"Vera," I say, but she doesn't look up from the screen.

"Did you know earthworms eat fourteen baby robins a day?"

"What?"

"Other way around. You know what I meant. Just, how many do you need?"

"How many of what?" I ask, my confusion distracting me enough to get to my feet.

Vera finally stops, looking up with a smile. "You scared the shit out of me." She walks over to the mini fridge she keeps behind the counter, and pulls out a bottle of water. She twists off the cap and hands it to me, and that's when I know for sure. It settles over me, all calm and shit, what a total head case I really am. My girlfriend gave her mom, like, a panic attack prevention plan for me. Fuck.

"Jubilee told me some facts just in case," Vera says, looking ridiculously proud of that. And now that it's confirmed, I want to crawl under a rack and melt into the floor. "She and Lil used to do that when she was little, too, you know."

"Wonderful." I know she did it out of kindness, but the fact that Peak and Vera definitely had a "my boyfriend is messed up and here's how to help him not lose it" talk just makes me feel worse. Dirty almost. Broken in a way I haven't felt in a little while. A very little while.

"She just wanted to make sure that if anything ever happened here, you would be okay."

"Right," I say, because still, it smarts, and I'm embarrassed, and also I get so tired after these things, I can't be bothered to say more.

"Ridley, I didn't mean to—it's just that, you're dating my daughter. My only daughter. And I care about you. You seem like a great kid . . ."

She pauses, and there's a *but* coming. I know because there's always a *but* coming, always an addendum, a reason why someone can love me but not unconditionally. When I die, my gravestone will probably say, *Here lies Ridley Oliver Everlasting. But . . .*

"But," she finally says, and I wince. "Jubilee is my priority. And I have concerns."

"Yeah," I say. "Makes sense."

"Ridley, look at it from my perspective. I don't know where you're from, or who your parents are, and Jubilee won't tell me anything. She's never shut us out like this. And maybe coming to you directly is a violation of her privacy, but she's put you at the center of her universe, and I just want to make sure that you deserve to be there."

"I don't," I say, biting hard on the inside of my cheek.

And she frowns.

I scratch the back of my neck. "But I'm trying to be someone who does."

She smiles at that, like it just assuaged all her fears or something. And I realize for the first time that this is someone who actually wants to be there, who wants to care about me. Who really wanted me to say the right thing. And I think I just did?

liar

"You're a good egg, Ridley." She comes up behind me, her hand burning into my skin when she places it on my shoulder. Because I think she just gave me her blessing, but also it's Friday, and I have to go write up another fake report for my dad.

I swallow hard, my skin crawling. I have to stop this. Today.

She squeezes my shoulder again. "I'm sorry for pushing. I just—I'm a mom. It's what we do."

I nod like I know what that means.

"I have to go." I grab my hoodie, push open the glass door, and walk the three miles back to my house, clutching my skateboard like a shield, trying to buy myself time to figure this out.

I want to say just the right thing when I get home, the thing to show that I'm mature, that I've thought this through, that I'm more than the inconvenience my mom thinks I am— she's barely called since I've been here—or the fuckup that my dad does.

That I've watched enough Captain America movies to know right from wrong, and this is wrong. That maybe if they let me, I could start a life here, maybe enroll in public school like a regular kid, even if I have to repeat my senior year. That it's not worth it to nibble on the scraps of their attention anymore, begging for it like a starving dog.

That I could have a life and friends and a future, and maybe that wasn't anybody's intention when I came here, but it could be the outcome.

But when I get home and I knock on the door to Dad's

study, he pulls it open like I'm bothering him somehow, and it all goes out the window. I stand there for a second, trying to steel my nerves—*What would Steve Rogers do?*—but he just raises his eyebrows and says, "I'm on a call, Ridley."

Like somehow that call is more important than finding out what I need. It's not. Not anymore. Because for this second, I have enough adrenaline coursing through my body to form words instead of excuses. For this second, I'm a Super-Soldier with a conscience, clutching his vibranium shield.

"Hi, Dad," I say, pushing into his office before I lose my nerve.

"I'll have to call you back," he says, and I didn't realize he had his Bluetooth thing in his ear. I hate those things; they make everybody look like sci-fi movie rejects. Nobody even uses them anymore except my dad and people like him, probably because they're also the only ones who even *make* phone calls anymore.

He pulls the device out and drops it onto the desk beside him. There are papers all spread across it, and he closes a file with a hard thud and then picks up his glass of scotch. "Okay, you have my attention." He leans against the desk a little bit, his legs angling out, taking up as much space as humanly possible. "What's so important that you had to interrupt me on a call to our German financiers?"

And I know I shouldn't be excited just by the thought of having his attention for once, his undivided attention, which I don't think I've had even once since I was born—stolen from German financiers, no less—but I am.

I am.

God, I am so screwed up.

"This is wrong," I say. And that wasn't how I meant to open, but it'll do. I tuck my hands behind my back and lean against the wall and hope my opening volley was a good one.

He blinks and then lets out a little sigh. "I wondered why you've been feeding us bogus reports. I should have anticipated this. You've always been the emotional one." He runs his hand over his chin. "It's just business, Ridley, glorified market research, nothing more."

"You knew?"

"I thought threatening to send you back to Seattle would bring you around."

Awesome, so his threat was actually a business strategy. He literally does not care. I swallow hard—I can't worry about that now—and steady my course.

"They're good people."

He turns around, shuffling some papers on his desk. "Why does that matter?"

"Screwing with good people is wrong." I can't believe I even have to explain this to him. This is like Being Human 101.

"Is that what you've been doing?"

"That's what you're making me do!"

"No, I brought you here, but everything else was your decision. All the nonsense you've been up to with Vera's stepdaughter—" He looks at my surprised face. "Did you really think I didn't know how much time you were spending together? I'd hoped you had learned from your last indiscretion not to get in bed with people we do business with. Your mother swore to me you wouldn't make this messy like—"

"Like what?" I shove off the wall and take a step closer.

He hesitates for a second, like he's trying to decide how far he wants to go, but then his eyes narrow and his cheeks kinda suck into this tight smile. "Like you're prone to do."

I nod, squeezing my eyes shut, trying to swallow down the anxiety coiling tight in the pit of my stomach. "Maybe if I had parents who—" But I stop myself. It's pointless. He's going to think what he thinks, and nothing I do will change that. "I've seen what a family is, Dad, and I know it's not this."

"Oh, that's rich coming from you," he says. "Do you know what you've cost us over the years?"

"Me?"

He pushes off his desk and takes a step closer. "We may not have had much time together, and I own that, but we gave you opportunities that most kids could never even dream of."

"I didn't want opportunities; I wanted parents!"

"We tried that, and you jumped off the roof, remember? This roof, actually. And then your mother made me buy her a whole new house across the country so you could have a fresh start. But you screwed that up by letting that boy take pictures of you. Do you know how much I had to pay that website to make them disappear?"

I shift uncomfortably. I didn't even know they existed until Chandler threatened to post them online, hoping it would derail his conservative father's political career. I guess queer kids hating their shitty dads is kind of par for the course.

"Who exactly do you think has been bankrolling all of your mistakes?"

I stare down at the carpet. "I just don't want to be a part of this anymore."

He scoffs. "A part of what?"

"Any of this." I gesture to the reports, to the room, to him.

He takes another step forward, and another, until my back is against the wall, and I wince from the smell of booze on his breath. Shit, it's barely afternoon.

"What would you do without any of this? You have no skills, no money, no education. You've been coddled to the point of uselessness." His voice changes, like he's letting loose years of pent-up frustration. "You are a black hole, Ridley. You always have been, sucking us all in with you. You want out? Nobody's stopping you. Not anymore."

I bounce my head against the wall a couple times, trying to ground myself, trying to put together the threat behind the words, to remember what's important, what matters, what I should do . . . but it's hard to remember when no one ever bothered to teach you.

"Yes," I say, and it comes out more like a plea. "I want to go."

He huffs out a breath like he doesn't believe me.

I spin off the wall and bolt to my room. I tear back the blankets to find my favorite pair of sweats and grab all the little notes that Peak left me whenever she came over, and the three hair ties she abandoned in my bathroom, and the little bit of money my dad has given me for my work. I shove it all in the black duffel bag at my feet, along with whatever clothes are within reach, and dart down the stairs.

My dad is standing in the doorway of his office, but he looks different. Resigned instead of mad. But if I think about that too long, I might stay to ask why, and I can't.

I can't.

"Ridley—" he says, but I don't look back.

CHAPTER THIRTY-NINE

Jubilee

RIDLEY IS LYING stone still on my bed, staring at the ceiling with his shoes still on. He never leaves his shoes on—he knows we don't allow it—and now they've left muddy smudges at the bottom of my comforter.

I'm too worried to care.

It has been exactly twenty-three minutes since Mom called me to the door with the tiniest bit of an edge to her voice. No one else would have noticed probably, but it's the closest I've ever heard her to panic. I didn't know what to expect when I ran down the hall, but it definitely wasn't Ridley standing on our doorstep with a black bag slung across his body and a haunted look on his face.

"I got this, Mom," I said, taking his hand and leading him back to my room.

She mouthed *Is he okay?* and all I could do was shrug because I didn't know. Our last texts had been about going to Stacks later today, and he'd seemed fine. Mom followed us to my room, lingering for a minute, and then shut the door behind us.

And now, with his heartbeat thumping in my ear like a metronome on speed, I know the answer is loudly and conclusively no, he is not.

I tried to talk to him at first. I tried to tell him some facts, to make him laugh, but he just lay down without a word, his eyes red and exhausted, his breath still hitching. I did the only thing I could think of: I curled up next to him, I told him I loved him, and I waited.

• • •

"I can't ever go back to that house," he says, and I startle a little. I thought he'd fallen asleep. I glance at the clock again; it's been two hours since he came to my door.

"What happened?"

"I got out."

I go back to stroking his hair, just relieved that he's talking. "What does that mean?"

He draws in a deep breath, holding it for a full beat before letting it out. "I told my father that I was done. He knew the reports were fake already. We got in a fight, and he said some stuff, and—it's fine." His breath hitches again as his words trail off.

I nuzzle in closer, kissing any part of him I can reach. "It's okay, Ridley. You're okay." When I stop, he looks down at me, frowning.

"He said I was a . . ." He's looking at me so intensely, it scares me. "Am I a black hole?"

"No," I say, sitting up. "I hate your father. I hate him. You are *not* a black hole."

He pinches the bridge of his nose with his thumbs and shuts his eyes. "But I am. I am. Look at what I've done to you."

"You haven't done anything to me."

"They're going to send me back to Washington, I bet. Back to that house, and it'll just be me and all those windows and a fucking housekeeper and nothing." He squeezes my arm tight. "I thought I could do the right thing for once, but it didn't matter anyway. I'll—"

"My parents will help us; we'll figure it out."

"No," he says, scrambling backward until he slams into my headboard. "Peak, if they find out who I am now, I'll have nothing. You were right; we can never tell them. I was stupid to think we could." He jumps up and starts pacing. I've never seen him this frantic. "What if my dad tells them now to screw with me? I can't—there's no—"

"It's going to be okay," I say in as calm a voice as I can muster.

"You don't understand. I can't go back. I'll—" And then, all at once, he goes completely still, and our eyes meet. "You could leave with me."

"What?"

"Leave with me, Peak. It's the only other option."

"Only other option than what?" I ask, the hairs on my arms standing up as I realize what he's talking about. I know exactly what he's doing: he's checking for emergency exits and coming up short.

"I won't go back to my mom's." He shakes his head. "And I can't stay here. Peak, if your parents—no, *when* your parents figure it out, it's all over for us anyway. Come with me."

"I have school. I have the audition for the summer program in, like, a week and a half! We can't go anywhere."

He scrunches his eyes shut, nodding in a way that feels more for him than for me. "You're right," he says, walking over to where I sit. "You're right. The audition. I'm so proud of you, Peak." He leans down and kisses me. It feels so right, so loving, that I almost don't realize what it is—a goodbye.

I grab on to his sleeve, but he shakes me off. "Ridley."

"It wasn't fair to ask. I'm not thinking straight."

"Ridley, stop. Seriously, you're scaring me. Stay here for tonight. It'll be okay."

He exhales, his nostrils flaring as he wipes at his eyes. "It will never be okay, Peak. That's the thing."

And then, before I even realize what's happening, he's shoved open my window and thrown his bag outside, putting his hands on the sill like he aims to follow.

"Wait." And I thought there'd be more time before it all came crashing down, that we'd get at least a few months of happiness. I thought if we could just make it to summer . . . I can't let him go out there alone, though, not like this.

"I'm coming with you." I glance at my cello; I can't help it, because leaving right now feels like losing it forever. Resentment rises up inside, choking me, but I swallow it down. There'll be time to be pissed—at his parents for failing him, at the world for putting us in this situation, at him too maybe—later. When he's safe.

He runs his hands through his hair, linking his fingers behind his head. "Peak," he says, letting out a hard breath. "This isn't—I'm trying to do the right thing here. I don't want to—I'm not going to be your black hole too."

And I swear to god, if I ever see his father again, I will claw his eyes out myself.

"I can decide for myself," I say, even though this is the definition of forcing my hand, but whatever. I grab my book bag off my chair and shove some clothes inside. I know this is a terrible idea, probably the worst I've ever had, but if I can get him through the night, then we can come back and fix it all when he's calmer and thinking straight. My parents are going to kill me, but I don't see any other choice.

I zip up my bag and turn to look at him, hoping I look more confident than I actually feel. Inside my stomach is churning. "Okay, let's go."

Ridley drops his arms and looks at me. "I'm not worth it."

"You are." I try to mask the annoyance in my voice. If he only realized that, we wouldn't be here in the first place. Why can't he realize that?

He turns around to hop out the window, but I pull his shoulder back. I nudge him out of the way, dropping my bag outside next to his. He looks at me, confused, as I walk to the bedroom door.

"Don't you think it would be a little suspicious if we jumped out of my bedroom window? We probably only have a few more minutes before they come open the door anyway."

"You're going to tell them you're leaving?"

"I won't tell them what we're really doing, but I'll say you're staying with Frankie for a few nights and I'm taking you to get settled."

"Get me settled?" He winces. "Like I'm a little kid."

"Ridley." I squeeze his hand. "I have to tell them something." And also, I'm kind of hoping I can convince him that Frankie is our best bet anyway, so it's not really a lie.

"Okay," he says, squeezing my hand back. "Okay."

CHAPTER FORTY

Ridley

IT WAS EASIER getting past her parents than I thought it would be, and somehow, even walking down this cold, dark street with the weight of both of our bags on my shoulder, I feel lighter than I ever have. I don't have to be a liar anymore; I don't have to pretend to be anything I'm not; I can just be a boy holding the hand of the person he loves and leaving everything else behind.

I look over at Peak, and she smiles, pushing some of her hair back and tucking it behind her ear. We've been walking in silence for a half hour, but if she's scared, she's not showing it. If I was one-tenth as brave as her, maybe—

"Where to?" she asks, her voice gentle, quieting all the noise in my head. Peak's magic like that.

"Just up here. I need to borrow something from my sister." Something flickers in her eyes, confusion maybe, or possibly relief, but I don't want to think about that too long.

"Oh, good idea. I was going to say we should go to

Frankie's for real, but your sister's is probably a better idea. Maybe she can help us figure it out."

I scrunch my eyebrows, shifting the bags up higher on my shoulder without letting go of her hand. Suddenly this seems so much more tenuous than I thought. If she thinks we're staying here, in town, that would explain why she's not freaking. Should I rip that Band-Aid off, or?

icantlosehericant

And shit. It feels so good walking here with her. So peaceful. Like in another life, it would be day instead of night, and our bags would have homework instead of clothes in them, and everything would be fine, and nothing would hurt. But that's a lie. And I'm done with lies, so.

"I'm not staying at my sister's, Peak."

"Okay," she says, and I almost believe her, until she says, "where should we go, then?" She pulls out her phone. "We could go to Frankie's or head to Jayla's basement for a few days. Her parents never go down there." I stop as we near the parking garage, and she looks up at me, confused. "What are you doing?"

"Borrowing something we need."

I cut across the street to where the valet parking is. I pull out a parking stub from my wallet and hand it to the attendant. Gray forgot it in Dad's car when he dropped her at the airport. I swiped it from him so it didn't get lost while she was gone.

"Normally, Ms. Everlasting has our driver deliver her car to her apartment," the valet says, frowning.

"She asked me to get it. She has a late flight tonight, and I have to get her." He looks me up and down, like he's not sure he should do what I'm asking, but then seems to decide I'm all right, or maybe that he doesn't care either way, and radios another attendant to bring the car around.

Gray's car appears a few minutes later, a shiny new Audi. The valet hops out, leaving the door open and even popping the trunk. He takes the bags from me and drops them in. Peak eyes me slowly before getting in the car.

I jump when the valet shuts the trunk.

"Is everything all right, sir?" he asks, coming around for his tip.

"Yeah." And god, I hope that's true. I really hope that's true.

I slide into the driver's seat, adjusting the rearview mirror and the blowers for the heat. Okay. I can do this. I had six hours of driver's ed last summer when I stayed with my aunt and cousin in Michigan because my mom needed a break from me. It was the best summer of my life. Best months of my life, really. And suddenly, I know just where we can go. She would definitely let me stay, probably Peak too. Maybe Peak could even fly back for her audition. Maybe it could be okay.

"What are you doing?" Peak asks, looking at me with wide eyes as she buckles up.

"Getting us out of here." I tap my fingers on the steering wheel. I can see the guys in the valet stand still watching me, and if I sit here for much longer, they will definitely know something is up. I try to shift into drive, but the gearshift doesn't move.

Peak stares at me, and as calm as she looked before, she seems really fucking concerned right now. "Sorry," I say, giving her a weak smile. "I forgot you had to be pressing on the brake. I remember that now." I push it into drive and ease off the brake, letting the car roll forward a bit.

"This is a bad idea. You don't even have a license." And she's right. It is a bad idea, but it's also the only other idea I have that ends with me still here.

"Do you want to get out?" I ask, my foot planted firmly on the brake again. And I mean it too. I might be running away from home, I might even be in the middle of grand theft auto as we speak, but. The valet guy knocks on my window; we've been sitting here a long time. But I can't go, not until she answers.

She hesitates and then shakes her head, and I could kiss her face—would be, actually, if the guy from the garage wasn't still knocking.

I lower the window. "Sorry, we were just trying to decide where to go eat. Am I in your way?"

I'm scared he's going to say something, like he realized something was up and called Gray or my dad, or that he could tell I didn't really know how to drive, or that the police were coming to arrest me for driving without a license. But he just says, "There's a great lobster bar down by the pier; it should be pretty quiet tonight."

"Thanks, we'll be sure to check it out." I flash him my

most winningest smile and hit the gas. The car jerks forward, and I ease it onto the road, tightening my grip on the wheel and saying a quick prayer that I can handle this.

"Ridley," Peak says, but when I look at her, she's turned toward her window. Whatever words she was planning to say dying on her lips.

CHAPTER FORTY-ONE

Jubilee

THIS IS BAD. I'm 99 percent sure that we just stole his sister's car, which is extremely illegal. Even more illegal when you don't have a driver's license, which neither of us do. I fight the urge to call my mom. She'd probably just call the police or something, not to be mean, but just to have them find me and give me a ride back home. But that would probably be worse in the end. The way Ridley is white-knuckling the steering wheel is already freaking me out. I don't know what he would do if we got pulled over. I don't want to find out.

Suddenly, I feel very small. Very small and unprepared. Running away seemed like a good idea when I thought it meant crashing in Jayla's basement for a day or two, or hiding out at Frankie's apartment and still texting my mom good night even though she was definitely going to ground me.

But this, this is completely different. This is so much bigger than me. Bigger than us. These are real problems, with real consequences, and I am not equipped to handle this. A few weeks ago, I thought if I didn't nail my audition, it would be the end of the world, but this night feels like it could actually *be* the end of my world, and that's scaring the crap out of me.

"Ridley," I say when I notice he's heading toward the freeway. He's been driving carefully until now, keeping to back roads and not going over thirty miles per hour. I can tell by the way he swerves and slows that we definitely shouldn't be going freeway fast. Not to mention it will have actual traffic, even late on a weeknight like this. I need to stop this; this is a mistake.

"What?" he asks.

"Watch the road," I say when he looks at me, but he stares at me for a beat too long anyway, and I feel like I'm going to throw up. "I was just going to say, don't get on the freeway."

"Why? It's the fastest."

Because we'll probably die, I think, but instead I say, "We can go the back way, take Route 9 all the way out. We'll see the coast and be low profile. What if your dad already called the police or something?" It bothers me, the ease with which I lie now. I've had a lot of practice since I met Ridley. I kind of hate that.

"Smart." He flicks on his turn signal and follows the Route 9 sign. I wait until we're a little farther out of town, driving through the woods on some back roads, to try again.

"Where are we going?" I'm trying to sound completely unfazed. I don't want to scare him again, not when he's driving, or whatever you want to call what we're doing. There's a reason people have to take tests to operate cars. I haven't even taken the test for my permit yet.

"I don't know." He takes one hand off the wheel and scratches the back of his neck. "Gray's on the other side of Canada, so I was thinking my aunt's?"

"Where does she live?"

"Michigan."

Okay, so that's not as close as Jayla's basement, but not as bad as driving to the other side of Canada. But still, I feel it settling over me, this feeling of doom, like it's all going off the rails and there's no way to stop it. I have to try, though.

"Have you talked to Gray about everything that's going on?"

"Uh, no, Peak, this was pretty spur of the moment. I came to you first."

I turn to face him, pulling one leg up on the seat. It's now or never. "Don't freak out, please. But this feels like a bad idea. I really think we should go back now."

He slams his head against his seat and looks at me, so hurt, so lost, and I wish I never said anything. "I told you not to come. And I gave you the chance to get out when we got the car. I can't stay. I thought you got that."

And he's so worked up, I need to adjust the timeline of my plan. I can't wait for him to calm down; cooler heads need to prevail now.

"I'm not asking you to go back to your dad's. We'll go to my house. I know my parents will let you spend the night." He makes a face like he doesn't believe me. "Just the night, and probably on the couch, but tomorrow we'll tell them everything. You've wanted to all along; you were right. Okay?"

"It's too late. I can't fix this. They'll hate me, especially now."

"They won't. They'll understand. Trust me, tragic origin stories are kind of their thing. Do you even read Vera's comics? And here I thought you were a superfan," I tease. I'm trying to break the tension; it doesn't work. "Fine, they'll be mad. But even if they're furious, they'll still help. I promise."

"You trust them way too much."

And oh, that breaks my heart. "You're supposed to be able to," I say. "Like, in a perfect world, everybody could trust their parents."

"Yeah, well."

"Bats." He looks at me quick and goes back to driving. "Please believe me. They might be pissed—they're definitely going to be pissed—but they'll help us. Tomorrow we'll call your aunt and your sister and figure everything out from there."

"I can't go back with my parents," he says, his eyes shining in the dashboard lights. He's slowed to twenty miles per hour, and if I can just keep talking to him, maybe I can get him to stop.

"You won't have to. I won't let that happen." He looks at me again, probably surprised by how intensely I said that. "Look, my mom will know what to do. Maybe she and Vera can even talk to your parents for you."

"They're mortal enemies," he deadpans, like this night hasn't been dramatic enough.

"Fine." I try to laugh, but it comes out more like a huff. "Then they'll call your aunt, and she can talk to your parents. Maybe you can even stay with her until you finish school?"

"You're here, though." He says it like it's the most important thing. And I thought it was too, I did, but this feels so much bigger than anything I've ever had to deal with. Somehow, I don't think grand theft auto with a boyfriend in crisis is what Mrs. Garavuso meant when she said I needed to live a little.

I tip my head toward him. "Michigan is a lot closer to Connecticut than Washington is."

The car slows to ten miles per hour, and then five, and then stops. "Why are you like this?"

"Like what?"

"Why are you so nice to me?" His voice sounds small and kind of far away, like his body's here but his head is not. "I cause you so much trouble."

"Not really," I say, acutely aware of the fact that we're now completely stopped in the middle of a dark road. "I mean, tonight sucks." I lace my fingers with his. "Which is why, right now, I need you to turn the car around. Please. You don't have to trust them, but please, trust *me*."

He stares out the windshield, out to where our headlights meet the darkness. The fingers of his other hand tap on the steering wheel. "I do."

He takes a deep breath, driving across the lane and then

shifting into reverse to do a three-point turn. For the first time tonight, I think things will be okay. Forty miles an hour toward home is a lot better than twenty miles per hour in the opposite direction, no matter what the outcome.

And that—that's the exact moment when everything goes to hell.

CHAPTER FORTY-TWO

Ridley

IT'S LIKE SLOW motion when the other car hits us, barreling in with its blinding headlights. There's no time to react. There's no time to do anything. There's no time at all.

Somewhere in the background Peak screams, or I do, and our car spins, and I think, *I always thought dying would be my choice.*

. . .

"Ridley!"

"Ridley, please, open your eyes."

"Yes, he's breathing. Okay. I'm putting you on speaker."

"Ridley."

I crack open my eyes, but it's hard. I'm tired, and something is making them burn. I reach up to wipe it away, and Peak grabs my hand and pushes it down.

"Ridley! Help is coming. Just stay still, okay?"

Help. Yes, Peak said we needed that. I'm glad. I turn my head a little bit, and everything hurts. Everything really hurts, but I need to see her. I need to know she's okay. She's clutching her shoulder with her left arm, her right arm gone totally limp. *That's not good,* I think, my eyelids drifting shut.

"Ridley, hold on."

Hold on to what? I wonder. But when I open my mouth to ask, nothing comes out.

"Shh, baby, shhh. You're okay. You're okay. They'll be here in a minute. They'll—"

She's still talking, probably. I think I can hear her voice somewhere in the distance, somewhere far away, somewhere I'm dreaming of, like if I listen hard enough, I can almost chase it back. I can almost get there. But I'm so tired.

She's crying now. I can hear that much, and I want to open my eyes. I want to tell her that everything is fine, probably. If only I could make everything less red.

We were going home. It was going to be okay. She promised.

I'm so tired.

I should sleep.

I should sleep now.

"Ridley, open your eyes."

"Ridley!"

CHAPTER FORTY-THREE

Jubilee

I'M STILL SOBBING when my parents burst in, pulling back the curtain as I'm trying not to hyperventilate while the doctor tells me that my shoulder's dislocated and I'll need surgery to fix the bones in my wrist. I don't even care, though—they can cut it off if they want—because Ridley wouldn't wake up and nobody will tell me what's going on.

A nurse told me he was okay when we first got here, but I've seen enough television to know that might not be the truth. They won't let me out of this bed, and the doctor is just droning on about how they need to stabilize the injury and I need to calm down, and I just want to scream at her to shut up, because WHAT DOES IT EVEN MATTER ANYMORE?

Ridley's hurt or worse, my audition is out the window, and I've been lying to my parents for weeks. I've lost everything that matters in one night. I'm hurt and I'm pissed and I'm scared, and I don't even know what to do with any of this.

"I'm sorry," I say when my mom and Vera wrap me tight

in a hug, uttering things like "oh thank god" and "you're okay." Their hot tears prick against my neck, and it reminds me of how warm his blood was on my hands, and I gag. My mom leans back and places her hand on my forehead like she did when I was little, and I just want to go home.

"What were you guys doing out there? Where did you even get a car? I thought you were going to Frankie's, and then the hospital calls!"

"He was turning around, Mom, I swear," I cry. "We were coming home."

"Jesus Christ, Jubilee. What were you thinking? And, Jubi, your arm! Your arm!"

"He wouldn't wake up," I choke out before dissolving into a fresh round of tears. The doctor stands in the corner, exasperated. "I was trying to help, Mom. I was trying to help! They won't tell me anything."

"Vera, go check on him," Mom says, sounding exhausted. Vera gives my leg one last squeeze and stands up.

The doctor—Dr. Philman, her name tag says—interjects, "The patient that came in with her is getting the care he needs. Only immediate family can see him right now, like I've already told her."

"He doesn't have a family," I sniffle. "He just has us."

The doctor's lips draw in a tight line. "I understand your concern for your friend, but I need to stabilize your arm and wrist before you injure it more."

"I'll go, honey," Vera says. "Even if they don't let me see him, I'll be there."

"Hurry," I say, but when she pulls back the curtain again

to step into the hallway, Ridley's father is standing there, looking down at his phone.

"Mark?"

"Vera," he sighs. "I don't suppose you know where my son is, do you? My wife is very upset. Apparently, she got a call he was here." He says it like it's no big deal, like it's a minor inconvenience, and if the doctor wasn't holding my arm in place, I swear to god I would slap him.

"Your son?" Vera asks, and I can't do this. Not now, when I just need to know he's okay.

Ridley's father glances up. "Don't play dumb, Vera. Do you know what room he's in?"

Vera and Mom turn back toward me, confusion covering their faces.

"I'm sorry," I say, and then it feels like the walls are closing in on me. The doctor gives me some oxygen and puts something in my IV, and everything gets kind of heavy and warm.

Somewhere, far away, people are shouting.

CHAPTER FORTY-FOUR

Ridley

I BLINK GROGGILY under too-bright lights, feeling pain in places I didn't know existed. Panic claws around my heart, sending its rhythm spiraling faster as I try to piece together where I am and how I got here. I turn my head, which, ouch, this is a headache like no other, and there's Gray sitting in the chair beside my bed. She sets her phone down, patting my arm with a sad smile.

"Hey, Rid," she says. "You're in the hospital, but you're okay."

"Peak?" I rasp. It hurts to talk, but I have to know.

"Peak's fine," Gray says. "She already went home."

"Fine?"

"Well, a couple broken bones, but nothing that can't be fixed." The relief mixes with whatever drugs they have me on, and I shut my eyes again, content to drift some more.

. . .

The next time I open my eyes, Gray's in different clothes and drinking coffee. I shift in bed, wincing.

"Hey," she says, scooting her chair closer and rubbing my leg. "Sleeping Beauty awakes."

"Am I . . . ?" I trail off, not sure what I'm asking. Alive? Okay? Still a part of your family?

"You're fine. Mostly. There are six staples keeping your brain from leaking out, and you have three cracked ribs, so nice work." She takes another sip of her coffee. "We're not even going to talk about what you did to my poor car. I just got that thing, Ridley."

I reach up and touch my head, wincing when my fingers ghost over the bandage. "How long was I out?" I ask, poking at all the holes in my memory. There was yelling, I think, and . . . Vera?

"You've been awake off and on for two days, but they doped you up really good, so I doubt you'll remember. I guess you were awake for part of World War Three the other night, but the nurses said you didn't make any sense. You just kept saying you were going home, but every time Dad said you would soon, you freaked out until they finally had to sedate you. They turned your meds down this morning. I think they're discharging you tomorrow."

"World War Three?" I rasp, and she finally hands me some water.

"Small sips," she says, and it's so automatic, I wonder how often she's been doing it.

"Tell me what happened." I focus on the feel of cold water sliding down my throat to stay awake.

"Apparently Dad was here, and so were Peak's parents."

"Vera." I huff out a deep breath.

"Yeah." Gray grimaces. "And from what I gather, it did *not* go well. The doctors ended up banning them all from your room."

"Vera must hate me."

"Actually, your night nurse said she was mostly ripping into Dad. I guess it got pretty vicious."

"Was Peak here?" I ask, because it doesn't make any sense that she isn't now.

Gray hesitates and then nods. "She stopped by when she was discharged. You were asleep."

"What aren't you telling me?"

"What matters is that you're here and you're okay. And we need to focus on getting you better right now. You—"

"Gray, just tell me. Whatever I'm imagining is probably so much worse." I'm so tired, but I can already feel the adrenaline kicking up.

tellmetellmetellme

"It's doesn't matter."

"What did she say?" The heart monitor starts beeping faster and faster; Gray stares at it, looking worried.

"All right." She shakes her head. "But you have to calm down."

"That's not how it works," I say through gritted teeth. "Just tell me."

Gray bites her lip, smoothing her skirt before looking back up at me. "She said she didn't know it was possible to love someone and hate them at the same time."

Oh.

I thought the staples in my head hurt, but this.

This.

"She was just upset, Ridley. People say weird things when they're in pain. Her arm—"

"Her arm?"

"I mean, I don't know the specifics or anything, but it was in a sling and her wrist was wrapped."

"Which arm?"

"I don't know. I wasn't paying attention."

"Think!" I shout. "Which arm? Right or left?"

"Left, I think." Gray closes her eyes, tilting her head back. "No. No, right. Definitely her right arm."

"Her audition is so soon." I'm going to be sick. Gray grabs the pan near my bed and shoves it under my face just in time. I've texted her so many clips of Peak playing, and we've had so many conversations about how important the audition is. She knows exactly what this means.

"Maybe they'll give her an extension," Gray says, rubbing my back while I try to get a grip. It turns out throwing up with broken ribs really fucking hurts.

"It's competitive," I groan when I can finally talk again. "Hundreds of applicants for eight spots. What do you think?"

"I think it sucks, but it could be worse. You guys could have been killed; you realize that, right?" She pauses, taking a deep breath. "Let's just all be glad it wasn't worse." She stares down at her coffee. "I think you're getting a ticket for driving without a license, but the other driver was speeding and had drugs in his car, so you got lucky."

I look at her and crinkle my forehead, which tugs at the bandage in an uncomfortable way, because seriously? Lucky?

"Well, not lucky," she says, but then she scrunches up her face. "No, it is lucky. You were both very, very lucky. What were you thinking, Ridley? Dammit." She stands up and slams her coffee on the tray hard enough that some of it splashes out. "Why didn't you call me? I would have done something. You promised me you always would. You swore!"

I clear my throat, and when she looks at me, her eyes are glassy. I hate that I keep hurting everyone I love. "I don't know. I didn't think you would understand."

"What?" she shouts.

"Dad's so different with you. I didn't want you to know how he really is, at least with me."

"I see a lot more than you give me credit for. I should have done something sooner. I just hoped . . . You're not dealing with this alone. We'll go back to Washington together. We'll—"

"I can't go back there, Grayson." I hesitate, searching for the words. "Whatever's wrong with me, Mom and Dad both make it so much worse."

"There's nothing wrong with you."

"There is."

She sits back down and grabs my hand. "It's different, harder maybe, I don't know. But it's not wrong, okay? So don't say that."

I shrug, because I want to believe her so much, but I don't.

"I was already looking at apartments in Boston. I'll get a two-bedroom; you can stay with me."

"You don't have to do that." I squeeze my eyes shut, because I know, I know that's not enough. And I don't want to screw up anybody else's life.

"I want to."

"I think I need help, Gray. Like more than you can give."

"Okay," she says, her voice sort of quiet and love soaked. "You'll get it, Ridley, whatever you need. We're going to work on this together, you and me. I don't even want to see Dad after some of the things he said, and Mom didn't even fly out."

"What did he—" I start to say, and then catch myself. "I don't want to know."

"Just, don't ever pull this again, okay? I'll—I'll teach you to drive myself. I'll buy us a car. Whatever you need. I'm gonna be there. Just don't make me see you banged up like this again."

"Promise?" I ask through my tears.

She grabs my hand and squeezes it. "Promise."

CHAPTER FORTY-FIVE

PEAK: I'm glad you're okay
and I love you, but I can't do
this anymore.

                                                   BATS: I know.

CHAPTER FORTY-SIX

Jubilee

"CAN I TALK to her?"

Jayla is at the door, blocking the entrance, but his voice still cuts through me, making me ache in places that I wish it didn't.

I am sitting on the couch, staring at the TV, trying not to think. Jayla's parents let her stay home with me today since my parents reluctantly had to go to work and I'm only two days post-op. They both wanted to stay home, but they've missed so much already and will miss more with all the specialist visits. Ironically, instead of going out to audition Monday, I have a surgical follow-up.

I glance down at the bandage around my arm, wondering what it's going to look like after this is all done. And then I think about how it used to look playing cello, something I won't be able to do for weeks.

"You have serious balls," Jayla says, and I sigh. I could just sit here and let her handle it, but I know I need to see him. I need to talk to him. It's been almost a week since the accident, three days since I texted him, and it still feels like I can't breathe without him. We both know this doesn't work anymore, though. And if we don't, at least I do.

I know it was my decision to leave that night, and my decision to get in the car and stay there, but I didn't feel like I had a choice, and I think a part of me will always resent him for that. No matter how much I love him and want him, I just can't anymore.

"Let him in."

Jayla looks at me like I've lost my marbles but steps back and opens the door wider anyway. Ridley walks in and I look up, fighting the urge to hug him. I take an inventory instead. He looks smaller somehow, more jittery. He's all bruised up, and there's a bandage on his head. A large chunk of his hair is missing where they had to shave it. There are dark purple moons beneath his eyes that suggest he hasn't been sleeping. Maybe his pain meds aren't as good as mine.

He walks slowly, gingerly, to the chair across from me, and I don't miss the way he winces as he sits down. Jayla comes and sits next to me, and I give her a look that makes her roll her eyes.

"I'm gonna go make lunch," she says. I know how much she hates him for this, and I know how much effort it takes for her to give us space. Jayla has been my rock, through the tears for the audition and even the tears for Ridley. I don't know which I cried harder for, anyway.

It feels like the silence stretches forever, but we're not even back from the commercial break yet. Ridley hangs his head, and every molecule in my body is begging to touch him, to hug him, to kiss his lips. I want things to be okay, but they never will be, and it's just as much my fault as it is his. He squeezes his eyes shut and takes a breath.

"I know you need time and space," he says. "I know that the rest of our lives might not even be enough time and space for you. I am so sorry for putting you in this position, and I'm not going to make it worse by asking for your forgiveness. I just came by because I'm leaving tomorrow, and it didn't feel right to go without letting you know."

"Thanks," I say, taking a shuddering breath because why is this so hard? Why does it feel like I'm dying, or will die, or have died without him?

"Don't," he says. "But thank you for trying to help me. For trying to be there for me. I'm sorry that you got hurt because of it."

I don't know what else to say. I'm sorry too. Doesn't change anything.

"I love you, Peak," he says, and then holds up his hands when I open my mouth to speak. "You don't have to say anything. I know what I did. But I'm so glad that you exist, and that you're you. Because you showed me there's more to this life than I thought. That it's worth trying to figure out." He takes a deep breath, and I look away.

"Where are you going?" I ask, praying it's not back to Washington with that thing he calls a mother.

"I need help, Peak. I'm staying with Grayson in Boston for a while. She found this place that specializes in this kind of stuff, and there are horses," he says, and I can tell it's hard for him to spit it out.

"Horses?"

"I don't really know." He ducks his head. "I don't know why I led with horses. There's just—" He runs his hands over his face, letting them linger on his mouth, as he looks to the ceiling. "There are people there who can help me figure this stuff out. Because the way that you make me feel, I want to be able to feel it on my own too. I know it's selfish, but god, Peak, I am so fucking glad I met you."

"Ridley." My heart is breaking, and he's saying everything right, and it would be so easy for me to give in to this feeling, but so wrong of me to ask him to stay.

He looks up, his eyes piercing mine.

"I want that for you," I say, "so much." And he shuts his eyes and nods.

We sit there for a while, until his phone goes off. He pulls it out with a sigh. "Gray's outside. She got the rest of my stuff from my dad's. I didn't want to go back there, you know?" He stands up and walks over, brushing his thumb gently down my injured arm. This time when he kisses me goodbye, I don't try to stop him. I don't beg him to stay or ask to go with him.

"Bye, Peak. Thanks . . . for everything."

And when the door clicks shut, the tears come in earnest because I know that he changed me and I changed him. We'll never be the same, but maybe that's okay.

I bet the horses will be beautiful.

CHAPTER FORTY-SEVEN

Ridley

"YOU READY?" GRAY asks, leaning in the doorway of our new apartment. Dad threatened to cut her off, but Gray called his bluff and things are mostly fine. I think Gray's even getting glorified child support now too, but I don't ask.

It took a little while for a bed to open up at Greenwild Acres, the ridiculously bougie therapeutic equine facility my sister found that specializes in teens with clinical depression and anxiety disorders. They don't just load you up on medication there, but that is part of it, and they've already prescribed some in coordination with my new doctor. I was always really weird about having to take stuff, but it actually does seem to help.

Greenwild Acres is located on a sprawling horse farm just outside of Boston, which is where Gray and I live now, and I've been doing outpatient services there while I waited for a bed. Everybody is pretty cool so far. I'm nervous about going inpatient for the next six-plus weeks, but I feel hopeful somehow too.

Plus, they have a skate park there, and I can bring my board, which is awesome—except they'll keep it locked up at first because skate privileges need to be earned. I know I'm lucky to be able to go to a place like that; most people can't. I told Gray I didn't think I deserved all this special treatment, and she said it's not about deserving it and to shut up and pack. So I did. But I still feel a little weird about it.

I miss Peak, like, so much, but my therapists have got me pretty well convinced that if we're meant to be, we'll be, and that the best thing I can do is get myself in order before I go charging back. I really hope someday we're meant to be, but if not, I'm trying to just be grateful for the time we had.

I stare down at the words across the screen of my laptop. I'm on the admissions page for a community college near our apartment. If things go well, I might take a class this fall. My therapist said starting small was still a start, so.

I wait for the words APPLICATION RECEIVED to flash across the screen, and then I click it shut.

"I'm so ready."

Gray twirls her keys around her finger and then tosses them in my direction. "You're driving," she says, and I catch them.

Because yeah, for once I am.

CHAPTER FORTY-EIGHT

Jubilee

I WENT TO my first physical therapy session today, and it kind of sucked, so Jayla and Nikki are over trying to cheer me up. I'm a couple weeks post-op now, and everybody's extremely happy with the results. I am too, I guess, but this big rush to get me back to playing just seems pointless now that I've missed my audition. When we told the conservatory what happened, they offered to reschedule to the end of the decision period, but I had to decline. I knew I wouldn't be ready. Even if I was cleared, it would still take time to get back my technique.

Jayla shoves open my bedroom curtains and pushes up the window. The sounds of birds and traffic flood my room. The brightness is nice, but when it hits my cello case—highlighting a thin layer of dust—I swallow hard and go back to fiddling with the straps of my splint.

"Come on, Jubi, let's go do something," Jayla says, but I ignore her.

I don't really *do* anything these days besides go to school and hang out in my room, and Jayla knows it. I haven't been back to the shop since everything happened. Memories of Ridley cover every inch of it and I'm just not ready, and without that or my rehearsals and lessons, I find myself with a lot of free time. Too much, really.

Nikki flops down beside me while Jayla moves to open the second window. "Okay, no more moping. We can do anything you want, you name it."

"I want my cello to not be covered in dust, and I want to play it."

"No actual playing for at least two more weeks, doctor's orders." Jayla leans against the windowsill. "But we can definitely help with the first part. I wasn't going to say it, but this room is disgusting."

And so that's how we end up spending a perfectly good Saturday playing "keep or toss" while cleaning my room. We toss all the old painkillers and antibiotics and keep the get-well-soon cards. We toss the now deflated balloons and keep my hospital wristband. We take it item by item until it looks less like a recovery room and more like my own space.

Jayla is just sorting out my desk, and Nikki and I have been spending an inordinate amount of time cleaning my case and polishing my cello, when it happens.

"Keep or toss?" Jayla asks, her voice hesitant.

I stare at the Batman mask in her hand. They're both looking at me, waiting for me to answer, but I don't know what to say. I should say toss, right? The scar on the side of my wrist should be a permanent enough reminder of our doomed relationship . . . but it doesn't feel like it is.

"Keep," I finally say.

Jayla nods, setting it on my desk, and I go back to wiping down my cello and waiting for her to find the next emotional land mine. I know it's waiting over there amid the piles of clutter and empty glasses.

I can tell the moment she does. She freezes and holds up the wrinkled envelope, the word *Peak* scrawled on the front. I try not to react.

Grayson gave it to me the other day when she was in town. We met for coffee, and she convinced me to go to a CoDA—Co-Dependents Anonymous—meeting with her. She said she was too nervous to go alone, which, ironic, but I think she mainly just wanted to get me there. There were other teens there too, which was kind of surprising. It was interesting enough, and I saw a lot of me and Ridley in the stuff people were saying. I might keep going, I don't know.

Grayson gave me that envelope right before she left. There wasn't a letter in it, just a flash drive. Apparently, Ridley's therapists thought it would be a good move for him to delete all the videos he took of me playing cello off his phone. I don't know how I feel about that, and I *really* wonder how he felt about it. At any rate, Grayson told me he did remove them but couldn't bear to delete them. Instead he downloaded them all onto a flash drive and asked her to give it to me.

It's been sitting untouched on my desk ever since. Until now.

"Keep?" I say. I'm not sure.

"Is this from him? I can take it home and hide it, if you want it gone but not *gone* gone," Jayla says.

"It's videos he took of me playing. I have no idea what to do with them."

"Can I see one?" Nikki asks, helping me get my cello back into its case and setting it in the corner. It's rare that Nikki and Jayla get to hear me play. I always practice alone—well, before Ridley came along, anyway—and their soccer stuff often conflicts with my concerts and recitals.

"Knock yourself out. I play like shit in half of them anyway."

"Doubtful," Jayla says, firing up my laptop.

I flop down onto my bed, dropping my hands over my eyes as the music floods my room.

"Look at you," Nikki says after the second one.

"Jubi, these are incredible, seriously incredible," Jayla says after the third piece.

"I missed a note on that last one. Delete it."

"Are you kidding me? These are awesome."

I start to protest, but movement in my doorway catches my eye. My mom is there, a wistful look in her eyes, listening to the music. "I miss that sound," she says when she notices me watching her.

"Pretty soon, Mrs. J," Jayla says, "she'll be back to playing so much, you'll be sick of it."

My mom smiles, but her eyes still look sad. I know this has been rough on her too. She's cheered me on at every competition since the third grade, carted me to every lesson, spent money on my music even when there was barely any money to spend. She's been almost as much a part of this process as I have.

I know this isn't the end of the world—it's one summer program—but I can't help feeling like it is. I've worked toward this for so long. And now—

"Will you please play the Bach? I don't have it yet."

Hearing his voice again, even through my computer speakers, cuts deep. I try to play it off but don't do a very good job.

"I'll stop it," Jayla says, rushing to shut my laptop.

"No, leave it," I say. "I want to hear."

• • •

Hours later, when Nikki and Jayla are both asleep on an air mattress and my parents have long shut their door, I open an email and I write.

CHAPTER FORTY-NINE

Ridley

THERE ARE TWO kids on boards when I get to the skate park, if you want to call it that—it was maybe slightly oversold in the brochure. It's more like a small area of concrete with a few rails and some wooden ramps, but it'll do. Earning board privileges at Greenwild feels like a huge accomplishment, and I've been chomping at the bit—pardon the horse pun, but—to finish my journaling work this afternoon and actually get out here.

I push off, picking up speed to slide a rail to shake off the day. It was a tough one, even with the horses serving as a distraction. My therapist met me at the barn for my morning session, and we talked a lot about my relationship with my father while I brushed Westley and Buttercup and cleaned out their stalls. I think she knew that wasn't a conversation I could handle sitting still.

I didn't have group today, so afterward I went to my room to do a journaling exercise, which was when my peer counselor surprised me by awarding me my board back and said I was making "exceptional progress." It was awesome, and now I'm here, the board dipping and swaying as I cut around the course, leaving it all behind.

I don't know what I expected inpatient therapy would be like, but it's not awful. Some of that is definitely related to the fact that Gray insisted I go inpatient at a place that feels more like a country club than a hospital, but still. It's more exhausting than I expected. Like sometimes I feel more tired from journaling and group than I do from spending a day mucking out all the stalls.

I haven't really made any friends, though. Not that that's the point, but we talk a lot about support networks and stuff for when we're back on the outside, and right now that list consists only of Grayson and the people she pays to care about my mental health—like the staff here. I've seen some of the other kids hanging out and making connections, but it's whatever.

I push harder, skating over to the ramps and doing a few kickflips on my way. The two other kids hop off their boards and walk over.

"You're pretty good," the first kid says. "You new?"

"Ish? I just got my board back today."

"Congrats, man, that's good. That's big. Where you from?"

"Boston," I say. "It's like twenty minutes from here."

"Yeah, I think I've heard of it," the second kid says, feigning surprise. He flashes me an easy smile, and it feels less like he's making fun of me and more like he's having fun.

"Right, yeah," I say, flipping my board into my hand. "What's your story?" I ask, wondering where they've been hiding. I'd think they just got here, but the fact that they already have skate privileges says otherwise.

"I'm Hector, and this is Quinn," the first kid says, holding out his hand. "I'm from Boston too, but Quinn's from here."

Quinn nods. "My mom's one of the doctors; she lets me skate sometimes when she's working, depending on who's here."

Hector thwaps his hat. "He's also an alumnus, which he should have mentioned because that's the real reason he gets to use the skate park. But that was before his mom came here. Now he's sort of an unofficial mascot."

"I'm the official mascot, asshole." Quinn laughs. "Me and Buttercup are on the front of the brochure. But yeah, he basically covered everything. My mom fell in love with the place when I was here for treatment. She started working here after, and I kinda became a fixture. My mom actually helped me petition to have this built."

"Well, thanks, because I was losing it without my board." I suck my lips over my teeth and shake my head, realizing what I just said. "I guess technically I was losing it before that, but."

Quinn smiles. "Hey, if we can have horse therapy, we can have skate therapy too, right?"

"Yeah."

"Why are we just standing around, then?" Hector asks, dropping his board and aiming for the ramp.

"Hey, what's your name?" Quinn shouts, barreling after him.

"It's Ridley."

"Okay, Ridley, let's see what you got."

CHAPTER FIFTY

Jubilee

"JUBILEE!" MOM CALLS from the kitchen, and I set down my bow, flexing my fingers.

I still get stiff, but the physical therapy is really helping and my playing is getting close to where it was before. I love my PT team, but I can't wait to be done.

"Jubilee, come here."

I hate when she interrupts me, but the urgency in her voice has got me curious. I slide my splint back on—I'm still supposed to wear it when I'm not playing—and head down the hall.

Mom and Vera are both sitting at the kitchen table, and they look way too excited for this early on a Saturday morning.

"What's up?" I ask, glancing between them.

"There's a letter," Mom says, pushing an unopened envelope toward me. "From the conservatory."

"Oh yeah?" My voice cracks from nerves, and Vera tilts her head, watching me.

"It's thick," Vera says. "Open it."

I snatch it out of her hand, tearing open the envelope and scanning the words on the letter as fast as I can.

"What does it say?" Mom asks, her eyes going huge.

"Dear Jubilee—" I clear my throat.

We would like to cordially invite you to attend the Junior Summer Orchestra Program at the Carnegie Conservatory.

While taped auditions are generally reserved for our international students, we were willing to consider your application, in light of your extenuating circumstances.

We hope you will be sufficiently healed to join us in this program next month, as the selecting committee was deeply moved by your performance.

Please review the tuition and fees breakdown and acceptance information provided in the enclosed packet. We look forward to a wonderful summer filled with music.

"Holy crap," I say, tears flooding my eyes. "I got in."

"You got in!" Mom shrieks. "How, though? I thought you withdrew!"

"Remember that day when Jayla and Nikki were watching those videos Ridley made?"

My mom's face falls; she still gets nervous when I talk about him. "Yes, but what does that have to do with anything?"

"He had my whole repertoire on that flash drive. I figured I didn't really have anything to lose, so I emailed it to them last minute and asked to be considered after all. I didn't tell you because I didn't want to get your hopes up. The application fee was nonrefundable anyway—I thought we may as well make them work for it."

"Oh my god, baby." Vera laughs. "You did it; you're going to the conservatory!"

And then I realize what the letter doesn't say, and my stomach drops to the floor.

"What's wrong?" my mom asks.

I flip the paper over and look in the envelope, but there's nothing else besides a brochure. I swallow hard. "I didn't . . . I didn't get the scholarship, though."

"Let us worry about that," Vera says. "You got in. You're going."

"It's too much."

"We've been setting aside little bits for this whenever we could, just in case." My mom gets up and kisses my head. "And Vera's been having a *very* good year on Kickstarter."

"Wipe that worried look off your face." Vera smiles. "Because you're going to the summer program, Jubi. You did it. You did it!"

"Oh my god. I'm going to Carnegie!" I squeal as they smother me in hugs.

CHAPTER FIFTY-ONE

PEAK: Are you still in Boston?

CHAPTER FIFTY-TWO

Ridley

IT'S SUNNY OUT, borderline too hot, but not too humid for mid-August, and I'm sitting on a picnic table, waiting. She's late. A part of me thinks she's not coming, but I am prepared to sit here all day.

I pull out my phone and make a note of that in the app. I should probably mention that in group, just to be sure. I think it's probably okay, though. I think some people are worth the wait. But what do I know? As my therapist says, I'm still "recalibrating my normal meter." I've graduated back to outpatient, but there's still a lot of work to be done.

It turns out I have a whole host of issues, which I knew going in, but there are also a lot of ways to manage them, which I definitely did *not* know. Apparently when you're the child of narcissists *and* not the golden child *and* predisposed to mental health problems, it kind of fucks you up extra. But we're working on it, and it's mostly okay.

My therapists know I'm here, and what I'm doing, and they don't think it's the worst thing, so that's cool. We talked a lot about boundaries and expectations, and I think I'm sort of prepared for whatever happens. And if I'm not, I've got all their numbers programmed into my phone. Plus Gray's. And Hector's. And Quinn's.

I'm still living with Gray and will be for the foreseeable future, my parents effectively cut off. We tried some family therapy with them, and it didn't work. Like, at all. So now it's just me and Gray mostly. It's a small family, but a good one. She still works for The Geekery, though, and managed to convince—okay, blackmail—my dad into calling a truce between him and Verona, which was pretty damn cool. She travels a lot less for work now too, and when she has to go, one of my friends stays over or my aunt Mary comes. It used to bother me that I needed a babysitter, but now I know what it really is: a solid support system, which is something that I never had before.

It's kind of nice.

I feel healthier than I ever have. Hector, Quinn, and I even started recording ourselves skating, and our YouTube channel is getting tons of hits. We plan to turn it into an actual web show once the new camera we ordered comes in. Who knows if anything will ever come of it, but it's nice to have goals and dreams of my own for once.

There are still a lot of dark times; there's no fix for that. But for the first time it feels like surviving them is an option—an option I really want, no matter what happens with Peak today, or anybody else for that matter. So that's new.

I run my hands through my hair and sit up a little straighter. I don't know how it will go when she gets here, but I miss her. Now that I'm sure I'm not just trying to fill up my empty spaces with her love, we all—meaning my therapists and me—thought it was probably okay to respond to the text she sent me the other day. We even had a plan for if she didn't text again after my response, which would have sucked but also been okay.

But I'm so glad that she did.

She's been in Boston all summer, and it's been hard knowing that she's been so close and still so far. We emailed a couple times in the beginning—she wanted to tell me she got into the summer program, and since I was still inpatient, I didn't have my phone. I was open about where I was and what I was doing. She said she was glad, because she worried all the time that I was dead. I said there was something really wrong about that, and I was sorry for what I had put her through. And then I didn't hear from her again. Until the text.

It's been hard not texting her—I know she still sometimes talks to Gray—but I wanted it to be her decision to reach out . . . Well, more like my therapists wanted it to be her decision, if I'm being honest. But they helped me see that I really didn't want to force my way back into her life; I wanted her to want me there. And if she didn't, that was fair and fine and valid, and I would work through it in my counseling sessions.

"Ridley?" she says, putting her hand on my shoulder, and I jump, because I was expecting her to come from the path in front of me and she snuck up from behind.

God, she looks so beautiful. Her hair is longer, and she's

got a bit of a tan. I notice a small scar on her wrist and fore-arm from the surgery and frown, but only for a second before it moves out of sight as she pulls me into a hug. And maybe I breathe in a little too deep, trying to memorize the scent of her shampoo. I had forgotten what it smelled like until right now, and I don't want to forget again.

"It's so good to see you," she says, stepping back and tucking some of her hair behind her ear.

"You too."

We both sort of laugh a little awkwardly, and she looks down, toeing designs in the sand with her white tennis shoe.

"I missed you," I say, and then clap my hand to my fore-head, because I didn't mean to be this obvious.

"I missed you too," she says with a little laugh.

"Yeah?"

She raises her eyebrows and nods, like I'm ridiculous for even asking that.

"Do you want to . . . ?" I trail off, not sure how to finish. Start again? Get lunch? Be my girlfriend? And shit, I wasn't going to be this eager; I wasn't supposed to push.

"Ridley," she says sadly.

"Right." I mean, she knows I've been working on myself, but she hasn't seen it, and that's fair. "I'm getting ahead of myself. It's really good to see you. I want you to know I get that we can't pick up where we left off. I've done a lot of work around understanding that."

"That's good to hear. I've actually been working on that too."

"Really?"

"Yeah." She takes a deep breath and unzips her messenger bag. "And I decided that I don't want to pick up where we left off. That was . . . bad."

"Right, no," I say, jumping down off the table, and I hope my voice doesn't sound like she just drop-kicked my heart into next week, even though it feels like she kind of did. "I talked about this in my session this morning. We made a list of outcomes, and you meeting me for closure was one that we put in the positive-outcome column. Although, I don't remember why. I did at the time, it made sense, but right now I—" I look down and shake my head. "I took notes, and I can email them to you if you want. They're actually right in the car. I could go grab them now. You know what? I'm rambling. Sorry."

"Wow."

"I'm really nervous," I say, because Dr. Gabriella says labeling my feelings is an important tool to help control my anxiety. If I address what's at the root of it, too, sometimes I can stop it from spiraling out. I suck at figuring that part out, but I'm working on it.

"Let me finish." She pulls the Batman mask out of her messenger bag and slides it onto my head. She stops short of pulling it over my face, and okay, I was not expecting this. "I don't want to pick up where we left off. I'd rather rewind farther than that."

"You want to—"

"Have a redo maybe and see where it goes," she says. "Slowly. Extremely slowly. Like glacial."

"I can do glacial."

"Like occasional cups of coffee as friends with several days in between."

"I love coffee," I say, a little too eager. "Are you sure, though?"

"No, but I want to try. I miss you a lot, and if you think—if you're in a good place, I thought maybe we could start talking again. Just talking."

"I would like that." I grin; I can't help it. "Hang on." I grab my phone off the table and pull the tattered feather out from the case, twirling it in my fingers.

"You've carried it the whole time?"

"Whole time."

She smiles so big it's blinding, and maybe my eyes water a little, but who's really checking, anyway.

• • •

Later, when she's back at her dorm and I'm cooking dinner with Gray, I text her a picture of a baby bat, and she texts me a picture of a ridiculous peacock, and . . .

I don't know where this is going. Maybe nowhere. Maybe somewhere. Life is an unpredictable and strange thing like that, but.

But.

It's also kind of amazing.

And I'm so glad I'm here.

RESOURCES

If you or someone you know is struggling, there is help available. Please reach out. The world is better with you in it.

National Suicide Prevention Lifeline:
1-800-273-8255 | suicidepreventionlifeline.org
The Trevor Project Lifeline:
1-866-488-7386 | thetrevorproject.org
Trans Lifeline:
1-877-565-8860 | translifeline.org
Crisis Text Line:
text HOME to 741741 | crisistextline.org

For more information on Co-Dependents Anonymous, the support group Jubilee visits to learn more about healthy relationships and setting personal boundaries, please visit CoDA.org

ACKNOWLEDGMENTS

I am so lucky to be surrounded by so many talented and hard-working people. This book would not exist without them.

A massive thank-you to:

My agent, Brooks Sherman, and my editor, Stephanie Pitts, who once again made this entire process a blast from start to finish. I am a better writer because of you both. Jen Klonsky for your support and insight, Lizzie Goodell for being my publicist extraordinaire, and Christina Colangelo, Bri Lockhart, Felicity Vallence, James Akinaka, Friya Bankwalla, and everyone at Penguin Teen and Putnam—*Verona Comics* truly could not have asked for a better home.

Jeff Östberg for once again bringing my characters to life with an amazing cover illustration. I am forever in your debt.

My writer coven, Karen Strong and Isabel Sterling—I would be lost without you two and definitely not still chasing that licorice candy. Becky Albertalli, my brain twin, for too many things to count, but you know. Roselle for just getting it. And Kelsey Rodkey for her eternal patience, advice, and beyond excellent friend and critique partner skills. Can you believe it's a whole book later and you're still reminding me to drink water?

Hannah Capin for her music expertise—anything I got right is because of her; anything I got wrong is on me. Sarah Grimes, even though Bucky is still mine, and the many writer friends who have been there for me this year—especially Erin, Meredith, Sophie, and my DVSquad pals.

And especially Shannon, my eternal BFF, and Jeff, who lets me steal her near weekly for horrible TV dates and laughter but is also a most excellent friend in his own right. My big brother and best friend, Dennis, for always, always being there—but stop saying we're twins when I'm four years and 364 days younger. My mom and family for their unwavering support, and Brody, Olivia, and Joe for loving me even when I'm cranky and on deadline.

And also all of my readers—your support means the world. Thank you.

READ ON FOR MORE
FROM JENNIFER DUGAN

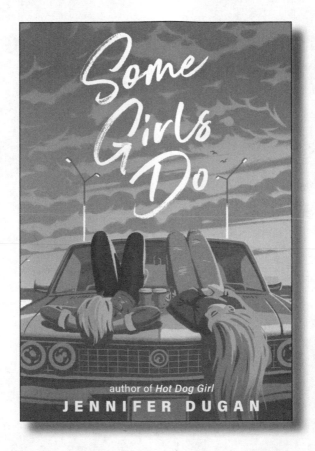

1

RUBY

There's an art to the extraction. First, I take Tyler's arm—heavy across my stomach—and slide my fingers beneath. I lift it slightly and move centimeter by centimeter to the right side of the bed. And when I'm mostly free, I grab one of his pillows—warmed by my own overthinking head—and slip it under his arm. If I'm lucky, he'll snuffle softly in the moonlight streaming into his messy bedroom, hug the pillow, and stay sleeping. If I'm unlucky, he'll wake up and ask me where I'm going: *Ruby, just stay. Ruby, please. Ruby, it won't kill you to cuddle.* I don't have the energy for that.

Tyler's messy brown hair falls into his face as he smiles in his sleep and hugs my pillow replacement a little tighter. I got lucky tonight—in every sense of the word. I grab my boots, leftovers from one of the ten million Western-themed pageants I've smiled my way through over the years, and creep out the front door barefoot, careful not to let the screen door slam and wake his parents.

The motion-sensor light clicks on as I shove my feet into my boots and beeline it for my car, my soul, my lifeline: my baby-blue 1970 Ford Torino. Yes, it's old as hell, but it's the one thing in this world that's truly mine. *I* bought it, rusted and rotten, off my great-aunt Maeve's estate for three hundred bucks. *I* painstakingly put it back together, scavenging pieces from junkyards and flea markets. *I* restored it to its current state of splendor. Me. I did that.

Okay, so maybe I had a little help from Billy Jackson, the town's least-crooked mechanic, but still.

I climb inside and shift it into neutral, taking off the emergency brake and letting the car coast backward down Tyler's long hill of a driveway and into the street, where I finally flick the ignition. It rumbles to life, the sound closer to a growl than a purr. I resist the urge to rev the engine—god, I love that sound—and point my car toward home, feeling loose and boneless, relaxed and happy, content in the way one only can during that tiny glint of freedom between chores and obligations.

Not that Tyler is an obligation—or a chore, for that matter. He's nice enough, our time together fun and consensual. In another universe, we'd probably be dating. But we live in this one, and in this universe, I love exactly two things: sleep and my car.

Tyler is a great stress reliever, an itch to scratch, a good time had by all. Nothing else. We have an arrangement, a friends-with-benefits sort of thing. No strings. If he called me tomorrow and said he wanted to ask a girl out, I'd say go for it as long as it isn't me—and I'd mean it. I hope he'd say the same. Which is why I'm driving home from his house two hours after getting a text that simply said: **big game tomorrow, you around?**

Be still my heart.

But then, a couple weeks ago, I texted him: **pageant in the AM, come distract me?** And he was crawling in my window within minutes.

See, it's not an all-the-time thing; it's an as-needed thing. Some people get high; Tyler and I get twenty minutes of consensual, safe sex—always use a condom, people—and a subsequent awkward exchange about how my leaving right after makes him feel weird. Thus, the sneaking out once he falls asleep: the ideal compromise, at least on my end.

I pull into the dirt-patch driveway in front of my trailer. It might not seem like much to some, but it's ours and it's home. Just me and my mom. Well, some of the time, anyway. The better times.

But the lights are still on in the kitchen, the TV flickering in the living room, and my heart sinks. Mom works the overnight shift cleaning offices, and her car's not here, which means this will not be one of those "better times." Literally nothing could drag me down from a good mood faster than having to be around her boyfriend, Chuck Rathbone.

Chuck and my mom have been together off and on for the past few years—and unfortunately for me, lately they've been more on than off. "Getting more serious," I heard her say to a friend. Which is why he has unrestricted house privileges. Along with *eating our food and wasting our electricity even though we can't afford it* privileges.

I get why Chuck can't help chasing my mom around—my mom is the kind of beautiful that even hard jobs and tough luck can't dull, a beauty queen and Miss Teen USA hopeful right up until that second line showed up on her pregnancy test eighteen years ago. (Sorry, Mom.)

But I don't really understand why my mom always takes him back. Chuck is, objectively, the worst.

I'd crash at my best friend Everly's house if I wasn't so sure Chuck had heard my car—my engine is less than stealthy, and normally I like it that way. But if I leave now, he'll definitely tell Mom, and that's one guilt trip I don't need. On a scale of "needs an oil change" to "engine's seized," being rude to my mom's boyfriend rates somewhere around "blown head gasket"—not a fatal blow, but like most things when it comes to my mother, expensive and difficult to fix.

I turn off my car, listening to the tick of the engine as it cools down in the spring air. The curtains in the living room move, no doubt Chuck stumbling around, trying to see what I'm doing and why I'm not inside. I reach into the back seat to grab the bag of stage makeup Mom made me pick up earlier and get out.

Our door creaks as I yank it open, ignoring the siding falling off next to it, and step over a particularly suspicious stain on the carpet. Five yapping Jack Russell terriers come tearing down the hallway. Mom's other pride and joy. Please, god, do not have let them in my room; they're barely house-trained—and by "barely," I mean not at all.

"Shut those mutts up!" Chuck yells from the kitchen as he pulls open the fridge, as if I have any control over them. As if anyone has control over them. Mom likes them a little wild; she says it's more natural that way. I'd personally prefer if their "wildness" could be contained only to the rooms with vinyl flooring.

I crouch down and pet as many of them as I can, as fast as I can, while being tackled by the others. Tiny paws dig into my sides and legs as they fight for attention. "Shh, shh, shh," I coax, calming them as much as it's possible to calm five under-exercised terriers that rarely see the outside of our home.

"Goddamn dogs," Chuck says, carrying two cans of beer over to the recliner in front of the blaring TV. Fox News. As usual. He drops into the recliner, drips of beer falling onto his faded black T-shirt, which reads DON'T TREAD ON ME. He looks like he hasn't shaved in days, flecks of gray poking through his brown stubble. "You're home late."

"Yeah, sorry. I was studying with a friend," I say, standing up once the dogs decide that sniffing one another is more interesting than tackling me. I wonder if they can smell Tyler's cat.

Chuck raises his eyebrows, the last wisps of hair on his head flopping comically. "Your mom might fall for that garbage, but I know what girls like you do at night, and it's not studying."

"What would you know about studying?" I say, hating that he's right but determined not to give him the satisfaction.

"I know you don't get hickeys from math homework." He laughs and his eyes flick to the talking head on the TV.

Goddammit, Tyler, no marks means no marks. My hand reaches up to my neck as my cheeks flame.

"Hey, hey, it's all right, I won't tell your ma."

I look at him, waiting for the catch.

"Come here, darlin'," he says, but I stay where I am, poised for a quick escape. He leans forward, a conspiratorial look on his face. "So, what did you really get up to tonight?"

"What time is Mom coming home?" I change the subject with a smile that shows too many teeth.

He frowns slightly. "I don't know. It's slow this week, she said. They lost another client."

"So anytime, then?" I ask, and he looks back at the TV. "I'm gonna head to bed. Night."

"You sure you don't want one?" he asks, gesturing toward the beer can beside his on the tray. And did he, what, think I'd get wasted and spend the night watching conservative shit-heads spout lies on cable TV with him? No, thanks.

"It's a school night."

"Does that really matter to you?" On the TV behind me the host blabs on and on. I stare at the wall, taking a deep breath.

I won't take the bait.

"This shit'll rot your brain, Chuck," I say, grabbing the remote and clicking it off.

Because I will not be intimidated in my own home. I will not take crap from any stupid man sitting on the recliner that I got Mom with my Little Miss Sun Bonnet winnings years ago. I will not be scared of the Chuck Rathbones of the world.

"Fuck off." He laughs, chugging his beer and turning the TV back on.

I scamper to my room and lock the door behind me, praying to any god that will listen: *Please don't let this be my future too.*

2

MORGAN

"Do you have everything?"

"Yes!"

"Do you have lunch money?"

"Yes, I have lunch money."

"Your track schedule? Practice goes until at least five thirty most days, they said."

"Yes, and then I'm gonna jog or walk to the apartment after."

"Okay, I'm usually at the shop until about six thirty, so if you beat me home and I'm not there, don't worry."

"Oh my god, I'm not worried. I can handle being home alone."

"I just want this to be good for you. You deserve it after—"

"Can we not talk about that? Fresh start and all?"

"Okay, well, what would Mom say?"

"I don't know. 'I love you'? 'Have a good day'?"

Dylan smiles, a serious look in his eyes. "I love you. Have a good day."

"Holy crap, Dyl, (a) your impression of Mom needs work, and (b) you're taking this 'in loco parentis' thing a little too seriously."

"I just don't want to screw anything up," he says. "Mom and Dad will kill me if I break you or lose you or whatever you do with kids."

"Dude, I'm seventeen." I groan, pulling my long brown hair up into a ponytail.

The car behind us beeps, and someone shouts, "The drop-off lane is for drop-offs. Get out or get moving."

"Yikes," Dylan says, looking into the rearview mirror.

"Yeah, hell hath no fury like a suburban mom late for her latte," I say. "But don't worry, I'm going to be fine. And you need to go." I give him a quick one-armed hug and then dart out of the car before he can stop me.

But despite what I told Dylan, I have no clue what I'm doing. A bunch of kids bustle past me, laughing with their friends, completely oblivious to the fact that I'm new. I shift my backpack higher on my shoulders—or at least I try to, which is exactly when I realize it's missing. Crap.

"Dyl!" I call, but of course he can't hear me on the other side of the parking lot with his windows up. So I do what I do best: I run, fast. I fly through the parking lot, weaving between rows, hoping to cut him off as he moves slowly through the traffic jam that's formed in front of the school entrance. I'm just about there, one more row to go, when a loud horn and the screech of brakes makes me freeze in my tracks.

And there, a foot away from my hip, is the bumper of a very shiny blue car. Seriously? I look back to Dylan's car just in time to see it pull out and disappear down the road.

"Dammit!" If it weren't for this stupid car, I would have made it. I wouldn't be standing in the middle of the parking lot of a new school without my schedule, a notebook, or even a friggin' pencil. "What is wrong with you?!" I spin around, slapping my hands on the hood of the car. "Watch where you're going!"

I look up to glare at the no doubt macho asshole driving this stupid muscle car and am struck with the brightest pair of blue eyes I've ever seen—which promptly narrow and glare back at me.

"You're the one running through the middle of a parking lot," she says, hopping out of her car and shoving me out of the way to inspect her car hood. "If you so much as put a scratch in this—"

"You could have killed me!"

"It would have been your fault if I did," she says, straightening up so we're nearly nose to nose. "Where were you even going? School's the other way, if you haven't noticed."

And oh no. Oh. No. She's . . . very . . . cute. And before I know it, my brain is unhelpfully making a list of everything I should *not* be wondering about. Like how her perfectly tanned hand might look linked with my lighter, peachier one. And whether there are tan lines underneath her fitted gray hoodie and obscenely tight jeans. And, oh god, I am a creep.

It would be so much easier to stay angry with her if she really were some asshole dude, but this is a complication. One that will require a full system reboot if I want to get out of this without embarrassing myself. Step one: close my mouth, which is currently hanging open like I'm witnessing a miracle. Step two: pull it together with a quickness.

Like, the objective part of my brain recognizes that she still technically sucks. But the nonobjective part of my brain still really wants her name and number, and to know if she's single and how she would feel about dating a marginally disgraced track star of the female persuasion.

"Hello! I asked you a question." She waves her hands in front of my face. And, yes, that was helpful. Please keep being an asshole, car girl.

"I forgot my backpack in my brother's car," I answer the second my brain comes back online. "I was trying to catch him before he left."

"Why didn't you just call him?" She looks pointedly at the phone sticking out of my pocket. And, okay, good question.

"Instinct?" I say. "I'm a runner. I run. It's what I do."

"Yeah, well, don't run here. This is a parking lot. For parking. It's what it's for," she says, mocking my tone.

"It was an emergency situation."

The girl huffs and pulls her hair—long dirty-blond strands that look like they've been highlighted to within an inch of their life—into a messy bun on top of her head. "You're lucky there're no scratches from you punching my—"

"I didn't punch your car. I lightly pressed my hands against it in frustration."

"Sure. Well, the good news is all it's going to cost you is a car wash to get your grubby prints off the hood." She smiles in a mean kind of way that should *not* make my stomach flip down to my toes but absolutely does. And seriously? Seriously?! Can I just for once not be attracted to someone who looks like they could eat me for dinner without batting an eye?

"I am *not* paying for you to wash your car just because I touched it."

She shrugs and walks back to her still-open door. "It was worth a shot. She's due for one anyway."

And now when my mouth pops open, it's with annoyance instead of awe. "Worth a shot? Are you— You almost killed me! You almost killed me, *and then* you tried to scam me into paying for a car wash you're already getting? What kind of a monster are you?"

"The kind that didn't forget her backpack *and* isn't going to be late for homeroom," she says, before sliding into her car and reversing down the row.

"Asshole!" I yell, flipping her off for good measure, but she just rolls her eyes and laughs.

I have the good sense to wait until she's out of sight before admitting defeat and pulling out my phone. Dylan answers on the first ring, sounding totally panicked. Once I reassure him that, yes, I'm fine, the world has not ended, nothing irrevocably bad has happened in the five minutes or so since he dropped me off—barring almost being run over by the rudest girl in rude town, which I definitely do *not* mention—he calms down enough to promise to bring me my backpack.

I find a bench near the track with a good view of the parking lot and wait. So much for coming early to find my classes. There are a couple girls running on the track, no doubt members of the school team, and I wonder if they're making up a practice or if they're running penalty laps. My old coach at St. Mary's was big on those. Coming in early was good for the soul, she used to say, although my body wholeheartedly disagreed.

I recognize one of the girls as she runs by: Allie Marcetti—we've run against each other a few times, and I kind of know her. She's fast, but not as fast as me, and definitely not for as long. No one is. Well, no one around here anyway. I heard a rumor she was switching to sprinting for her final season anyway.

They rush past me, their matching ponytails streaming behind them, and I bounce my leg, wishing I were running too. I can't wait until later, when it's finally my feet slapping the track, pushing myself until my muscles burn and my stomach shakes and . . . I stop, reminding myself I'm technically not an official member of the team yet, not until my waiver comes through.

If it comes through. But with my past ranking, Coach had no qualms about letting me practice with them for the last couple months of school. I even signed an early letter of intent to run for my dream school—although at the moment it's "on pause" while they "evaluate the incident."

I've spent a lot of time convincing myself this is all fine and none of it hurts. That going from star athlete to high school scandal is a totally normal progression that I am both equipped for and totally saw coming. But, yeah, I look away as the girls cross the finish line, trying really hard not to think about how that should be me, at my old school, with my old friends.

My mom keeps saying it's just a matter of time before I'm cleared to compete again and everything is sorted with my college. Apparently, being given the choice to withdraw or be formally expelled from your old school—a school your parents are currently suing for a myriad of reasons including but not limited to discrimination and harassment—makes it seem a lot less likely that your new school is poaching elite athletes. Let's just hope the High School Athletic Association agrees when they finally rule on my case.

Coach didn't poach anyone. We both just got lucky that my brother has an apartment in a school district with a decent running program in the same conference, and the school happens to have a spot for a distance runner. If it were up to me, I'd still be racing with my old crew at St. Mary's, but it's not.

That's what happens when you lose it on a teacher who tells you that being queer is against the code of conduct at your stupid private school . . . and then decides to make your life a living hell because of it.

We tried the homeschooling route when everything first went down. We naively thought we could just remove that one part of my life and everything else would still be the same. But then the local news picked up the story, and I started to feel like everyone was watching me or something. Maybe it was in my head at first, but then my friends stopped calling, and their parents stopped texting my parents. And then I just had to get out of there.

Whatever. No wallowing. Fresh start. New me. Out and proud. Taking a stand. So fun! This waiver just better come through before states, or they'll have to chain me to the bench to keep me from competing. I will not miss the final track season of my senior year, so help me god.

The first bell rings, and everybody rushes inside, the parking lot and school grounds becoming a ghost town in seconds. And I stay sitting, waiting for Dylan. Late for my fresh start already.

DON'T MISS
THIS HILARIOUSLY AWKWARD ROMANCE!

"Funny, joyful, bighearted."
—Becky Albertalli, bestselling author of
Simon vs. the Homo Sapiens Agenda

"A great, fizzy rom-com."
—*Entertainment Weekly*

"Both classic and new, hysterical and heartfelt."
—Mackenzi Lee, bestselling author of
The Gentleman's Guide to Vice and Virtue

"One of the best reads of the year, hands down."
—*Paste*

"This laugh-out-loud debut stole my heart."
—Rachel Lynn Solomon, author of *Today Tonight Tomorrow*